Praise for Colin O'Sullivan

"A hard, poignant novel of great humanity ... remarkably well written ..."

—*Rolling Stone* (France)

"O'Sullivan's voice—unique, strong, startlingly expressive—both comes from and adds to Ireland's long and lovely literary lineage. Like many of that island's sons and daughters, O'Sullivan sends language out on a gleeful spree, exuberant, defiant, ever-ready for a party. Only a soul of stone could resist joining in."

—Niall Griffiths

"His words swagger with purpose, never meandering too long on a scene, always moving the story forward, even when it goes back in time, like a faded photograph coming into view. Lyrical to a point, one word flowing to the next, hardly stopping. I read this novel and saw a movie in my mind – that's how each page appeared to me – and that's a good thing. This story reminded me of a beautiful vase, now shattered to pieces on the floor. But with each piece picked up and glued back into place, a narrative came into being, with each piece representing a character, beautifully written with all their flaws and realism, broken by their own imperfections and weaknesses. But most of all, the dropping of the vase, once beautiful, representing by the act of a man, long gone, though his actions reverberate through the years, waiting, waiting for those sunny days in Killarney, when the sun finally gets to shine on that long buried seed, giving it the energy it needs to bloom – for good, and for evil."

—Love, Sex & Other Dirty Words

"A cathartic novel that ultimately creates positive emotions, like the blues can do. Poignant."

—Book Node

"A luminous novel that chases away the darkness … All its characters are at a crossroads and they will either meet the Devil himself or find a way towards a new life."

—Appuyez sur la touche lecture

"Carried by a genuine writing talent, *Killarney Blues* is a Noir novel full of melancholy and unfulfilled dreams with a surprising glimmer of hope at the end. Without the slightest naivety. A revelation."

—Le Soir (Belgium)

"*Killarney Blues* is a Noir novel – but not only – at the farthest reaches of love, desire and loss."

—Lettres d'Irlande et d'Ailleurs

"A novel of great finesse and humanity. Perhaps, sometimes, there is a glimmer of hope in the blues?"

—Action-suspence.com (Starred review)

"In a style that is sometimes luminous, sometimes direct, sometimes poetic, Colin O'Sullivan traces his narrative path, creates incredibly vivid and appealing characters and brings the reader, to the 12-bar beat of the blues, towards a heart-breaking denouement."

—*Le blog du Polar de Velda*

"This first Noir novel from Colin O'Sullivan is magnificent, very finely written, and profoundly sad. To be savoured while drinking a Guinness and listening to some old blues, by Muddy Waters or Bessie Smith. And if rain knocks on the window glass, like in Killarney, it's even better." —*RTL (Radio Télévision Luxembourg)*
"Moving, tragic, masterly crafted."

—Lea Touch

"*The Dark Manual* is a mature rounded work, assured and confident, at times lyrical and beautiful but also punchy and sharp. […] engaging, inventive and thought-provoking."

—*Nudge-Book.com*

"Colin O'Sullivan is a lyrical master of the written word. There are sections of the book that are heart-breaking, in their emotional and physical sense of loss, and moments of humor, surprise, suspense, pure sudden horror, and stark naked joy."

—Marvin Minkler, *Modern First Editions*

My Perfect Cousin

COLIN O'SULLIVAN

BETIMES BOOKS

First published in the English language in Dublin, Ireland, in 2019
by Betimes Books

www.betimesbooks.com

ISBN 978-0-9934331-8-4

My Perfect Cousin is a work of fiction. Names, characters, places, and
incidents are either the product of the author's imagination or are
used fictitiously. Any resemblance to actual persons, living or dead,
events, or locales is entirely coincidental.

Cover design by JT Lindroos

For the Ardshan boys and girls,
70s, 80s, 90s

Each knew, almost within a breath, what the other was thinking and wanting to say; each of them almost wept for the other."

Shirley Jackson, *The Haunting of Hill House*

The hills are far away. They rise up
blacker than childhood.
What do you think of, lying so quietly
by the water? When you look that way I want
to touch you, but do not, seeing
as in another life we were of the same blood.

Louise Glück, "The Pond"

PROLOGUE

Do you believe in monsters?
          I do.
     I am one.
     A human monster.
     Do you know what that is?
     We do exist, and we always have a story to tell.

I am the product of madness. The madness of love. The product of youths that bucked against what was right and proper; two that had bright hearts but cast themselves in shadow, bright souls that succumbed to dark or foolish deeds. The madness of love? Maybe it was all just the madness of madness.

Despite everything I turned out all right. I have no disabilities, am level-headed, clear-thinking, and for the most part law-abiding – if you'll excuse a few parking tickets and one or two illegal music downloads; I seem to have none of their waywardness, that flicker they both had that seemed so quickly to spark, so quickly to ignite.

I am doing all right for one born of such ignominy.

I remember hearing the word "stigmata" for the first time in one of Fr. Kavanagh's sermons – it was a God-fearing village for the most part, the one from which we hailed, and I listened rapt, and always a little unnerved — but I took to that particular word right away. Stigmata: it sounded so foreign, so loaded with mystery. I began to think that I was a persecuted martyr, suffering in some vague way, but the holes were never in my hands, the holes were in my heart, empty spaces I didn't yet know how to fill.

Fr. Kavanagh often looked down from the altar upon me with pity, and that ancient Sister Margaret too, her poisonous eyes, sometimes the slightest shake of her head; but the kids in school, they never really bothered me all that much: an occasional jibe, but nothing that stung, nothing that stayed. Village people can surprise you sometimes, their hearts more often than not are wholesome, even if what comes out of their mouths is sometimes coarse, or hurtful.

Everyone knew about our situation. That is the way it is in a small village. Everyone knows everyone else. You can't escape. Not as a child at least. It takes time, time to grow up, and you can get out if you make the right moves — I'm just not sure my parents ever did, if they ever truly knew how.

When they spoke to me about it all eventually it was not really with regret —perhaps they were beyond all that, or it was just too late — but all their words were tinged with a kind of sorrow; they were aware of all the wrongs they had committed and they managed to come to terms with things, if not able to account for them all. Things could have been otherwise — what life cannot say this? They understood that the sins of the fathers weren't nearly as bad as their own, but, like I say, too late, perhaps it was all just too late. They escaped punishment, the lashes of the law certainly; perhaps it would have been better if Fr. Kavanagh's notions of hell had turned out to be actual. Sin, sin: did anyone in the village even know what that word meant?

None of it hit home until I was maybe eight or nine, that age when a child becomes more aware of what family is, who fits in what place, who is related to whom, what role each has to play in that structure, that tree. What is an aunt? What is an uncle? Cousins. What those are? You begin to tease things out, you begin to put things together.

I certainly didn't deserve any of it.

You just get born.

There's nothing you can ever do about that.

They deliver you, kicking and screaming into the world; the nurses wipe you off and give you a gentle slap: that's your introduction, see how you fare.

And then you get held … and they tell you who they are.

Mommy.

Daddy.

Both of them.

MommyDaddy.

DaddyMommy.

They were always together, for me, as much as they could be; good and loving, playing their part; let us not judge too harshly the sins of youth, so much can be shed with the wisdom of age. There it is again, that concept, sin. Perhaps my story is all about just that, trying to understand what that sin means.

Then you get held … and they tell you who you are.

I managed to go to a good university, studied English and Philosophy – the latter certainly useful when pondering the uncertainties of life, the big questions and the lack of answers – and I have found myself a decent man, David, who manages to make me laugh at my odd predicament, the way I got here – he's a psychiatrist, has a trick or two up his tweedy sleeves, I could've done a lot worse.

I like music as much as my parents ever did; I even have cassette tapes that still work on a cassette player, vintage things, maybe worth something, maybe worth nothing at all, anyway, they're part of me, they're part of this story, too.

They are quite charming, my parents, as I'm sure many would attest, and they are still youthful, vigorous, middle-age having not really yet set in. I go over their story a lot, wondering how things could have been different. If they hadn't made the choices they had made. If they had stayed away from that pond. Stayed in their own rooms with their own separate sounds, licking whatever wounds they had, and they did have them: wounds, troubles. In teens, as we all know, they often treble in size anyway, bulge out of all proportions, what hope did they ever have?

I just noticed in the newspaper today that they are stopping the cultivating of peat in the bogs of Ireland. Did you know that? All of course in accordance with EU regulations, environmental laws. Back then, in the eighties, our village was surrounded by bog: black, thick, wet land; you could stumble and fall right in if you weren't careful, could get subsumed right into the muddy puddles. Or you might climb out of it, like a creature from the black lagoon, declaring yourself, yawping about your sins. This is actually how I write my poems, they are often declaratory, often a little insane.

I'm not a published poet, there's no book, not yet, unfortunately, but I get the occasional one into a notable magazine and this sustains me, for now. David says it's a form of therapy, all catharsis. He may have a point.

Here's one I've only recently started. It goes like this:

He has music. She has monsters.
She has music. He knows of monsters, too.

His music is not hers. Not yet.
The music is not theirs. Not yet.

And the monsters, the monsters, the monsters will be *their* monsters.

This fragment feels like the beginning of something. It might even be an epic! Who knows? The creativity is the thing. I have that in my blood.

And at least I am sure of the theme: Monsters.

It'll take time to expand, to see where I'm actually heading with it.

But the theme is there all right: Monsters, where they come from ... where they go ... and sins ... and understanding ... and ...

Don't judge them too severely.
Like I said: wisdom. Age.

I am the product of some kind of madness, and this is its tale.

TELL ME YOUR TROUBLES AND DOUBTS

1

He has music. She has monsters.
She has music. He knows of monsters, too.

His music is not hers. Not yet.
The music is not theirs. Not yet.

And the monsters, the monsters, the monsters will be *their* monsters.

2

They take turns kicking a stone along the dirt road. The mud is unusually dry and it cracks and breaks under their tread.

This is a place of crops and stone walls, of livestock trudging languorously in fields, the livelong rural quietude only ever perforated by unseen trilling birds boldly claiming their territories, or some big-wheeled machine out turning and churning, raking and breaking. All these things occur in their appropriate season, without fuss or fanfare, a good ten miles from the nearest sizeable town, the nearest thing Laura and Kevin refer to as *civilisation*.

This is their neck of the woods, a neck they'd like to grasp and choke, and not just on this particular almost-autumn day, but any day, or *most* days. Laura Maloney is fifteen years old and her cousin Kevin O'Brien matches her for that. They are on their way home from school again, together again, on this unusually dry trail, and even their strides now match, causing tiny wisps of fine brown dust to sweep over the toes of their black brogues. They are bemused by this fortnight without rain, the hot and splendid simmering September sun, the rarity of it all, bemused they are, and quite rightly so.

෨

Dark green and grey school uniforms – a recent addition to the school and compulsory now for each student – say nothing about their personalities, but their schoolbags do: Kevin's scrawled all over with band names and badges, rock music buttons proclaiming that he is a serious music fan with serious alternative tastes and everyone should be made aware of it; Laura's bag is impeccably clean and cared for: no signs, no scrawls, no hanging trinket or badge, not even a wayward chocolate smudge.

They walk along the lonely laneway like this. Like they always do. Side by side. Thrown together in the cosmos. Fated.

They wear identical Sony Walkman headsets, bright orange foam pieces covering their ears, and their tastes cannot be more different. In Laura's ears "Girls Just Wanna Have Fun" contrasts sharply with Joy Division's "Dead Souls" thundering in Kevin's, and to anyone passing by in the stifling afternoon – there is no one passing by in the stifling afternoon – the sound would appear tinny and irrelevant. In their ears however, the sounds are anything but: they colour in their young and fertile imaginations, they colour life.

Laura begins to move her muscles to the music, her hips in sudden sway to the pop grooves, and she is soon pulling away from her companion and dancing ostentatiously in a shimmying Lauper parody.

"They just wanna, they just wanna…"

Kevin feels his face reddening, embarrassed for her and her corny, uncalled-for movements, and for it to be such an atrocious choice of music to boot. He pulls his headphones off his ears, and on hearing her awful attempts at accompaniment, curls his upper lip in derision.

"Shit song. Cut it out."

Laura pulls her headphones down and glares at him. "What?"

His message has the blunt brevity of a telegram: "Shit song. Stop."

"It's not shit."

"It fucking is. It's a shit song. It's stupid. Grow up."

She shrugs.

Kevin puts Joy Division back in his ears, nodding in time to the heavy bass, the industrial thrum, and nodding too, as if to acknowledge the rightness of everything he does, the decisions he makes, especially the tunes he allows to soundtrack his life, what he is free to choose – those tapes he pesters his mother to order in for him because the pokey shops around the village are never going to have them and he rarely gets all the way into the town.

They are not used to these days without rain. So often have they walked this same path without umbrellas and have been soaked to the bone before ever getting a foot inside the cosiness of their homes. What is up with the weather this past week? An *Indian summer* they heard it called, though they don't know exactly what that means. Summer was well over, calendar-wise, September nearly done and dusted too. They have heard their teachers going on about the ozone layer; the science experts harping on about it every other day, telling them not to be using hairspray anymore, or air-fresheners either; they have to become responsible for their actions now, no CFCs. Do they want the whole planet heating by degrees? Do they? Is that what they want?

Laura has no intention of giving up on her array of sprays, and Kevin isn't surrendering his underarm deodorant – the scientists can sort it out themselves. Who cares if the weather gets a little warmer in the decades to come? It isn't going to herald the end of the world, now is it?

Laura hangs her headphones on her neck and Kevin, sensing that she wants to talk, groans and makes like removing his is extremely bothersome, the way only a hyperbolic teenager can.

"What?" he says.

"Can you play it?"

"Play what?"

"'Girls Just Wanna Have Fun'. On the synthesizer?"

He considers. He considers like a great maestro would consider: affectedly, his lips pursed and his mouth twisted as if to show he mulls and he muses. Even though he knows that this all is beneath him, he is still prepared to give her a moment of his time, just because they are related, because they are first cousins, his mother a sister to her mother (although estranged, direct opposites, the two women, only a stone's throw away, but more like magnets, ever-opposed) and they are bound by loss, by both absent fathers – where did those two go? They can perhaps understand the mothers, two sisters who have never really gotten on, but the fathers, completely gone, upped and left, where ... or more significantly: why? The mystery and misery has made these cousins close, tight and forever together like this, and this is the way their conversations often go on days like this, meandering, digressions into pop songs, and whether the boy can play them on his instrument ... if it wouldn't trouble the maestro too much ...

"Maybe I can. But it's a shit song. Who'd want to? It's already dated. How many years ago was that piece of shit anyway?"

"I like it."

"You would. You like all kinds of shit songs."

"No, I don't."

"Yes, you do."

He wants to ridicule her for her love of The Bangles, for Madonna, for George Michael and Spandau Ballet, for Nick Heyward, for those gay blond brothers (he wouldn't even dignify by naming) but he refrains, or maybe the school day has worn him out and it would take too much energy to get him risen and riled; instead, affectedly again, trying for a twist of bitterness, but with actual sincerity, says:

"You need a proper musical education."

Laura sighs. She knows her cousin is sometimes a bit on the pompous side; a bit of an arse at the best of times, no denying it. But she is used to him. So many days on the same trek, you get used to a person; you get to know them intimately, for good or bad. She *knows* him. Good and bad.

Kevin pats his pockets and roots around in his natty schoolbag.

"Got any food on you?"

"Food?"

"Like chocolate or something?"

He is imagining an un-melted Dairy Milk to suddenly appear, or something cheaper, chewier: a sticky pink Wham bar, to cling to every tooth, fill him with fizz.

"No. Come to my house and I'll make you some toast."

She clutches her stomach and swoons at her own suggestion. Toast. So simple. And lashings of butter spread right on top of it. The way she always does it. Her culinary skills are quite limited, her taste buds unrefined, but she doesn't care, the thought of toast divine. Nor does she particularly care if what they say about butter now is true, that it is bad for you, makes you put on weight, or worse, clogs up the arteries – she is not prepared to substitute it for the fake stuff that was appearing on the shelves in supermarkets these days. Only the real stuff will do for her, the thick, hard blocks of pure yellow stuff. No half-hearted measures. If you are going to have toast, then you need real butter. Simple as that. As long as there is always a sliced loaf in the house, Laura will not starve. That toaster gets used about as much as her Walkman. Even the TV seems to get more respite.

"My mother's at work. There won't be a scrap in the house. Lazy bitch rarely goes to the supermarket these days."

This is another thing Kevin might go off and get riled up about, the fact that since his father had left – and that was years ago – his mother has gotten lazier, less inclined to do the most rudimentary stuff, like shopping for food. Or even taking the hoover out once in a while and giving the carpets a bit of a going over. He could swear the dust was playing havoc with his breathing, and often he has coughing fits in the middle of the night, keeping him awake and frustrated. She makes endless cups of tea, his mother, and if she isn't drinking them herself, then she is bringing them meekly up to him, a polite knock on the door, a tentative enter, as if apologizing for all that has gone wrong, as if she is shouldering all the blame. Kevin doesn't want to think of the family's unexpected dismantling. He is aware of the rumours. Some villagers say things out loud, not even bothering to whisper. He doesn't know who to believe, what to believe. Sometimes he thinks ignorance might be preferable, better being kept in the dark. What was it he overheard one of the boys in school say? Existing *like a mushroom... kept in the dark and fed a load of shit.* Kevin doesn't want any tea. And he wants no intrusions on his kingdom. Of course he doesn't. He is an adolescent boy. He wants a little more privacy, a little less of the bungling mother with another cup of Barry's, barging into his lair and mildly (passive-aggressively) complaining about the loudness of the music. What would be the use in explaining the sheer genius of *Psychocandy* to her, how the album needed to be heard loud, that was the point of the chaotic thrust of the feedback, the hidden pop melodies strangled or suffocating but trying to break through a wash of glorious noise. She'd never get it. His mother likes Daniel O'Donnell.

Kevin sighs to the stillness of the afternoon, the fading light, the sense of perpetual doom.

It is as if she can read his thoughts.

"At least your mother is young," she says. "And not sick all the time."

This often happens, as if some kind of telekinesis is involved, or connections through their separate headphones, or maybe it is just the fact that they are cousins, and are always together, perhaps it's only that, in tune with one another.

She side-foots the over-kicked stone into the ditch as an attempt to get his attention. That little game is over.

Her mother's sickness weighs upon her. How can one woman get so many illnesses? And her own serious illness, epilepsy, those furious fits that strike her with severity when she least expects it – has that all been passed down to her? DNA: another hot topic in her chemistry class that she rarely pays any attention to. There is so much she doesn't understand. So much still to get a handle on. But she is young. Confusion is to be expected. She hopes it will all someday make sense to her, understanding life, understanding herself and the quagmire in which she is so often sunk.

She tries another attempt at conversation:

"Are we the only children in the village with single mothers? How unlucky is that?"

"Nope, Margie Cummins," he says.

She is always surprised he can ever manage this: somehow able to balance heavy bass, spiky guitars and the doleful mutterings of Ian Curtis in his ears with the ramblings of his cousin, somehow able to hear and make perfect sense of both.

"Margie Cummins," he reiterates. "She lives with her mum. Single mother. The father went off to Australia with some big-titted slut from the creamery."

"Big-titted slut from the creamery!" Laura can't help but parrot the phrase and let loose a raucous laugh that rises from deep down in her diaphragm, certainly the heartiest of her ordinary day. It is much better than thinking about her mother and her ever-nausea, or the worry of her own affliction, better than considering DN-bloody-A.

"And Margie herself. She has huge tits an' all. I wouldn't mind getting my hands on …"

"You're such a pervert," she says cutting him off, but the laugh still present in her reproach.

"I'm fifteen," he says, matter-of-factly, conclusively, and it is hard to counter that.

He stops walking then, comes to a sudden stop and takes his schoolbag from his shoulder. He dumps it into Laura's hands.

She knows what is coming now. They've been through this little routine once or twice before.

He moves to the side of the dirt road, looks around cautiously, and then unzips his fly.

"Need a slash. Won't be long."

Laura slings Kevin's bag onto her free shoulder. For some reason his is always heavier than hers. Perhaps it is those music magazines that he carries around and furtively reads in class: *Hot Press, NME, Melody Maker,* hidden in Geography books, scanned with relish when he should be doing History or Irish.

He sighs, the relief apparent.

"Could you not have waited two more minutes? We're nearly home."

"Sorry. Bursting."

She wonders why he has been keeping it in all day. Is there a reason why he doesn't do it in the school? Is it because of the fellas who hang out there between classes, fearful of what they would do to a music-loving boy with alternative tastes... is that it? Or is it that he just likes exposing himself, flaunting the fact that it can be whipped out and all over and done with so easily. It is a dare: *go on look if you want*, which she would never do of course, this filthy habit of his, no, she wouldn't ever.

Steam rises from the pee in the sultry September air, and from the few steps behind him Laura can smell the ammoniac tang of it permeating. She retreats a little to the other side of the narrow road where she picks a blackberry off a bramble, examines it for insects, and pops it into her mouth.

"Could put these on toast," she mutters.

His back is still turned to her, he is nearing the end of his flow, content with the letting go; he hasn't heard her.

"Blackberries," she says.

"I'd give them another week. Hardly ripe yet."

"They look full and black enough to me."

Kevin zips up his fly, faces her again: there is so much that he has to always explain to her, what would she do without him?

With delicate fingers Laura picks off another berry and offers it to him. He shakes his head, stands his ground.

"Someone will catch you someday…with your lad hanging out," she says, and she eats that picked berry too.

"Who cares?"

"I do. It's disgusting."

"You're just dying to see my big cock."

She gasps.

"Yeah," she says then, giving in to laughter once again, "I'm sure it's a fecking monster."

He nods as if agreeing with her, as if she has hit the nail right on the head.

"Anyway, we're cousins, not supposed to be showing each other anything, certainly not…"

She cuts herself off, aware her tone is unnecessarily overwrought.

He is not listening to her anymore. Instead, he is examining the same bramble and the blackberries bountifully sprouting there. Softly then, he starts to sing:

"She's lost control again."

"Don't you dare! Not with that fucking song."

He baits her with the Joy Division lyrics, a song about losing bodily control, the scourge of epilepsy; singing flatly:

there is an unfortunate lack of lilt in his singing voice too, and he murders what little melody the morose number ever had.

Laura dumps the schoolbag back into his arms and thumps him hard on the bicep. For one as wiry as him, his body is tough, surprisingly strong, and the boy hardly feels it. Or maybe it is just the fact that he *is* a boy, and they are all like that, vigorous when they want to be, tougher than you think, coiled tight, at any minute ready to spring.

"Horrible song," she snaps. "And wash your hands before I give you any toast."

They stand in the middle of this quiet country road. No car passes. No farm machine rumbles. No one takes a dog for a walk. There is hardly a sound at all save for a couple of distant crows circling and cawing up the sky, and the sound of Kevin now ransacking his bag.

He pulls out a packet of cigarettes and with it a cheap, garish pink plastic lighter, and when he is sure that he will not be spotted, he lights up.

"You're just full of bad habits, aren't you?"

The boy shrugs.

"You should stop," she says.

"But I've only just started."

She looks at him disapprovingly.

"If you're trying to be ultra-cool like Aidan Carty, it's not working."

"Cool? Just because he's got blond hair … fuck him."

"I would," Laura says, and as they resume their walk she allows herself a little dream: Aidan Carty, strutting down the school corridor, his longish blond hair blowing back like in an American rock video. The camera turns from him to show a mechanical wind-blower and two of his friends – clearly sycophants in awe – gaze adoringly up at their lion-maned messiah.

Laura giggles.

Kevin looks at her, miffed at not being allowed in on the private joke. The sooner he gets to the sanctuary of his own bedroom the better. Perhaps he'll write a new song, or at least jot down a few thoughts in his notebook. He has been creatively bereft of late, and it is something he needs to sort out. Get back into the swing of it: writers' block, perhaps that's all it is. He is still peckish, and the idea of toast has taken root in his mind. His stomach's rumble is as loud as anything Peter Hook has to offer on his cassette tape.

They walk on, their headphones hanging around their necks, buzzing against the hush of the country afternoon. They aren't far from her house but Laura is intent on obliterating that hush with conversation.

"Learn any new song?"

"Don't You Forget About Me."

He pauses to see if the title registers. It doesn't.

"Another shit song, really," he adds, "but it's easy to play."

"I don't know that song."

"Yeah you do. Everybody does. It's on the radio the whole fucking time. For years!"

"Nope. Doesn't ring any bells."

Kevin shakes his head.

"*The Breakfast Club*?"

"Haven't seen it. Video's broken. Who sings it?"

"Can't tell you. You wouldn't understand."

"What?"

"You're a simple mind."

"What?"

Kevin stops abruptly and looks at her, hardly able to believe her ignorance.

"That was a clue, dumbbell."

"What?"

"You're so fucking thick."

"I don't get it."

"A *simple mind*? The band? Simple Minds?"

"Oh, right."

"For fuck's sake."

She tries to hide her embarrassment by pretending she doesn't care.

"It's just a fucking song."

"Because you're retarded."

"Fuck you. I'm not retarded. That's a nasty word."

They bump shoulders as they lumber on, Laura looking increasingly irritated – Kevin has that way of annoying her, and she has promised herself countless times that she would not let it get to her … but it always does. *He* always does. She loves him, as a family member, as a companion even, as someone she is stuck with, he even helps her in so many ways, when she gets trapped in her affliction, but he annoys the fuck out of her too, his haughty attitude, his pomposity, not to mention his frequently explosive temper.

"I'm not retarded. You know I hate that word. Take it back."

He lets a few seconds of silence ring and just when she thinks he'll relent, he fires back:

"But you are … kinda."

"Fuck you."

"And your language is atrocious. You've got to stop the fucking swearing."

She tries hard not to lash out and smack him one. She won't, she won't take the bait, not this time.

"I'm not retarded," she says, aiming for seriousness and for an end to the argument.

"A spastic then."

She elbows him hard.

"Fucking hell!"

"Your language is atrocious," she says, her voice an almost perfect imitation of his. "And it's epilepsy. I can't help it, can I? So fuck you!"

Kevin does not want to lose. Even in this, the final stage of their saunter home, he'll fight for the last word:

"That hurling helmet you used to wear in class, now, some may have laughed … but I think it rather suited you."

"You're such a dick, do you know that? I had to wear it. I was young. In case I fell and banged my head on the desk. I don't wear it anymore. You know that. You're such a dick."

He smiles to himself, knowing how easy it is to get the upper hand, loving the feeling of victory, of superiority. He is mean to her at times, and at times he even feels guilty about this. He does care for her, really, he does, more than she will ever know.

"Why do you walk home with me then, if I'm such a dick? Why not with your *own* friends?" he says.

"Why don't *you* walk home with *your* friends? Or is your only friend your little pen pal in America?" she snorts, cynically. "Still writing gay letters to him? Jason, is it? Sad. Fucking sad."

"Fuck you."

It's true, he does have a pen pal, and Jason, a couple of years older, who of course he has never met, seems cool, talks about American bands: Pere Ubu, The Replacements.

He even has his own shotgun; his grandfather takes him hunting in the woods – once he shot at a deer, but apparently he missed, inches. He saw a mountain lion too; Jason wrote how he had nearly shat his pants.

Kevin's pen pal. The phrase sounded so quaint: *pen pal.*

Laura has him on the ropes now: it's all over Kevin's irked face – such a quick turnaround – and she is not prepared to let him off so lightly.

"Or you'd rather be playing your gloomy little pop songs in your room, thinking you're Nik Kershaw."

"Nik Kershaw!"

"Howard Jones, then."

"Fuck me, where did you pull those names from? They've already got their feet up in the retirement home."

"Well, I don't know the names of the boring fuckers who play keyboards in The Cure, of the Talking fucking Heads, do I?"

"No, you don't … but you should."

Turnaround.

Then turnaround again.

Every day.

Same path.

This is the way their arguments go.

The quarrel takes them all the way around the bushy corner to the gravel drive of Laura's home, when they are suddenly, without warning, stopped in their tracks.

What they see shocks them to their very core.

Their feet become stuck, like they've been suddenly glued there with some industrial-strength adhesive, or hypnotized by some ostentatious stage showman. They cannot move.

What they see is a dusty white ambulance starting its engine and driving slowly past them. No siren. No fuss.

An ambulance?

In the middle of the day?

Tom Dennehy stands solemnly waiting for them at the front of the house.

Kevin, breaking out of his spell, quickly flicks his cigarette into the dry bushes.

Tom's arms are behind his back and his stiff comportment is that of a man with serious information to impart.

"Uncle Tom? What's going on?"

Kevin can't keep the surprise and worry out of his voice, but there is also a sense of awareness, a sense of knowing, that this was always going to be the case, that one day, this ... an inevitability.

"Laura, love, I'm sorry, your mother, I'm afraid ..."

Tom's bushy eyebrows furrow. He doesn't really know how to go on; all the practiced solemnity so soon has withered away.

The cousins look at each other, a riot of emotions overwhelming their features, as if a selection of dark-coloured dyes has just been added to tumblers of the clearest water.

"No," says Laura, trying to put order to the chaos of her colours, and then with more obvious distress: "Fuck! No!"

Tom goes to her in an awkward attempt to embrace, but she pulls away briskly, almost violently. As she does so her Walkman slips from her hip and the cassette flips out when it hits the stony ground.

Frantically she falls to it, wrapping the brown, shiny, ultra-thin tape around her hands, unravelling it the more she draws on it, watching it twisting and folding upon itself, and the central tiny wheels of the cassette turn in tiny spins.

Kevin looks down upon her sympathetically. His poor cousin, his friend, the one he cares for when she is in the mad grasp of her grim enchantment, now like a mad surgeon pulling the intestines out of an open torso in some gruesome Grand Guignol. Mad, maddened cousin, unable to control this moment too: this derangement.

His earlier scoffing and derision have transformed utterly. He's sorry. Guilt grabs him. He's always sorry. Poor thing: Laura. Now there is nothing but pity. Now only that for her: purest pity.

For his cousin on the gravel.

As he watches her unravel.

A PRAYER FOR SOMETHING BETTER

3

The clothes he wears are not his funeral clothes. His funeral clothes are hung up neatly on a hanger – his mother's doing – ready for the following day, or is it the day after that? Kevin is unsure how many days it takes to get a funeral underway. Are they able to organise it all so quickly? Is that how fast things happen in a village? In a place where so few remain, that when one departs it is all *business*, the hole dug before you are even cold? Is that how it goes?

Won't they have to contact Laura's father?

Won't they have to find him first?

Bring him back?

No one knows where Declan Maloney is, so … how do you do that? How do you find someone who does not want to be found?

Kevin looks at the hanging funeral suit his mother has borrowed – how quick she was to run over and get it from Mrs. Nolan – Mrs. Nolan who always seems to be ready with supplies for any occasion: birth, marriage, and most of all death, as if crisis is her business and not the little bakery she runs, not custard slices and chocolate éclairs. Kevin's mother had hardly heard the news about Dymphna, her very own sister, and already she was going through the gears, no time for grief, there had been enough of that over the years; organisation: that was what was needed. Action stations. They hadn't really been close, never felt the need to be, had nothing in common from the earliest age, and with the husbands gone they just saw loss in each other's eyes, only that, gargantuan loss, the only things they really had in common then: loss, and *their* failure, which was obviously dispiriting for both; thus they kept themselves to themselves.

Kevin looks at the stiff black suit hoping it will fit; he does not want to look like an idiot, standing there, amid the mourners, amid the glut of gossipers, no, not with everyone gawking at him – you still wanted to look cool, no matter what the occasion.

He is used to wearing dark colours. Kevin always wears black when he can. When he isn't in his school uniform – or his *prison garb,* as he snidely calls it – he wears dark garments: trousers, long cardigans.

He should at least try it on though, see how the suit looks on him, but as vain as he is he doesn't bother, succumbs to the evening's languor. Instead he sits at his bedroom desk and fiddles with the synthesizer that lies large and heavy there. He feels no love for any of the sounds he absentmindedly creates, other things press upon him: everyone expected Laura's mother to go … and she just did. Just like that. Like a candle snuffed out with spitted fingers. Was she old? Laura thought so. How old *was* she, his aunt? How old is Kevin's own mother? He doesn't even know.

Kevin thinks of his cousin now and he knows she will be crying throughout this night, another adult has gone from them, or *taken,* as is more common local parlance, like it is actually the shenanigans of some thief out there, some Bogeyman doing all the damage, operating when the sun sets, whisking bodies away, a stealer of souls.

He wonders what it is with this family, with this village on the whole. Their grandparents, Kevin and Laura's, those who had lived in the village, they had all died young, hadn't they? What is it with this place … is it cursed?

Laura knew her mother had been sick for a long time – that at least was no family secret, everybody knew that much – and now she is set to join the rest of the ghosts; the village growing only ever sparser, more space for the lonesome winds to blow around the forlorn fields, more space for desolation, for silence, for feelings of emptiness. This is no place for youngsters. This is no place for those who want out and elsewhere, who are growing up on pop music from London and New York – they want elsewhere, anywhere at all, anywhere at all will do.

It is still a shock though. Dymphna gone. Laura's mum. Death has the ability to do that: even though you know it is on the cards, when it comes, it is never the right time. There never *is* a right time, Kevin thinks, and he needs no song to verify that.

He thinks about calling Laura on the phone. He can picture her trampling down the stairs to the hallway to cancel that obnoxious resounding ringing; he can even see her wet cheeks rubbing up against the receiver, can see the sour scene all too clearly.

He chooses not to call. He is not sure if he'd even have the right words. It's different when you write them in a notebook, different when you sing them in a song, however badly, or when you trial your own notes on your own instrument. But on the telephone? Different matter. You are expected to know what to say. How to handle yourself.

The voice unadorned. The sentiment naked. He isn't ready. He'll see her the next day. He'll be better able to deal with her then. He'll sympathize. He'll console. He'll offer commiserations properly. This is all going to be new for him. A funeral, or wake, or whatever is going to happen, it is going to be a new experience for him; he was too young to remember those stricken elders.

It will be new for Laura too, a funeral. But not *loss*. Not *absence*. There is nothing new about those things. These teens are well acquainted. The absent fathers have seen to that. Kevin in his quiet bedroom shakes his head sadly to himself, and then shakes his head with added vigour, as if to dispel the very absurdity of it. The absent fathers. It has the ring of a band name about it. *The Absent Fathers.* It could be a glum Goth band from the north of England, their promotion videos full of arty mist and insinuating shadow: The Absent Fathers might even be the band he will someday form and front himself, all white face paint and spiky gravity-defying hair, platinum-selling records. A tribute, maybe, to Tadhg O'Brien and Declan Maloney. The Absent Fathers. Where are they now exactly? Where are they now?

He tries a few more notes on the keyboard, but they sound hollow. He tinkles a few more times, but no lines stick, no melody climbs out of that muck to attract any attention. It is all random, inchoate, it is all rather pointless.

A cry sounds from outside the house, and he thinks it might have been a cat, or maybe one of the many foxes who seem to be multiplying at a rapid rate, the only population increasing round these parts. They get closer to the houses too, incrementally, out of the forests and their secluded dens, braver, banging around dustbins when the sun goes down, flashes of rust, sightings of scampering brush.

Kevin thinks of the cry of the banshee. Local lore has it that an old wailing woman crying in the night is a harbinger of death. But he is pretty sure the only wailing woman this night is a young one, his unfortunate cousin. He knows the sound of her every sob, has known each one since they were infants; he could write the sheet music for her every single sigh, knows the shape of her salty tears, his first cousin.

He finds and opens his notebook. This is the one that sits alongside his collection of cassette tapes, the copybook marked "Lyrics". He goes to a new, crisp page, presses down hard upon it so the book stays flat. His pen hovers over the page … but he only gets as far as the title: Laura. This is the heading. This is to be the title of a new poem or perhaps a new song. Right there at the top of the page: one word. Her name. The rest of the page is blank.

He sits back in his chair, swivels, then puts the Bic biro into his mouth and sucks on it, chewing on the hard plastic cap even when it hurts his molars reminding him he needs to brush more often, needs a visit to the dentist – they told him as much in his last school check-up. He will get no further with his creativity tonight and he knows it. There is way too much sadness stultifying the air, a sadness that hangs heavy: it does not even have the grace to mould into melancholy, it is just pure sorrow. Every breath he takes seems stale; there is something wrong with the day, obviously.

A fox outside – it must be, mustn't it? A fox? That strangled cry. It cries again and sends a shiver down his spine.

The poster on the wall has the only banshees he really believes in. Siouxsie and the Banshees. She stares down upon him, her dark eyes, her messy Gothic get-up, Siouxsie: his post-punk queen. This is how a woman should be: sulky, angry, defiant, and yet romantic when she needs to be. Deep. That's it. Deeper than the rest of them. Girls do not *just* want to have fun.

Someday he will convince Laura that this is the kind of music she should be soaking up and not the base nonsense that usually fills her ears. Yes, he knows that he is a musical snob, but he can't change any of that. Music to him is like religion – or in his case atheism – you make your mind up firmly about these things when you are at his age. You make your big decisions or you have your big realizations then. Fifteen. Sixteen years old. Belief in God? No, thank you. Siouxsie, yes. Bauhaus, yes. The Birthday Party, of course. Or the more recent Bad Seeds, sure. Why not? And that is that. There is no going back. The idea of God just never seemed to fit. Why, when He had so many of them on their knees in St. Finbar's church of a Sunday morning, should He treat them all so badly, take away their loved ones? Put them in boats to better places. Why would He do that? It makes no sense. He does that because He is not there.

Kevin gets up and goes to the stereo that sits on his little bedside locker. He presses play and waits. It only takes a couple of seconds for The Cure to start in with "One Hundred Years" and this all makes complete sense to him. It is as far from Cyndi Lauper as he can possibly get. The edginess of it, the galloping of the drums and Gallup's rumbling bass, the swirling synth. Robert Smith's perfect lines of poetry. Every line. Every bloody line. As if they are not only the lines of songs but actual physical lines running through Kevin's mind when he hears them, lines that somehow transform to be wires, high wires running across a dark circus tent, a Big Top say, and he becomes an acrobat swinging there, from one to the other. Or no, Laura. Laura swinging in his mind. Laura on the wires. Sequined. Better. He should write all this down. Laura. It could be his poem. Or a new song. The bones of it anyway. On the wires swinging. A girl. He has the title. His cousin. Her name. *Laura.* That's the title. His cousin crying out. Crying out into the night. There is no ghost. There is no God. There is no … there is only a tormented girl. Anguished. Her dead mother. Dead now. And Laura crying too for her absent father. Where is he? Where did he go, that Declan Maloney? Where did any of them go? Crying for an uncertain future. And swinging. Swinging high upon the wires. Heaven forbid that she might fall; there is only ever one to catch her. Yes, he is mean to her sometimes, but there is only ever one to catch her when she falls. Kevin's open arms.

He pleads with his silent Siouxsie. *Help!*

The rock star glowers.

He takes a look at his empty notebook. Just one word on top. His cousin's name: Laura. And the rest … the rest of the blank page glares back at him, intimidating. Empty. This place. Empty.

Although he writes nothing down, he nods to himself, telling himself that he is satisfied with these musings. Something will come. Something proper. Something better will come, no doubt. He hopes that in Laura's bedroom, in her gloom, that she is all right, that no fox cries outside her window, nothing that might scare her. She's unlucky, his cousin. He knows that much. Laura is terribly unlucky. Crying into the night. She probably is. Crying away into this awful night. Probably.

He recalls her on the ground outside her house, pulling tape from her Walkman, the tape, coming faster and faster out of the machine, little toothed wheels spinning.

He recalls her wearing the hurling helmet in the classroom a few years ago – doctors recommended it, the authorities insisted on it, the fits that came upon her, they were just too regular. And just last week, daydreaming she was, looking out the window and far off into the distance, not paying the slightest attention to the teacher, Mrs. Kane, and her rattling on and about the formation of oxbow lakes in front of a cloudy blackboard.

Laura's daydreams soon started to fade that afternoon and a whole other story whelmed.

Her eyes began to roll around in her head, her body began to tremble and she fell hard to the floor. This was her curse. It was there again. And nothing she could do about it, nothing at all. When it came, it came. Her eyes were open as if she stared her demon right in its face. And it horrified her. It made her body gyrate and shake right then and there on the dirty classroom floor. She could see dust motes and a chewed blue biro cap – was that Kevin's? – and there was the plastic transparent corner of a protractor; but even as she saw those things, even as they somehow registered, her curse didn't allow her to fully engage, she could not reach out for anything, not even for herself, could not break the trance. She never could. It was what it was. The happening. That regular happening. When she least expected it. It had nothing to do with the formation of oxbow lakes. The formation of oxbow lakes had happened millennia ago. This was right now. *Again* and *right now*. Epilepsy is always about the *again* and the *right now*, and when you least expect it.

Kevin ran to her from the back of the classroom and without panicking seemed to know exactly what to do. He cradled the back of her head in his hand and let her head – it was hardly a lift, so tender was the motion – gently up and onto his lap. He was calm and he was in complete control. He had been there before. They all had. The other students looked unsurprised at the proceedings, the drama not so much a drama at all – there were other things going on in their teenage lives that demanded their attention, and mad Laura shaking on the floor again was nothing to get excited about. The teacher watched on too, leaning forward, her chalky hands on her desk, another spectator, hardly alarmed, nodding assuredly, letting her cousin Kevin take care of the situation with typical aplomb. It's what he did. It's what he always did.

The Cure play on the stereo in his bedroom.

The night is still the night, still a day or two before a funeral, a day or two before a wake, or a gnashing of teeth.

Time sometimes goes incredibly slowly. Anticipatory nights. Or nights when you don't know what's what. He listens to the music.

If Laura listened to this type of music, then maybe she'd be better able to deal with the pain that she is in no doubt immersed. That's what all those songs are about. Pain. Even the songs that play now. Pain and how to deal with it. Rage at it. Defy it. That is what he thinks about on so many nights like these. Pain. The absent fathers. *The Absent Fathers!* He is the frontman, imagine that now. He moves towards the front of the stage, moves towards his window, spiky, gravity-defying hair – maybe it's green, or pink. He looks out at the crowd, the fans, the darkness, mostly it's his own face coming back at him … it's just a window … you have to focus to see beyond your own reflection.

His arms are folded now and he moves his hips gently to the music. This band he adores. Obsesses over. The way music should be: obsessed over, the way a girl should be.

The Cure. It is a name he has often pondered. Because there is none, he thinks, for so many ailments, no cure, only the music itself: *that* is the cure – it's a super clever name if you gave it any thought, though Kevin doubts anyone ever has. He should sleep. But he is not tired. And this band, this band is so damn good. He does not want to sleep. He does not want to sleep at all tonight. Keep sleep away, more time; give him more time with this.

Rain droplets slide down the window and his eyes follow one droplet in particular making its course down the pane. He sniggers to himself – he is like one of those sad-eyed romantics in an *MT-USA* pop video, the type Vincent Hanley would introduce, and the video's lovelorn hero pining, wondering if she'll ever answer his phone call again, how could he have been so stupid to let her go; he's sorry, so sorry, darling. *Hello, is it me you're looking for?* Kevin sniggers again.

He turns away from the window and goes to his desk. He sings along with the track, doing his best Robert Smith impression, trying to inject as much cavern and hollow into his tone as he can muster.

He picks up his pen again and goes to write something in that blank notebook, but just as swiftly he changes his mind. Instead he drops the pen on the desk, sits back in his chair and just listens to the music.

It is enough.

It is, really.

His music.

It is enough.

For this night at least, it is enough.

There is a knock at the door.

A second or two later the door slowly opens and there stands his mother, with a cup of warm milk and a plate of Bourbon biscuits. She tries to make eye contact with him but he is intent on ignoring her. This is an art much practiced, maybe he has perfected. She enters slowly, putting the glass and plate on his desk, careful that the slightest drop of milk won't escape and make its way towards the synthesizer. She goes to the stereo and turns the volume down, glancing at him to see how he will react, whether he will let loose his temper, let childishness get the better of him, again, and explode in a tantrum – he has done this many times before. Once he lashed out and put his fist through a framed picture on their wall. A family photo. His father in it. He had cut his knuckles badly, but didn't need stitches, the blood though, the blood poured from him, and the incident stung more than the wound. He wants to lash out again. Boy, does he want to react to this right now. The imposition. The touching of his things. The entering of his room. *His* room. This is the room they gave to him, allowing him to fashion it as he saw fit. But in that giving of it, there is an implied contract, a *giving up* of it. It is now *his* and therefore a private realm. Knock or no knock. Biscuit or no. They gave him his room. They. *They*. The pronoun seems oddly archaic now, a word uncalled for. For there is only *she*, his mother, only *she* now and ... yes, of course he wants to react, wants to let loose, to say that this is not right at all, none of it is right, that she *has no* right, it is his private place for his private moments. And his music. His creativity. His thinking.

But he knows that this will just start an argument, and that that argument could go on and on. On and on: there is rarely any true victor in the ons and ons.

It is better to stay silent.

Better to accept this.

Accept her offering.

Her milk.

Her biscuits.

Her little chats.

She will go away soon enough, give her time.

This has all happened before. He is only fifteen, but so much of what happens to him all seems to have happened before. The repetition of things. Life in a village. The dreadful repetition of the dreadful repetition.

Maura O'Brien bends to her son and kisses him on the cheek. His neck flushes with embarrassment, but again, thinking on it, he is prepared to accept it. Better the peace tonight. Better for all their sakes. Accept it. Better for everyone. Or Laura at least: better for her. That's a mature thought that has just come to him and he is instantly proud of it. He can be mature when he wants to be. He can be good like this. Like the way he keeps Laura's head from hitting the floor, because he knows how to … he knows how to take care of her, and he knows *her*, and he is there when she needs him. Good. He can be a good …

"You OK?"

"Yeah."

They hardly look at each other anymore: the wrongs they keep doing to each other. The wrongs. Repetition. When did the rot set in? This is no way to be. Mother and child. It all went horribly wrong.

"Poor Laura."

He maintains his deliberate silence, he's very good at it, practice makes…

She doesn't even mourn her own sister. What kind of a woman…

"Well, I'll leave you to get back to whatever it was you were doing. Writing a new song, is it?"

She puts the music volume back up, but not as loud as before. She looks at her son and she smiles meekly. There is perhaps hope in her that all of this will someday thaw, possibly, ironically, in the winter, though she does not know why that is, or how to go about it, she does not know, but things cannot go on like this, they simply can't: it'll be the death of both of them.

When she is gone from his room he goes to the machine and turns the music up loud again.

His room.

His music.

Let's be clear on this: *his* music.

His room.

4

People mull around the umber living room in murmured conversations, eating sandwiches. Some of the men hold glasses of Guinness, the off-white tops of the stout seeming yellowy and sickly in the dim lighting – there are not many electrical appliances on at all, respect for the dead, respect for departed Dymphna, only a few meagre lamps, and music doesn't play.

Sammy McCreary – a little stooped, a little drunk – approaches Tom Dennehy, grabs his hand and shakes it sincerely.

"I'm sorry for your troubles, Tom."

"Thanks, Sammy. Thanks for coming."

They had all stood in the afternoon rain – at last it had come, a salve to the burnt and yellow grasses, the thirsty roots of oak or beech, the dried-out husks of earthworms and to the parched, blind burrowers. The rain had come. It didn't mince its drops, meant every one and they thundered down on bent and mourning heads.

The rain seems to have stayed inside them: the gathered grim group feels saturated still; feels heavy, clammy, like sodden blankets.

"She was way too young for this, Tom. Way too young."

Tom remembers Sammy saying this before. He was quite well-known for saying it about every cold corpse laid out at every funeral, at every country wake. *Way too young.* They were all *way too young.* Tom wonders what is *not.* A hundred years old perhaps? A hundred might be about right for Sammy. *Not* way too young. If you got to be a hundred years old then you deserved your right to go to Heaven or Hell or whatever other dimension you had in mind. Until then you had work to do; Sammy himself might be the only one with zest enough to reach such an age, despite his stoop, despite his failure with the opposite sex, his never-very-busy painting and decorating service, his rusty van – you had to hand it to him, this constant sense of surge, the appetite, the rest of the villagers couldn't quite account for such sanguinity.

Tom reaches out to get his glass of Guinness from a nearby table and he sips from it, for something to do, something to occupy himself with.

Sammy remains, half-swaying, rocking a little on his heels, intermittently sipping from his own. He looks a little distracted, like he is itching to say something and is trying to weave in at the appropriate moment.

Tom is wise to the stratagem; he'd prefer it if he'd just spit it out.

"It's all right, Sammy, say whatever it is that's on your mind. If it's about our poker nights, then no, they won't be cancelled. They'll go ahead."

Yes, much better when you laid your cards on the table, metaphorically speaking, thinks Tom to himself, and liking the link.

Sammy shifts on his feet. He has developed a nervous tic, his left eyelid madly fluttering and the more he tries to blink and suppress it, the worse it seems to become.

"Right, yeah, I was just wondering and all … like if you have too much on your plate. I know how it is."

"We'll have a game next week, Sammy. Don't worry about it."

Sammy is pleased with the information but tries not to show it. It is no time to be showing any kind of pleasure. He sips at his drink again and searches for something to say, to distract from his own selfishness.

"Might be good for you, Tom. Take your mind off things and all."

Tom nods, and would be glad to let the conversation simply dissolve. It had been a long day, a trying day. There had been many such days in his life. In anyone's life. Especially when houses and people are bunched so close together in one area, so tight, on top of each other. Long. Trying. Indeed.

Laura passes the men with a tray of sandwiches, offering them to guests, doing her best to make herself busy, and she smiles benignly when receiving sympathy, accepting the gentle pats on her shoulder.

Sammy is not ready yet to let the conversation go. He wants to be of comfort to his friend, and he has questions, like all the villagers, no harm in asking about things, no harm … is there?

"And what is to become of the girl, Tom? She'll be a pity. What with the handicap and all."

Tom becomes immediately rankled, but he is in enough possession of himself and the occasion to not let it get the better of him.

"No handicap, Sammy. Just the fits that strike every now and again. But they've been few and far between lately. The medicine is good. Thank God."

Tom blesses himself, looking over at a picture of Christ on the wall, his arms out, beckoning the children to him; the soft colours, the radiant halo, the soft beams of light.

Sammy nods, but can't let it go. He's always like this. Never can he let anything fully go.

"And will she be sent away, like?"

"She will in her arse be sent away anywhere. She'll stay right here. I'm moving in proper. I'll stay with her. Give up my own shack – it's fit to fall down any day anyway."

Tom looks at Sammy gauging his reaction, and Sammy of course is taking it all in, soaking up the information, just like his old yellowy moustache soaks the froth of each poured and promising porter; gathering, like his cradling arms gather in all those chips when the poker hands occasionally go his way.

"I'll become her, whadaya call it ... her guardian. Who knows if that fecker, that gobshite brother of mine will ever return from wherever he is. This place has loads of room: why waste a big house like this? Better if I move in. It'll be left to me anyway ... in the will ... if there was a will ... if ..."

It is as if the thought has just occurred to him; there is probably a lot that he hasn't thought through. How can any of it go to him or Laura if the father is still alive? But *is* he still alive? The brother. And where? Where is he? Tom needs to spend a few evenings poring over these facts, the possibilities, the outcomes ... needs a bit of time to figure things out.

Sammy raises his glass and Tom clinks his up against it.

Tom drinks and can see over the glass-rim as it fits there on the bridge of his nose that Sammy is still not quite done. There is a little more of the gossip that he needs to acquire, for wherever he takes it, for whatever he does with it – maybe it's just to satisfy his own curiosity; he is like that little dog of his, Lucy, always sticking her nose into things, sniffing about at everything: she jumps right up and into your crotch when you least expect it and has a good snuffle around. Maybe Sammy enjoys that kind of thing.

"She's a fine young girl," Sammy says eventually. "No doubt about it. Fine strong girl. You'd never think she had any problems."

Tom does his best to ignore.

"She'll make a grand wife to someone someday."

Sammy is watching Laura still doing the rounds with the sandwiches, providing top-ups for the quickly diminishing drinks.

"Grand hips on her. Childbearing, you know."

Sammy tries to smile innocently, as if he meant nothing at all by it, but he is unable to make up for this mistimed, misjudged and blatant lecherousness.

He has no other option but to excuse himself now, to say how his prostate has been acting up again, another flare-up, and how he's been peeing round the clock … but Tom doesn't give him time to make any excuses, for he has already put his glass firmly down on the side table, and has walked right away from him.

5

Kevin sits on Laura's bed. The same long day. The same long-faced mourners drinking the same drinks downstairs.

He had been unsure as to whether to enter or not, hadn't actually been inside this bedroom since they were both much younger, with their infant toys: his dinosaurs, her dolls. But here he is, perched on the edge of her bed, quite at home, flipping through a large hardcover (and, he has to admit, rather childish) book called *Myths and Monsters*.

He looks up every now and again, keeping vigilant – if they catch him in here they might wonder as to what the young scallywag is doing in a girl's bedroom all alone, and no sign of her about.

Not that Laura would mind that much. She lets him get away with quite a lot: a visit to her room is hardly a crime. At least none committed yet.

This reading material, however … is this the book she actually has on the go? She actually went to the local library and was brave enough to take out this?

Kevin is open on an illustrated page with the title "The Loch Ness Monster" emblazoned on the top in slimy green. The infamous "monster" has been spoken about on many TV shows and everyone has seen the famous photographs.

Everyone. Even the youngest of the schoolyard kids, even they know too that it has to be a load of old rubbish.

But maybe not Laura.

Maybe Laura believes in this stuff.

Well, well, the things you don't know about the people you think you know.

She appears then at the doorway. She has crept stealthily. She was half-suspicious and so she is not all that surprised to find him there, loitering. He is a boy after all, worse, he is a *teenage* boy, and she knows that curiosity will always get the better of them. A movie came out the previous year: *The Lost Boys,* and although Laura hasn't seen it, she thinks it the most apt title ever. For her, *all* boys are lost. All are lost and looking for something – it was the hormones that made them that way. They couldn't help it. No surprise then to find a lost boy here. So often they are found in places they shouldn't be, and so often doing things they certainly shouldn't, and here is the proof yet again. Red-handed.

"Feel free to come in and use my bed, why don't you? And why not take a book from the shelf and have a read. Are you sure you wouldn't like a cup of coffee or a foot massage while you are here. Anything I can do for you at all."

"Sorry."

Her face softens, although, in fairness, it hadn't been all that stern to begin with.

"It's OK. I'm not upset … I'm not exactly myself … I …"

"You don't have to explain anything. Or apologize. I'm the one who … I just shouldn't be snooping around here."

"Snooping?"

"You know what I mean."

He continues to flick through the book, amazed at the childishness of it. This is a library book, the stamp on the card in its paper folder inside the front cover makes it clear that it was recently taken out, and it must surely be for eight- or nine-year-olds, not the kind of material a teenage pop music fan should be reading. Not for someone who usually reads *Smash Hits*. Not for someone more interested in what Madonna is wearing in her latest pop video … but who is Kevin to say? Who is he to say anything about anything?

"Do you actually want something? Like a tea or coffee or something? I can sneak some real drink if you want? No one will notice. Whiskey?"

Kevin laughs at her sudden maturation, all adult-y now, at odds with the Kappa – a Japanese river monster with a flat-top head – that glares comically out at him from the glossy book.

"No, I'm all right. I might nip out back for a smoke soon though. Might steal a drink for myself on the way out, too."

He prefers the notion of stealing a drink rather than being handed one. It is one of the only joys of being a teenager, that sense of rebellion, even criminality – if you were handed a drink it would be way too easy, wouldn't it? Where would be the fun in that?

Laura isn't listening to him. She is holding the empty sandwich tray, unsure as to why she brought it upstairs with her, unsure as to what she is to do next. Her mother is gone. She has not prepared for any of this. Her mother is completely gone: the absence is suddenly astonishing.

"You doing okay there?"

"I suppose so. Hardly the best day of my life, is it?"

She mopes around the room, picking up clothes from the floor, putting them back into drawers, hanging up shirts in her wardrobe. One pair of white knickers peaks out from the bed and she kicks them back under hoping he hasn't spotted them.

She picks up a wad of tissues from beside her pillow, and Kevin sticks his foot out on onto the silver pedal of the little dustbin near him, opening the cover of it. She fires the messy ball in. It doesn't even hit the rim.

"Nice shot."

"Thanks."

"Lots of tears?"

"Yep. Lots. A night's worth. Coupled with great globs of green snot. Lovely mix, eh?"

"Well, different to what I usually fill my tissues with."

She rolls her eyes. Why do so many of their conversations return to his *thing* and its emissions?

"Seriously though … rough night was it?"

"I knew it was coming. I just knew it. I knew something … she was so bloody sick so fucking often and …"

She shakes her head, unable to continue, then looks to the Minotaur on the open page of the book.

"Why are you looking at that?"

"I just saw it on your shelf."

"Yeah, I know, childish. You can just say it. Or what's that other word you use … *puerile?*"

"No … actually … it looks kinda …"

"Dumb?"

Kevin laughs.

"Yeah … a little … I suppose …"

She turns from him, her shoulders hunched, her brow furrowed. She looks at herself in the mirror and then back at him again, as if she is about to …

"What? What is it?"

So many things she wants to say.

So many things she wants to shout out.

Or to have explained to her.

"What? What is it? Tell me."

"Never mind."

In order to distract herself – or distract both of them – she goes to the stereo and inserts a cassette tape into it. She presses play. Terence Trent D'Arby's "If You All Get to Heaven" begins.

"This was the last tape she bought for me."

Kevin says nothing; taps his fingers on the side of the bed.

"I suppose you are going to tell me how shit this is, yeah?"

"No, not at all. Actually I have only good things to say about this album, and this guy," he says.

"Seriously?"

"No shit. This guy's got it all. Great voice. Great moves. I read how he used to be a boxer. Interesting lyrics."

Laura looks at him as if waiting for the punchline, but none comes.

"No, really. I mean it. Some fine work on this. I tip him for great things. Not usually the kind of stuff I go for myself, but yeah, he's got something. Will rival Prince and Jackson for sure. Gonna be huge, this guy."

"Wow. That's the first time you ever said you liked my music."

"Because you usually listen to absolute shite. This is the first time you got it right. Like I said before. You need a proper education."

"You're such a pompous dick."

Kevin is nodding, even enthusiastically.

He gets off the bed and looks at a framed photo she has on the wall: Laura, as a two- or three-year-old, her father and mother.

"Happier times," he says.

"They got married too late. I think I was a mistake."

"Don't say that."

"Well, I wasn't born normal, was I?"

"You were."

"You call epilepsy *normal*?"

"I don't call anything normal. Fuck it. C'mon, let's go get a smoke. And a drink too. Fuck 'em all."

"I don't smoke … or drink."

"There's a first time for everything," he says. "About time you learned some new bad habits."

They bound down the stairs, Kevin already putting his trench coat on. They hurry past dark-suited mourners and well-wishers, and Laura flings the tray aside when they get to the kitchen. It clatters on the table but lands neatly.

Tom, stocking the fridge, is startled, by the noise.

"Jaysus! What was that?"

"Sorry, Tom. I dropped the tray."

He harrumphs and goes back to what he was doing, putting the newer bottles of stout in at the back, pulling the colder ones out to the front.

While his back is still turned Kevin sneaks up beside him, takes a bottle from the box on the floor and slips it into his coat pocket.

Laura is watching the theft, impressed by his bravura.

They go to the back door, Laura taking her coat from the hook on the wall.

Rows of jam line the left side of the wall, their squat jars moody and suggestive in their dark colourings – her mother had made them when she was in one of her sprightlier moods, Laura can't remember how long ago that was. Have they gone off? Does jam go off? Isn't jam a preserve, does that mean that …

Only now does she truly notice Kevin's coat.

"What the fuck are you wearing?"

"I got it at Lenny's."

"Lenny's?"

"The guy with the second-hand shop in the town. Where I get the books and the cheap tapes. Haven't been there in while though. Mother doesn't really drive there anymore, says the local shops are enough. He's a wealth of knowledge that guy. Taught me a lot about 60s and 70s rock music."

"That shithole? That creep with the long hair? You bought a coat there? From him?"

"It's not a shithole. The guy has some good stuff, if you just root around."

Laura shakes her head as if she is revolted by the notion. She wishes that he would take some of her advice for a change, at least when it comes to fashion sense.

"Ian McCulloch has a coat just like this one. Wore it on *Top of the Pops.*"

"Who?"

"Ian McCulloch. Echo and the Bunnymen?"

She shrugs: no idea.

"Never mind."

Outside in the cool night two men are smoking. One takes deep pulls of a Major cigarette, the other constantly lights and re-lights a short, stubby pipe that sends forth bursts of grey plume to rise above their heads. They watch the flaws dissolve into nothingness – it could be a metaphor for the lives they have seen disappear before them, it could be themselves soon enough: if they don't have a foot already in the grave … they certainly have a few toes already dipped.

Behind the two men the back door is slightly ajar, and this is where Laura slips on her coat in front of Kevin and the jars of strawberry and blackberry jam.

The men neither see nor hear their preparations, they concentrate only on their smoking, not knowing fully how the addiction will kill them both in just a manner of months – or maybe they do know, but they go right ahead and smoke away regardless.

"If she didn't have that child so late in life she might have been all right."

The voice rings out in the quiet of the country night. The words cannot help but be heard. Kevin reaches out and grabs Laura's arm.

"Don't. Ignore them. Not worth it."

But he cannot stop her.

Laura is not the type to sit and take such slander.

Like one of Kevin's own temper tantrums – perhaps it runs in the family – she rushes out, swinging the old door on its hinges. The two men splutter their smoke in utter surprise when they see her emerging. They quickly extinguish their smokes and start to make their way towards the door, their faces searching for excuses, but they have nothing but the air of men caught, and they fumble and falter.

"Laura, love, didn't see you there, where did …"

"Fuck you," she bellows at the first, and to the second she bellows as loudly, "and fuck you too!"

The pipe man, his hand reeking of tobacco when he sticks it out before her, tries his luck:

"Laura, I'm sorry for your ..."

"Troubles, yeah, I know. Fuck off the pair of ye. I'm sure you've had your fill of free booze and sandwiches. Off home now with the pair of ye. Fucking disgusting."

They scuttle away, more like reprimanded street urchins than men with years of life experience – so badly they have let themselves down with their careless tongues.

They barge past Kevin, mumbling incoherently, clambering in the backdoor to their safety.

"Fucking cheek," says Laura.

Kevin can't help but agree. He hadn't expected any of that, the way they threw about their words so easily, it all seemed so unnecessary.

When he sees the coast is clear he lights up his own Marlboro Light cigarette – a pack Lenny had given him merely for sitting and chatting with him one boring no-customer day several months ago as they listened to Suicide – he still has two or three cigarettes left.

He reaches into his deep coat pocket and pulls out the purloined bottle of Guinness.

"Shit. No opener."

Laura produces one from her pocket.

"Been using this all evening. And serving fucking ham sandwiches."

"You should be a Brownie, you're so helpful, and resourceful. Not such a retard after all."

Laura allows him his joke.

"You do say the kindest things."

He opens his stout and drinks from it, sighing with feigned contentment. He passes it to her and, hesitatingly at first, she takes a timid sip. Quickly she spits it out.

"Jesus. How do they drink this shit?"

"You get used to it. Before my father ran off, even when I was very young, he used to give me the odd sup. Said it would make a man of me someday. Put hairs on my chest, the usual guff. I still have no hairs on my chest, just for the record."

He takes a manly slug.

"The taste kind of reminds me of him. Or the smell of it. I don't know."

Laura rolls her eyes.

"Fuck's sake. What are we like? Fathers gone. My mother gone now too ... and we're just beginning our teens. Rough or what? Fucking unlucky or what?"

"I know. I know. I don't know whether to laugh or bawl."

Laura giggles at his word choice – he always does that, throws in a word you wouldn't expect. *Bawl.* Must be a talent.

"We may as well laugh," she says. "It can't get much bloody worse, can it?"

They gaze out at the darkness, Kevin trying and failing to blow smoke rings, and Laura attempting another go at the Guinness. Nervously she takes another mouthful. This time she does not spit it out but swallows it down. He mimes clapping his hands in mute applause.

She takes one more drink for good measure and is able to hold this one down too. She hands the bottle back to him, enjoying the intimacy and the fact that it clears the funeral out of her mind.

"You know that book?"

"Book?"

"The one you were looking at in my room."

"*Myths and Monsters*?" he chortles.

"Yeah. That one."

"What about it?"

"Do you believe in any of that stuff?"

"What? Like ghosts? Vampires? Fuck, no…you don't…do you?"

"Look, you can laugh all you want, but…I mean, I know you're not going to believe this but…"

He seems to remember the same kind of conversations when they were younger, when they were in primary school. But now? Now? Now they are supposed to be teenagers, supposed to be mature.

He tries to muster up a serious face, gives her the benefit of the very big doubt.

"Go on," he says.

"Look, I'm just gonna say it, and you can laugh all the fuck you want, but…"

Kevin turns his face away from her abruptly. He is surprised by something he sees in the kitchen window.

"What?" she says.

"Fucking hell! What's he doing here?"

"Who?"

"Carty. Your dreamboat."

She nudges Kevin aside to take a peek into her own kitchen. Her cousin is not lying to her. Carty is there, the blond locks of him, like he's some sexy Swede visiting from Stockholm, and not an Irish country lad at all. His father, Donal, stands next to him and is shaking Tom's hand. Tom goes to get the man a drink, and Aidan, seeing something moving outside the window, flashes a look their way.

The cousins collapse to a squat.

"Jesus, why's he here?"

"Why do you think? Paying his respects. Go in and say something."

"Like what?"

"Like … anything."

Laura stalls for a second, then takes a deep breath and goes back into the house.

Donal Carty goes straight to her, all funeral frown and forlornness. He shakes her soft hand and Laura marvels at the strength of his, the hard bones of it, the skin too, the callouses of a tradesman or a farmer – she remembers then that he deals with farm machinery, makes sense.

"Sorry, Laura. Our sincere condolences. She was a great lady."

Laura mutters a thank you in humble response.

It's the turn of the young Carty now and the embarrassment of being a teenager unaccustomed to such formalities is etched all over his face, but the boy has enough gumption to stick out an awkward hand.

Laura swiftly seizes it, her lips twitching as she tries to suppress a smile.

Kevin watches all this from outside the window, curious and interested in the proceedings, and not without a hint of jealousy, as if he is to make do now with a surfeit of affection, that it is to be directed elsewhere – quickly he shuns the notion, becoming more worried that he might be mistaken for a Peeping Tom: the raincoat isn't doing him any favours.

When Tom, Donal and Aidan leave the kitchen Laura goes for the sandwiches. She has hardly eaten anything herself all day. Too busy. Too bunched up inside with nerves, with worry, with confusion. She munches on a sandwich she herself had made that morning; it wasn't half-bad either.

Her cousin appears beside her then, nicks a triangle of sandwich and munches too. He knows he should say something about the blond beautiful boy and his unexpected appearance in her kitchen, but he doesn't, preferring to veer Laura away from him completely, distract her from the image of blond locks with small talk.

"Enough butter on these for you?"

"I made them myself. Loads of it. Naturally."

"What are you going to do tomorrow?"

"Same as today. Mourn. And it's a Sunday. Perfect."

"I'm going to help Tom tomorrow with the moving. Maybe we can do something after. A walk? Or something?"

"A walk?" she asks, unable to mask her surprise.

Kevin knows he shouldn't say it, knows how quickly he can bore her with his music "asides", but he does so anyway:

"You know Morrissey and his female friend – can't remember her name – go walking in the graveyard quite a bit. That's what the song 'Cemetry Gates' is about."

He immediately regrets it. She's got her couldn't-give-a-shit face on, which Kevin has seen more than once before.

"Firstly, I'm surprised to hear that Morrissey has a friend, and secondly…don't you think I've had quite enough of graveyards?"

"Yeah, well," he stammers, shamefacedly, "let's go to the woods then, get some fresh air."

Laura looks at him as if he has gone completely mad. Where have these ideas sprung from? From where this sudden affection? He does nothing but take the piss out of her on the way home from school every day. And now *walks*? Together? In the woods?

She decides to acquiesce though, nodding at him, letting him know that she appreciates the gesture. She takes another sandwich and wolfs it down.

"What was it you were going to say to me, earlier?"

For a second Laura looks confused.

"Oh, that? Yeah … well … laugh if you want … I don't give a shit really."

Kevin leaves the empty Guinness bottle by the sink, goes to the fridge and takes another. Already his head feels a bit woozy, but he tries not to let it show. Laura finds the metal opener again and cracks the top off for him, letting the serrated beige bottle cap fly into the sink.

She bites her bottom lip summoning the right words to explain herself.

"You know the Loch Ness Monster?"

"Not personally, but I know what you mean."

She pauses, gathering her thoughts; she does not want to appear foolish.

"Well … there's a monster in ours too."

It is Kevin's turn to look at her as if she is the one who has lost her mind. He takes a deep slug out of the bottle, all the while keeping his ear cocked – the last thing he needs is Tom coming into the kitchen and catching him with the beer in his hand. He buttons up his trench coat as if he is preparing to leave.

"You're just going to go? You're not going to say anything?"

"Bedtime," he says. "Cocteau Twins to lull me to sleep, or maybe This Mortal Coil."

"Tissues more like."

"Yeah, well, maybe a moment or two of that and all."

He walks away from her, out of the kitchen, leaving the bottle behind – he's already had enough – and leaving her to shout after him:

"Are you not going to say anything … after what I just told you?"

"Go to bed, my dear," he shouts back. You've had a long day. Your brain's not working right."

Laura is left standing there, looking at her hand. The one that shook Aidan Carty's hand. She has that at least. That memory. That moment of … something … what does it feel like … promise? She smiles gently to herself, and she looks down at her hand again.

How I dearly wish I was not here

6

In the morning Tom had shown Kevin how to drive his van (Tom Dennehy Hardware Supplies DIY, written elegantly on the side of it), and he told Kevin that he should take it as an honour to be allowed sit behind the wheel of such an esteemed vehicle. Kevin didn't know if this was a joke or not, though he suspected it was – the van was older than himself, and had the rust to prove it.

It hadn't been as difficult as the boy had expected, this driving business; when he learned not to be so heavy with his feet he found that the rest was easy enough, the steering, the indicating. He just had to remember not to *step on it*, to ignore the American movie tropes, be a bit lighter with his touch, careful with the clutch: balance; that was what he had being taught, not to flood the engine. It was like with Laura, when she thrashed about, caught in her cataclysm of her curse, all you had to do was be gentle with her head, cradle, balance her, not be too heavy-handed, guide her back to safety.

Kevin was grateful for the lesson, and delighted in driving, however slowly, around the house, and Tom also enjoyed the experience – it gave him a feeling for what fatherhood must be like; he had had chances before, but on every occasion he had just seemed to blow it. There had been Maggie, there had been Joan, even a brief fling with an American woman, Mildred "Millie" Carter from Pennsylvania, but he had not been prepared to commit to any of them, and the relationships inevitably ended. Now the closest to being a father is having Laura with him, caring for her, loving her, yes, *loving*, and this young lad too, Kevin, son-like, if he could be so presumptuous, it is enough at his age, at his stage in life, yes, it isn't too bad at all.

Kevin helps Tom load boxes out of the back of his van and into the house. Tom does his best to stifle his moans and groans, trying to convert the huffs and puffs of his exertions into shows of strength, but it is hard to be convinced by them.

"Be careful with your back there, son. These are heavier than you think."

Tom knows all about bad backs, has been having jolts and jabs and disc problems since he was a teenager himself. He even had to stop with the hurling earlier than he would have wished, early retirement from the pitch when he would have loved a few more years running around with the lads of an afternoon. But there was just too much pain in the bending to retrieve that tricky sliotar, and too many times the lash of the ash across his body too – a rough game to be sure, but it hardened him, it made him tough.

"And those fingers, be careful ... I hear you're good on the piano."

"Well, maybe. It's the synthesizer I usually play."

"The what?"

"Keyboards. Electronic."

"Oh, right."

They lift one particularly heavy box together with a one, two, three and into the entrance of the house, and when done Tom takes a moment to raise his arms towards the ceiling, then hang them loose by his side and shakes some semblance of life back into them. The nerves in his shoulders and neck are pinching, little currents of electricity running up and down.

"'Tis no fun getting old, Kevin. Enjoy your youth while you have it."

Kevin does not want to ever be that old. How old is Tom anyway? He cannot tell the years of anyone over a certain age: a forty-year-old is the same as a fifty-year-old is the same as a sixty-year-old. Grey hair: is that how you tell? He'll die before any of that. "Rock 'n' Roll Suicide" perhaps, and the Bowie song immediately starts up in his head.

"If you could take those few upstairs, to the first room on the left, there's a good lad. That's the room I'll use from now. I'll fix myself a cup of tea. Have a break then yourself. Whatever you want."

"Right-o," says Kevin, as he continues with the boxes, lifting, heaving, sweating it out – the driving had been more enjoyable.

The last box has been laid down on the carpeted floor of Tom's new sleeping quarters. Kevin takes a moment to stretch and rub his muscles – perhaps Tom is right, he should enjoy his youth while he is still young and vital. Though he'd have to get out of the village and into a city if that is really to happen: "fun" and "this shithole" aren't exactly great bedfellows.

As he prepares to exit the room he notices that the scotch tape has peeled a little from the centre of the box, the cover-flap opens only to reveal a pile of pornographic magazines inside. Kevin gasps. Fuck me, what have we here? The motherlode.

He is suddenly panicky, nervous, as if they are his own illicit materials and he might at any moment be discovered, shackled, marched-off to some dark dungeon for his trespass; he is a sudden torrent of guilt, shame, edginess and wicked excitement. He rifles through the box, leafing through the magazines hurriedly, drinking in the images there and soon quite visually drunk on the excesses... the excesses... and the variety. He had no idea there were so many different kinds of beauties; it's just when you have them lined up like this, page after page, page after page, different body sizes, even ordinary women in the back pages described as "Readers' Wives" in dodgy amateur shots with poor lighting as if taken in an ordinary bedroom, and how open they are! These women! These actual women! He feels like he is about to faint... or vomit... or both.

Kevin's concentration is broken by footsteps outside on the landing and quickly he packs the magazines back into the box.

A knock on the door.

"Kevin? You there?"

Phew. Only Laura.

"Need a hand?"

He opens the door to her, grabbing her by the arm and yanking her in as if he has some incredible secret to divulge, something she will never believe... well, she might not!

"Where's Tom?"

"He's down in the kitchen, drinking tea," she says. "What's the matter with you? You look all flustered."

"Check this out," he whispers, unable to contain the febrile excitement that throbs through him, the hard pounding beat in his chest. He opens the box and she gasps in pretty much the same way he did.

"Bloody hell!"

A fit of nervous giggling then, she can hardly contain herself either.

"The dirty old devil. I didn't think he'd be able to … you know … at his age."

"Why not?"

"How old *is* he?"

"I don't know."

"Disgusting," says Laura. "Imagine his limp old dick trying to get hard."

"Shh," he says. "For fuck's sake. He'll hear us."

Laura leafs through more pages, becoming more tremulous at every turn. She stops and stares at one picture in utter disbelief.

"Jesus Christ, look at the thing on this fella! It's like a bloody arm!"

Kevin laughs but quickly stops himself, growing ever more fearful of alerting Tom.

"You may as well keep one," Laura says. "For your own pleasure. He's got more than enough. Wherever he got them. He's hardly going to miss one."

She hands him a selection of magazines. He looks at them, agog. No Siouxsies here. No Goths. No pale-faced post-punk priestesses. Just beautiful models, suntanned, lithe, each more flexible than the last. It's not like he is not attracted to these kinds of girls, these voluptuous beauties, of course he is, the more he ponders it actually, the more he finds he is attracted to *all* kinds of girls. He's fifteen, for God's sake, of course he is. There's a black girl here, too. He's never even see one in real life, not in actuality, not even on his one visit to Dublin, but here's one for him now, with amazingly muscular arms, not the grass-skirted kind he's spied in *National Geographic* magazines, no, this one could be an athlete, a basketball player, someone who throws a discus, look at the biceps on her, the ropey arms.

"For fuck's sake, hurry up! He could arrive up the stairs at any minute."

Laura starts to pack the rest of the magazines back into the box, but she soon changes her mind and pulls one back out.

"I'm keeping this one."

There is a sense of nonchalance and cheeky pride in this proclamation.

"What for?" There is only bafflement in Kevin's question.

"Because I'm curious."

The boy does not know what to say. He has just seen a naked black girl for the first time ... and now this, her insouciance.

"I've never really ... studied ... one of those before," she says.

Kevin doesn't know if she means the magazine or the body part.

"Am I not allowed a little pleasure too?"

Kevin does not know what words will come out of his mouth, but he sputters anyway:

"I didn't know that girls ..."

"Did you not?" she says, pretending to sound surprised. In their daily battle of wits the boy is usually the victor, but that's when it comes to banter about bands no one cares about, or the foolish pride in being able to pee against bushes: this was altogether different terrain.

Her sense of achievement only grows when she looks at his trousers and sees the tent that has formed there. She smiles. How sweet.

"Let's get out of here," he says, his voice at last reclaiming something close to conviction.

He leaves the room as fast as his wobbly legs can carry him.

Laura, still smiling, walks calmly after him.

At the bottom of the stairs Laura slips the magazine into her bag. This is the little satchel she carries everywhere when she is not in school. It is just as clean and well-kept as her schoolbag but bears the slightest whiff of some perfume she sprayed there months ago. The scent reminds her of her mother. The scent reminds her that she should be mourning, should be wailing, flailing, and she feels a flowering of shame that she is doing none of these things.

She makes Kevin stand still and pulls the magazine out of his shirt. His body is as rigid as a mannequin.

"Very stiff-looking you are today," she says to him, and she slips *his* magazine into her bag too. She tries to read his face, which seems just as frozen, and he tries to avert his eyes, looking anywhere but into hers.

"Right. We're ready."

"For what?" he asks, the second time in as many minutes, equally confused.

"For that walk you promised me. You didn't forget, did you?"

He shakes his head. He would have a hard time remembering his own name right now.

"You did. You feckin' liar."

She puts on her light rain jacket and the cute satchel on her back.

"Tom!" she shouts in the direction of the kitchen, "we're heading out for a minute! Just for like … a breath of fresh air."

"Right you are," is Tom's reply, as he drains the last of his mug of tea. "Be home for six though," he adds. "I'm cooking tonight."

Laura and Kevin look at each other, dubiously – at least it won't be platters of cold meats and cheese sandwiches. Something … anything different would be lovely.

"And tell your mother to come too, Kevin! The more the merrier!"

Laura winces and whispers to her cousin:

"The *merrier*. Would you hear the feckin' eejit. On the day after a funeral."

"Right-o, Uncle Tom!" Kevin shouts back: "we're off now!"

And it is Laura who leads the way into the unexpected afternoon.

And it is Kevin who will have to get used to falling behind or following his cousin's lead sometimes.

So he trots subserviently after her.

This walk could be the walk they take home from school every day, everything about it familiar.

"You got through last night all right?"

"I suppose," she says. "It's going to take a while to get used to the fact that she's not here anymore."

Kevin nods, getting it, trying to be as sympathetic as he can, but Laura is in no mood for sombreness – she's already had an adventure with the pornographic magazines, there should be more of that in her life now: adventure, more excitement, will she have to leave the village altogether to truly find it? Is that what has to happen? So often they talk about their futures, but it is always hazy, the future being some amorphous, inchoate thing they can never get their young minds around.

"And what about you last night? New songs? Or just tissues again?"

He does not want to tell her about the poems he tries to write. The blank pages. Her name across the top. The otherworldly cries of a fox.

"Tissues."

"Jesus, it's like some kind of disease you've got. Some kind of mania."

Kevin shrugs. What can he do?

Identical Sony Walkman headsets, bright orange foam pieces covering their ears, but the music is not yet switched on. In Laura's machine today: Rick Astley. In Kevin's David Bowie's *Low*. The songs are queued up and ready to play. They need to just hit the button when ready. They are wired for sound, and after the magazines, well, a bit wired generally, other parts of them, as if electric currents push through their every nerve and their pulses madly race. Kevin recently checked his dictionary to see what the word "ostinato" meant. It said: "a continually repeated musical phrase or rhythm". Somehow this word gives him great solace, as if it adheres to his life or provides some insight into the meaning of his existence. He hasn't it all figured yet, like so many things, he's only fifteen – he'll be sixteen in January – but he feels he's getting there. Ostinato. Continually repeated. Life.

Usually on this track they see no one.

No car chugs over potholes.

No dog scampers or no rabbit runs.

No friendly farmer ever tips the beak of a flat cap in passing.

That's usually the case.

But today is different. Today there *are* some people on this track. There they are, right there, right at the bend where the road rises to become a bump of a bridge over a small stream; stone walls on either side of this. Perched on these stone walls are three fellow students that Laura and Kevin immediately recognize. Fellow students, though in no way *friends*. They know each other because in a school of their size, well, how could you not?

Helena O'Dowd, fair-haired, languid-looking, forever an aura of torpidity around her lank locks, she's there idling lethargically; Brian Donnelly, quiet-spoken, largely timid and ineffectual no matter the endeavour, he's there too; and then there's the leader of the pack, Orlaith Crowley, brash, brusque, squinting now to try and make out who approaches on their dull-as-ever Sunday.

"Oh for fuck's sake," says Kevin. "This is all we need."

By the time they reach the stone wall, Orlaith has already leapt off of it and is blocking their way, squaring up, all sass and sway.

"Well, well, if it isn't the happy cousins out on an afternoon stroll."

Laura and Kevin are clearly in no mood for this, though Orlaith patently is.

"Leave 'em alone, Orlaith," says Helena, her manner of speaking as lazy and loping as her gait. "They've had a tragedy in the family."

The cousins shift uncomfortably on their feet, itching to move on and away from these cretins, away from Orlaith at least, and whatever bullets she has locked and loaded.

Their passage is still blocked.

"Is that right? A tragedy? How come I didn't hear? Sorry for your troubles."

Kevin nods and his lips tighten. He just wants to move on, does not want to lose his temper today. Just get out of here. Keep moving. *Continually repeated musical phrase or rhythm.*

"Looking very cool in that raincoat, Kevvy. Nice and light too, not too hot in it? We don't want you heating up. Good for this weather though I suppose, showers of rain. Always showers, eh? Even though summer was long and good to us, wasn't it lads? Is it The Cure today, Kevvy? Or something deeper and darker? Goth shit, is it? Is that it? Sure … isn't a tragedy right up your alley!"

She pauses, swaying her hips from side to side, as if she's paid far too much attention to Pat Benatar videos; she's waiting for him to bite, but he holds his tongue, the bigger person.

"Love is tragic, isn't it, Kevvy? That's why people run away, with their real lovers. Doesn't matter how against nature that is. Burn in hell they will."

"Let it go, Orlaith," says Brian, though without any great conviction.

And surprisingly Orlaith does back down, but with one last lash of vindictiveness before she lets them off the rack.

She "whispers" loud enough for them to hear, as the cousins move on, shuffling past, a parting shot:

"Spastic girl. Loves a bit of sympathy."

Laura starts to turn around but Kevin drags her away by the arm, focuses her on the road ahead. So often he has to do this, pull at her, tug at her, steer her clear. Ahead only, he is thinking. Don't look back. Don't give them the fucking satisfaction.

They walk on, both trying to breathe deeply and get Orlaith out of their heads. It isn't all that easy.

"They're not worth it," says Kevin. "They've got fuck all going on in their lives. That's why they start in with all this shit."

He is pleased with himself for showing this calmness, this maturity. He could lose his cool altogether, open the stable door and let loose the spooked stallion. He has been known for this, this lashing out, and Laura is no stranger to the giving or receiving of it either, but most of his ire of late has been directed at his mother, and for this he should be ashamed of himself; it's people like Orlaith, the tiresome bullies and their jaded malevolence, they're the ones who should be getting the brunt of his bile. Maybe he will lose it completely someday. Maybe he will lose the run of himself, go nuts, go erratic, go insane – these creative types, they have it in them. These teens, they have to direct their pent-up emotions at something, don't they? For now though, he is happy, to be walking with his cousin like this, rain so far keeping at bay, and the day still with a stretch before them.

When they are far away enough from their leering peers they're much braver in talking louder and with more confidence.

"Can you believe Aidan Carty is shifting that bitch?"

"Was," says Kevin.

"Was?"

"It's all over … from what I heard."

"Really?"

There is surprise in Laura's voice, but more than surprise there is possibly ... hope.

"Apparently. Haven't seen him with any girl in ages. Mostly he's alone. Bit of a loner, Carty. Have you seen him on his bicycle? Quite the brooding, mysterious type. Like River Phoenix."

Laura turns her face from him so Kevin can't see her beaming.

"I haven't seen him no. Just when he came to the house, that's all. He shook my hand. Sympathized. Maybe he'll give me a bar on his bike sometime."

They both put their headphones back on, talk has been quite enough. It's time they engaged in their music, time to get away from everything: they march forward to their own beats, their own playlist, their own passions.

They pass fields of cows and sheep, reminding them where they are and where they come from, and, most pertinently, where they are *not*. They are *not* in the trendy bars of London or New York. They are not in live venues in Dublin even, toilets with peeling rock posters on the walls, sound checks. They are not in huge record stores, Virgins or HMVs, hanging out at listening posts where they can check out all the latest tracks, run their fingers through the albums in their stacks. They are far from any of that, and only have their machines to get them away from their predicament.

Today: Rick Astley, a performer who has been topping the charts.

And for Kevin: *Low,* and right now "Sound and Vision", which Kevin could make a case for being the greatest pop single ever, for its sheer ballsiness, its effortless cool, its oddness, its blend of perfect melody, existential ennui and …

But who would listen to him?

Never gonna give you up.

Neither sheep nor cow nor cousin could give the slightest shit as to what Kevin thinks about Bowie's masterpiece.

A cow moos.

Another five minutes of walking and they arrive. They take their headphones down and click "stop" on their machines. They gaze out across the water.

"Never fails, does it?"

"What?"

"The lake. It's always lovely. In any season."

"It's not a lake. It's a pond," Laura says.

"Yeah, I know it's a pond. But everyone around here calls it a lake."

"Yeah, but that's just wishful thinking, isn't it? They call it a lake because they want it to be a lake. As if to make it bigger would make their lives somehow bigger. Somehow special. Give them something to boast about. But it's just a pond. No point in making it more than it is. That's just bullshit. They should call it what it is. It's just a fucking pond. A pretty big pond, sure, but it's just a fucking pond."

Kevin is nodding in surprised agreement. He hasn't heard her rant about anything in so long. What was Rick Astley doing to her head?

"I didn't know you felt so strongly about this place."

"I don't. I'm just tired of all the bullshit. Like all the mourners pretending they were sad and sorry, and yet none lifted a finger to ever help her when she needed it? Who took her to the hospital if she was ever in trouble? It is what it is. It's a fucking pond."

They make their way down the sloping path to the pull of the pond.

They sit on a large, flat rock, only a few meters from the edge of the water. A brisk wind has risen up and whispers coldly around their ears, signs that real autumn is at last here, often stern, often changeable, and they pull their clothes tight around themselves to muster a bit of warmth.

Laura takes some wrapped sandwiches out of the bag and hands Kevin one.

"Jesus. Again with the sandwiches."

"If you don't want it I'll have it myself."

"No, no, I'll have it."

They stay silent and thoughtful as they look out across the still water, wondering about its depths, wondering how many have swum here, have skated here when it froze over in winter, and how many have sadly perished. It doesn't take much to send thoughts down that road, any body of water will trap you into thinking it, and the teenagers have a propensity for morbidity, their haywire hormones harassing them, but they are not here to be glum, they are here to…

"So, tell me, Laura, why *are* we here? My *walk* was to be in the woods…I said nothing about coming to the la…pond."

"I wanted you to see for yourself. The monster."

She looks at him, daring him *not* to believe her.

She doesn't blink.

She doesn't budge on the hard rock beneath her bum.

"You're not joking, are you?"

Laura shakes her head. Not in the slightest. Why would she? Why would she lie about this?

They gaze out across the water again. As if an answer will come at any minute, as if something will arise and prove everything. But the water is absolutely still, and because the wind has died down again there is hardly a ripple.

"And you saw it, yeah? It just appeared, yeah?"

"Maybe. I mean, yes. It did. Before. Once before. Yes."

He takes a minute to take it in. He knows the strain she has been under. He knows that the epilepsy can rock her hard, and who knows the damage it does inside that brain of hers, it must surely take its toll. Or the medication she takes for it – sometimes it works, and sometimes it is no good to her at all.

"And you're sure it was a monster. Just like The Loch Ness Monster. Not a floating piece of … whatever … drift-wood … or something."

"It was hard to see clearly, but yeah, I know what I saw. Like a dinosaur neck, sticking out."

Kevin is trying hard to believe her; he's doing his best, really, but he is not succeeding.

"So, one minute you're telling me not to fall for any bullshit, that *it is what it is* and *a pond is a pond*, and *not* a lake. Then the next minute you're telling me that there is a monster inside it. So, which is it, girl? Are you a truth-teller, no-nonsense type, or just a big fat liar?"

He immediately regrets the "big fat" bit.

Laura doesn't seem too concerned one way or the other what way he chooses to perceive it. He can believe whatever he wants at this stage. She has explained it, her experience, as best she could; she's wanted to say it for a while, since she first saw it, months ago. If Kevin stays long enough he might see it for himself.

"You'll have to decide," she says, and she balls up the foil wrappers of the eaten sandwiches and throws them at his head. One bounces off into the water and he has to go and fetch it before it sails away.

"Careful now," she says, "he might come out and grab you."

"It's a *he*, is it?"

"Course it is. Aren't all monsters?"

"I suppose."

"Well, the ones in my book are anyway. The library one, I mean."

"Yeah. The baby one."

She throws another tin foil ball at him and he has to retrieve that one too.

Back on the flat rock beside her he reaches into his large coat pocket and produces a bottle of Guinness and an opener.

"Wow, this is becoming a bit of a habit. And you've fags too I suppose?"

He reaches into his other pocket, takes out a packet of cigarettes and the same pink lighter and lays them on the rock. He puts one in his mouth and lights it, then offers it to Laura. Tentatively she takes it, taking a nervous puff, and she splutters and coughs and spits into the water.

"You'll get used to it," he says.

"You're a bad influence."

Laura lies back on the rock, putting her bag underneath her head as a pillow. Her skirt rides up around her thighs.

"I hope you're not looking at my fat legs," she says.

"You should have warmer clothes on. Jeans for days like this. The winds can get cold."

"Very considerate of you to say so. You're like old Tom, very concerned about my welfare."

Kevin reaches down to pick up little pebbles and fling them out to the glassy surface.

Laura stares up at the flocculent clouds, the darkening sky.

"See anything yet?"

"Like a monster? Like a great ancient underwater beast?"

"Yeah. Like a Kraken."

"Nope. Just your fat legs."

He is *not* staring out at the water now, but deliberately along the white flesh of her thighs instead, just as he has owned up to – why lie? He stares as far as he can go, as far as the clothes allow.

Laura is unruffled. She does not move a muscle. Her eyes stay on the clouds, making shapes of them, making faces of them. *Pareidolia* is what it is termed: the making faces out of inanimate objects, like rock formations, tree barks, washing machines. She read that in a different library book.

"Right, well, you've probably seen enough for one day. We'd better head back. He's cooking tonight. Should be a treat."

Kevin pulls the ends of his coat over his crotch.

"Yep. A treat."

Laura sits up.

"Are you all right?"

"Yeah, I think I just need to pee."

"Right, well, not in the pond. You'll kill the fish. You can find a bush on the way back. Like you usually do."

She stands and slips her hands through the straps of her bag, jostles it into position on her back. Kevin stays put.

"Aren't you coming? What's the matter?"

"Nothing, just need a minute to … adjust."

She looks at him inquisitively, shrugs and moves off. He follows her a few seconds later, trots again: this too is becoming a bit of a habit.

Tom is standing at the cooker stirring a pot with a wooden spoon. The radio is playing "Everybody Wants to Rule the World" and he turns it up, moves his hips to it as he stirs some more.

He takes a sip from the broth and is pleased with himself. He turns around when he hears the sound of the teenagers returning, their usual bustle, their vigour, the energy he envies; what he wouldn't give to be back to those days again, to give things another go, maybe with Maggie, or Joan, or Mildred from Pennsylvania.

"Right on time," he shouts over Tears for Fears. He whistles along with the song. He knows it well now, a popular hit. He is already getting used to the sounds of modern pop music around the house, Laura's influence: it makes him feel younger, and he believes that is a good thing.

"And wash your hands, you filthy buggers! The downstairs toilet is blocked up. Use the upstairs one."

Message received, even over the loud pop music in the kitchen, even over bubbling and simmering pots and Tom now singing full-throated and joyously; they thunder up the stairs.

Myths and Monsters is on the bed. They both notice the book but decide to say nothing.

Laura takes the pornography magazines, the empty Guinness bottles and the sandwich foil wrappings out of her bag, and shoves them under her bed.

"We should've dumped them somewhere," Kevin says.

"I'll sort them out later," she tells him. "Don't worry, Tom doesn't enter here."

"Better get ready for Tom's delightful dinner. I'm going to go home, and change my shirt. Freshen up."

"And don't forget to bring your mother back with you. She was invited after all."

He could do without all that to be honest. Could do with a night off from his mother, a chance to be with other people, and not get into any discussion with her. They have lost something, and he doesn't know how it should be recovered. Or if it *should be* recovered. Perhaps he does blame her for his father's absence. He's got to blame something. Got to lash out at something. He'd probably be much better off just staying in his room altogether, having no dinner and no chat with anyone, just playing *Station to Station,* or *Tender Prey,* or *Songs of Love and Hate,* or *Seventeen Seconds.*

But he'll do it. He'll bring her back with him. He'll try not to overthink things. He'll be with Laura at least. That'll be enough. He enjoys his time with his cousin. Fuck Orlaith and those fuckers. Fuck them.

Have they gotten closer? These cousins. Have they gotten closer? Perhaps.

Maybe he will have lines for his poem after all. Something about a monster, bubbling under, something about a monster that wants to rear its head, spew forth something, spew forth … something … just spew.

Perhaps he will.

He needs to get these things out.

It's not good if he keeps things all bottled up inside.

7

The family is gathered around the kitchen table.

A family ... of sorts.

Tom faces Maura.

Kevin faces Laura.

It is a small table, and a small gathering, and while they sit close, only two of them, at this moment, really are: Kevin and Laura, the cousins. Close. Always like this. Fated. Thrown into the cosmos and ...

The older two ask them about school, about what they did that day, but the responses are monosyllabic, full of shrugs, often incoherent. More than once Maura and Tom have rolled their eyes to the heavens and tut-tutted, but they were teenagers once too, and they know the score.

"You've done a great job, Tom. This meat is delicious, so tender," says Maura, pleased to be out of the house, and secretly hoping it will make Kevin more talkative, communicative – he might open up in company, if not alone with her. Too often he prefers to lock himself away in his room, music blaring, no one for company but his morose self. It can't be good. It can't be healthy. At least this is an occasion, albeit coming on the back of a rather sad one. Yes, it is odd that Tom is trying all this now, this social gathering so soon, incredibly soon after a tragedy, yes, very odd, to be honest, but maybe his thinking is that it will begin a process of heal-ing, of helping Laura through it all. Maybe that's his think-ing. It might work. The poor thing. Maybe having loved ones close by, however they are coddled together, yes, there might be something to it; Tom is at least giving something a go.

"Only the finest beef served in this house, my dear."

"My husband never bothered his arse to cook. Never even skinned a bloody potato. I hope he's enjoying all that American meat, piling on the pounds – I hope he bloody chokes on it."

She had not expected such venom, and for it to come out of herself so quickly and easily, so soon. Perhaps it is because she feels so relaxed: Tom is good at that. A little rigid perhaps in his way, but friendly, affable, makes people relax and be comfortable quickly – a talent that is, for sure. Still, they all could have done without that little outburst of hers just now, where had that come from?

Kevin's eyes are on her, narrow and cold, but she chooses to ignore him.

"Well, our families haven't had it easy," says Tom. "But I suppose we should be grateful that we are here today … and now that Dymphna has gone, God rest her soul … we just have to get on with it."

"You have this fine house for the two of you now, Tom," says Maura, her eyes going round the table in the hope that no one gets offended. She is unsure as to the legal position, who has rights to what; she knows that Laura's father, Declan, is as unlikely to come home as her own fella. Good riddance perhaps. If you aren't prepared to stick around … and if a woman isn't good enough for you …

And she knows that there was no love lost between her and her sister, so the chance of being left anything at all …

"Laura is still too young to live on her own …"

Tom's attempt at surmising trails off. He's not sure how they will proceed with the official side of things, but he'll get them through it, he will.

Kevin is pushing peas around his plate, the names *Laura* and *Maura* rhyming in his head, he will not, however, include his mother in any poem or in any song; there's more to the art of poetry and songwriting than just rhyme, there's structure, and more importantly there's feeling, there's spirit and love and …

Laura too is fiddling with her food, bored with the occasion already, and wondering how long it will go on. She had enough of the adult world at the funeral, and the carrying of plates of food around for them, and the limp handshakes and the fake sympathy, and their nasty comments outside the house – at least when the Cartys arrived, at least that sparked something, something positive.

"Look, we'll make the best of it. We will, surely. Isn't that right, Laura?"

Laura looks up from her plate and nods at him. She has only been half-listening, but has enough to go on – it's not like the adults ask them anything really significant anyway, and she's still thinking of those two outside the house, the smoke rising in the night, and Aidan's soft hand on hers, and her blood rising, her blood rising, so quick it happens, like Kevin, his too, his blood quickening, two sides of the same coin, kissing cousins – what? – anger and attraction, the things those two old cunts said about her mother, and Kevin not believing in the monster, and the blond locks of that boy, like he's not even like an Irish lad at all, so exotic, Swedish or Finnish say, anger and attraction, maybe not so different after all, not so different in the stir of the pulse, the pulse, the rush, the pulse, the stir, the frenetic beat of the heart, hot and visceral and …

"You seem to be enjoying that meat, love," says Maura.

And their ease with endearments: *Love.*

Her mother used to say it all the time: the lilting Ls. *Laura, Love. Laura, Love.*

Laura nods again.

"I didn't know you could cook, Tom," says Kevin, a half-hearted attempt at conversation, his little input into the evening.

But actually, he is beginning to notice the scrunch of Laura's face, knowing her signs, her signals, knowing them all too well.

"When a man lives on his own for so long he gets used to things, Kevin. Picks up a few good habits."

"And a few bad ones too I'm sure," says Maura, trying to bring levity to the evening, as well as sounding a little risqué.

She doesn't get out of the house half-enough, thinks her son. And those British soaps on television only give her bad ideas, full as they are of closed encounters (everybody screwing everybody else in the neighbourhood) and endless arguments (everyone looking for everyone else only to pick a bone, start an altercation): Kevin is no fan. The best things to come out of Manchester were the bands: The Fall, The Smiths, Joy Division, and now the new wave of them, The Happy Mondays, The Stone Roses, Inspiral Carpets.

Kevin and Laura trade looks, not enjoying the flirtatious vibe that has started up between Tom and Maura. Not enjoying it one bit.

Putting it down to another bad day.

Tom's eyes linger on Maura, a little too long, at least for Kevin and Laura, and realizing this himself, he switches his attention to the youths.

"And how's school, you two?"

Hasn't he asked this already?

"Fine," says one.

"Fine," mumbles the other.

"Jaysus, they're a wealth of information, these two. You wouldn't want to be stuck for a bit of conversation, would you?"

"Teenagers," says Maura, "weren't we that way ourselves? Long ago."

"For me *long ago*," says Tom, quickly, "not too long ago for you, Maura. Aren't you still looking young and fresh and everything."

Kevin and Laura look at each other again; Kevin does the finger-down-throat-puking gesture for Laura's amusement, and it goes unseen by the adults.

It is all a tad claustrophobic, this family situation: Tom had been Declan's brother – *had been?* – and Dymphna had married Declan, and Dymphna was Maura's sister ... and the men, the married men, they left and ...

Too close.

It is all too close for comfort.

Too close.

"Get away outta that, you old charmer," says Maura, reddening, clearly delighted at the first compliment in ... who knows how long?

Tom eventually picks up on the kids' awkwardness and changes the subject.

"You know, Maura, we have poker nights once a week, great craic. You're welcome to come along."

He turns to Laura for permission.

"That's if you don't mind, love. The lads coming here, once a week, I mean, for a game. Couple of hours is all it is. We won't be too loud or anything. Just a few drinks and a game of cards. We won't interrupt your studies or anything like that. The Junior Cert or the Leaving Cert or whatever you are preparing for."

"I don't mind," says Laura, unwilling to get into any kind of discussion about upcoming exams; she doesn't want to think on that stuff at all; the meat on her plate is enough for her right now, it really is quite good, kudos to Bernie the butcher in his ever-blood-stained striped apron. Tender stuff indeed.

"Wonderful," says Tom. "It's not exclusively a male club or anything like that, we're very progressive around here, so feel free to join us whenever you want. We're no experts or anything. Just a bit of craic, like."

"Sounds like fun," says Maura. "It would get me out of the house anyway. I think I might need a few lessons first, though. Was never the best at card games; I don't think I even know the rules of poker."

Kevin looks at her suspiciously.

"I'll teach you, no problem. And don't worry, it's not strip poker."

Kevin nearly spits his water out over the dinner table. Jesus Christ! Imagine if it was! Four or five crusty old men gathering round his mother. Fuck's sake! He feels a sudden desire to be out of there and in his own room listening to Dave Fanning on the radio, even if he is playing one of those lauded Irish bands that really aren't all that good, Something Happens, or the putrid The Stunning. There aren't that many Irish bands that ever get Kevin excited.

He has a lot of time for A House though, and when someone on the radio said they were like an Irish version of The Smiths – though this was wildly inaccurate – he could *kind of* see their point. And anything Cathal Coughlan does is interesting, he is one of the few…

But what is happening to Laura?

Her eyes seem to go distant; her head rolls around on her neck as if it is too heavy to be attached there.

The three of them look at her.

And then the two adults look to Kevin.

"Shit," says the boy, "it could be happening."

Laura's head rolls around faster and her eyes roll up like manic marbles for a quick second and then leave nothing but frightening whites. She falls heavily off her chair and onto the floor.

Kevin is quick out of his seat and over to her. He places his hand under her head to stop it from banging on the floor.

He crouches down to her, almost genuflecting, and allows her head to rest on his thighs. Her head bounces and her body gyrates uncontrollably, but Kevin gently rubs her forehead with his hand in a calm and soothing manner.

The adult spectators seem to be holding their breath, until Tom lets out a gasp:

"What should we do?"

"Nothing. It'll pass," says Kevin. "She'll be fine. She's not so uncomfortable. This one isn't such a big one. She's had worse. Isn't that right, Laurs? We're nearly done, aren't we?"

Maura has her mouth open, shocked at the occurrence, but maybe even more so at the confidence and complete control of the situation her son displays. She had heard about Laura's affliction, but in any of the accounts she has never heard about the calm of her own boy, his reading of the situation, his reading and reacting, his legerdemain.

"Maybe it was the mention of strip poker that set her off," jokes Kevin, trying to put everyone – so obviously uncomfortable – at ease.

But the situation isn't over yet.

Laura continues to convulse for another minute or so until, gradually, the tremors begin to wane. She lies stiffly in Kevin's arms, oddly serene now, more like she's just had a relaxing nap than the trauma she's just been through, or ... the trauma *the adults have been through* – they seem to be the ones more visibly shaken now: Tom is drumming his fingers on the table not knowing what best to do with them, he's better at pulling bottles of stout from the fridge, serving drinks, cajoling; he knows nothing about how to deal with the kind of medical drama that has played out so vividly before him. It was like something on TV.

When she comes around completely, Laura looks up and into Kevin's eyes.

"Again?" she says.

"Again, my dear."

He always says this phrase in his "Big House" voice, his just-back-from-the-perils-of-the-trenches voice; as if he is a swashbuckling lord just returned to the sprawling estate to take care of all the winsome-but-wilting lasses that were lost without him and have left the grounds – as well as their own mental state – fall to disrepair; he allows himself these very grand thoughts of himself: voluminous, vain, especially in these, his moments of heroism.

"I'm all right though, aren't I?" she says, playing her part too, the distressed damsel.

"Yep. No blood. No bruises. You're in safe hands."

She keeps looking at him, deep, deep into his hazel eyes, and she starts to cry – there is no acting in this though, no deceit whatsoever: these tears are all unreservedly genuine, too hard to fake.

"Thanks," she says.

Kevin smiles down at her; with the cuff of his sleeve he wipes away her tumbling tears.

Heroism, yes, sure. Cockiness too. But more … more … affection than anything else. That also, too genuine to fake.

"Better get you up to the table if you want to have some dessert."

Laura manages a little laugh, and so too do Tom and Maura, out of sheer relief.

"Well done," Maura says to her son, but Kevin shakes it off, as if to suggest it happens all that time and he knows exactly what he's doing. He knows his cousin. He does. He knows her very well.

Outside the house, although the night has grown cold, their faces are flushed from the warm plum pudding (Maura had been making some for Christmas, and decided to take one bowl of it to Tom's: a trial, and it worked, compliments all round) as well as from the good conversation (post epileptic episode) when praise naturally went Kevin's way again, and when they were sure that Laura was sound and unlikely to relapse.

Maura goes to hug Tom.

"It's been a lovely evening, despite the little drama. Thank you for having us, Tom."

She stands on her tiptoes to reach him and kiss his (especially) shaved cheek.

"Anytime," he says, trying to sound as smooth as his skin.

And then a thought suddenly occurs to him.

"Actually, you know what. Instead of you walking home, why don't I give you a lift?"

"It's only down the road, Tom. No need. It's no bother. We'll walk."

"There's a bit of a chill in the air. And it'd be nice to talk some more. It isn't too late, is it?"

Kevin and Laura are standing watching this. As much as they don't know what is going on … they think they know *exactly* what is going on.

A quick thought of the porn magazines flickers across Kevin's mind and he shudders. Where had he gotten those? They were all UK publications. Were the poker players some kind of collector's group? Aficionados of smut?

Laura is hoping the whole night finishes soon, she wants to be done with it; she has no jacket on and the brumous breeze is hatching goose pimples on her arms.

Kevin has his long raincoat on and is ready for the road; enough of this, c'mon, enough now everybody.

"Actually, I have another bright idea," says Tom.

His voice is too high for the time of night, too high for the enveloping darkness, too high for a man of his age in a most unbecoming mood of fervour.

They wait, not knowing what to expect from him.

"Kevin, you can stay here for the night … if you like. Sleep in the spare room!"

His audience looks bewildered.

What on earth is he talking about?

He only had a glass of Guinness or two. Whatever she had put in that pudding has made him loopy, or is it senility creeping in on him?

No one knows quite what to say.

"It'd be good for Laura. You know, if anything happens to her … you could … you know … help her again."

"I'm fine," Laura says. "I don't need a private nurse."

"Well?" says Tom persisting, hopeful, denying that he sounds just a little on the foolish side.

Maura looks concerned:

"I don't know. Kevin doesn't have any of his stuff."

"What stuff does he need? He's only going to bed. I'm sure we'll find a spare toothbrush."

"My school uniform for tomorrow," says Kevin. "What about that?"

"I'll drop you back early in the morning and you can change then."

Kevin would prefer to be in his own room, with his own music, but he is veering towards succumbing to the whole daft notion. As long as it means no more chatter, he is tired of listening to them all, standing out here, his legs tired after the day – let's all just fucking say goodbye then.

Laura might be in the same boat, looks like she doesn't care either. She'd rather sleep. She'd rather rest her tired legs too. The fits, when they come, no matter how short an episode, take quite a lot out of her, as do the after-dinner pills she takes, and she wants to rest, and begin a new tomorrow, a normal day at school, hopefully able to go the entire day without a flicker, without a single problem. Normalcy: that's what she wishes for. Even to be like Orlaith, or the long lanky one, Helena, that might be enough. To get by. To get on. And then to get out. But there is not a lot of *normal* going on around her: her superhero cousin in his superhero cape – that weird raincoat – Maura jittery and slightly aglow from the evening, unused to alcohol or attention;

and Uncle Tom, quite beside himself with enthusiasm for plans that don't make much sense – unless he has ulterior motives, which he probably has, he is just a teenager too, grown older.

"Fine," says Maura, too tipsy to argue the point, "as long as you're not up late talking all night."

"We won't," says Kevin.

"We won't," says Laura, still thinking of sleep and how fast she wants it to come and assuage. "Promise."

"Laura has her baby monster book to read anyway, no time for talking."

He gets a dig in the ribs for this comment, and he groans.

"That's it then, settled," says Tom, pleased with his powers of persuasion, or just pleased with how quickly everyone has capitulated. He jangles his keys to let Maura know it is time for off. The white van will get her safely home, for the all of two minutes the drive will take.

Maura hugs her son, to his infinite embarrassment, and she whispers in his ear:

"Good job tonight. Well done. She's lucky to have a cousin like you."

She pulls away and speaks loud enough for them all to hear then, as Tom opens the car door for her:

"And no loud music. Don't drive Tom batty. He needs his beauty sleep!"

When Tom starts the van "Everybody Wants to Rule the World" plays again. How lucky is that? Twice in one day. A song he loves. Things must be looking up for him. Luck on his side. Luck. After all that has gone on these past few days … already into positive thinking and … well, things looking up.

The cousins watch the van pull away. They turn around and head into the house.

Into the warm house.

Out of the cold.

Into the warm and welcoming house.

Warm beds.

Soft.

Inviting.

And the sleep they crave…if it all goes according to plan.

But so little ever does: the cousins know this well enough, already in their young lives. Already they have seen so much: what else is there to experience?

8

Both driver and passenger face forward into the night and the road before them as the pop song plays.

He decides not to show off his singing voice, but Tom hums along, and Maura says she likes the song a lot too; it's been going solidly on the radio for two or three years now, and you'd never get sick of it.

"It's a strange old name, isn't it?" Tom says. "Tears for Fears. I wonder what it is all about. Who is tearful, and what have they to fear?"

Maura is sure that her son might have an opinion were he with them, it was those kinds of musings he cared for – whatever other mysteries were going on in his life she knew that much about her teenage son. But he's probably sleeping in that spare room already, with his own morbid music playing in his head.

"I don't know, really," she says. "But they all have strange names now. Duran Duran, what could that even mean? And what is a Kajagoogoo?"

Tom hasn't heard that last one.

"Things were much simpler in my time," he says. "The showbands were called after a place, a town, or village, or after the bandleader. It was much simpler."

"I suppose so," says Maura.

The drive is over before the next song has even finished. Tracy Chapman's "Fast Car" – which they might even consider ironic – but pulling up outside Maura's house there is something else entirely on her mind.

"It's good I've got you alone actually, Tom."

Tom keeps the engine running; he brightens, his own engine beginning to purr a little too.

"There's something I want to ask you about. Advice, like."

His face falls fast, and he hopes she doesn't see it in the dark of the van.

"For a few months now," she continues, "I've gotten letters."

"Letters?"

"From Tadhg. In America. San Francisco."

"Oh? And what does he have to say for himself?"

His tone is dismissive, displeased.

"I don't know. The letters aren't for me. They're for Kevin."

"So you haven't read any?"

"Not a word."

"And why haven't you given them to the boy?"

Maura thinks hard for a moment, biting her lower lip. She had one too many glasses of wine at dinner and is not used to such consumption. Now she is in a van with a man she hardly knows and she is confessing to something she hadn't expected to.

"Fear, I suppose," she says. And the band name comes back to her again. Fears. Tears. There had been a lot of those over the years.

"I don't want him to have any relationship with Kevin. He left us."

"I get that. But Kevin has a right to read his own post."

"But I'm still his mother. And I'm still the one looking after him. He's not yet a man. He's just a boy. Don't I have the right to protect him?"

"Protect him or protect yourself?"

"You think I should give them to him."

"Of course you should. Kevin is mature enough to know what to do. He's a sensible lad. And he'll only resent you if you start keeping secrets from him."

"You're right. You're right. I know it. I just don't…"

She reaches out and touches Tom's hand on the steering wheel. His grip has been so tight on it, white-knuckled. Now it relaxes.

"Thanks," she says.

He brightens again.

She is standing in her pyjamas ready to get into her bed. It has been a long day. It has been a long couple of days. She does not know if she is grieving or not. She heard Maura talking about Kevin going to school in the morning, but surely she isn't obliged to go. She is mourning for her mother, surely she has more time to … she *is* mourning, isn't she?

So why has she not cried?

Why has she not broken down?

Maybe because it is easier in the long run. Maybe it makes sense that her mother is not suffering anymore, and deep down she knows that. And maybe it makes sense that she is with Tom too, a good and caring gentleman who needs a bit of company and will look after her well. Look after her better perhaps, for the few years she needs, before she is able to go out on her own. Start college. Be a woman. Do her own thing. Whatever that will entail.

She will have to make career choices. They talk about it all the time in school. The career guidance teacher. The ambitious pupils. The girls who want to become nurses, head off to foreign lands and help the poor and the needy. The girls who want to do business courses, run their own companies, or study Psychology, or Graphic Design or get into the hotel trade.

Laura has no idea.

She has no idea what she wants to do.

What does she like to study? Nothing in particular.

What is she good at? Nothing in particular.

How come she has gotten to this stage of her life and not really thought about any of this? How come she has left it all so late? *Is it* all so late?

Kevin is good at music, a talented piano player, he's got that going for him at least. He will surely go on to do something with his skills, a professional musician perhaps, or a sound engineer, or a … fucking pretentious critic. Ha, that's more like it.

As if to stop her line of thinking there is a knock on the door. Kevin does not wait to be invited in this time. He enters, wearing only a T-shirt (The Cure's *Boys Don't Cry*, bought in Dublin on his one visit last year) and underpants.

Laura tries not to look surprised, and she tries not to look at the white underpants.

She is surprised to see him there. And, actually, she does sneak a look at his white underpants after all, which do look a little on the pathetic side in all fairness. He's all manly when he's whipping out his yolk at the side of a field, when there's no one around on the way home from school, but catch him like this in his Y-fronts, his twig-like legs sticking pitifully out of them, it brings him right down to size.

She manages not to laugh, and silently congratulates herself on this achievement.

"You don't like the spare room?"

"Did you not hear me coughing? I can't stay in there. Too much dust. I'm allergic."

He has no scientific, no medical proof of this, he has never been tested. He is not asthmatic as far as he knows. But it feels right to say this. He is not lying.

"It hasn't been cleaned out in years. Mom was too sick to clean anything. And I couldn't be arsed."

An awkward silence rises like a swarm of dark insects in the middle of the room, and hangs there in front of them.

What should they do now?

It is her house, it is her call – so what is she to do? What should she say?

She says nothing at all, she is struck dumb.

The boy in the embarrassing underpants tries instead:

"Can I stay here with you?"

Laura looks straight into his eyes, the eyes she trust so much, she really does, she'd trust him with her life. But she cannot help but feel a little sceptical, and a little scared too, of this new unfamiliar scenario, of this unchartered land, she does not know how to respond at all. Dumbstruck indeed.

Tom opens the car door for her and Maura steps out.

"It's been a long time since I've been treated like a lady. If ever I was."

"You deserve it," he says.

They walk to her front door, the light over it automatically coming on and limning. Spotlighting them. As if they are on a stage suddenly, or are being presented to the world.

She is embarrassed to notice that the paint on that front door is peeling. Could do with a lick of some good strong colour, or a whole new door even. A whole new house. But fat chance of that. Since she has been on her own she has had enough trouble making ends meet. The job cleaning in Cronin's Bar of a morning isn't too bad – Marty Cronin, not short of a bob, is always good to her, enough to provide Kevin with a pound or two of pocket money, and for him to buy his precious cassette tapes; and Tadhg had left some money in the bank, he hadn't gone with it all, took only what he needed, the cunt.

Needed?

Needed for what?

To go where?

Why doesn't she really seek the answers to these questions? She is quicker to let them dissolve, easier that way, much easier. Isn't that all she wants for the remaining years now: an easier run of things. If she can get Kevin to college, then she'll be all right. If she can get past that hurdle, then maybe he can get a good job himself, maybe look after ...

"Thanks again, Tom. For dinner and everything. And what you're doing for Laura, it's wonderful, it really is. I know I'm her aunt but ... as you know, I've got my hands full with Kevin, and ... well, you stepping in like this to take care of everything it's ..."

She stops herself from going on any further and instead reaches up to him on her tiptoes again, this time kissing him softly on the lips. It is a kiss as much to wipe away thoughts of Tadhg, Kevin and college – all of that, money thoughts, it is a kind of cleansing kiss then, to just focus on something else, a reprieve – as much as it is an affectionate token of gratitude to the man who has been nice to her these last few hours; he really has.

They shouldn't be doing any of this, not so soon after a funeral. But the rules of this family were truly broken a long time ago; when she was left on her own to look after a young boy. And she doesn't mind breaking a few rules herself now. She is long past caring. And if Mrs. Nolan is watching from her window, then Mrs. Nolan knows full well what she can go ahead and do to herself.

She turns from him, from this good man. She opens the door and sends him off with a little wave. She shuts the door as gently as she can, to let him know, that even though this is a literal shutting of the door, it isn't a figurative one, and she hopes he will have the wisdom to receive that.

Two faces look up at the white ceiling.

Two bodies are lying side by side in the narrow bed.

"Are you not cold?" she asks.

"No, I'm all right."

"Not too hot?"

"No, I'm all right."

Laura is concerned about him, his bare legs in the bed, his light T-shirt – she is more snug in her pyjamas.

"I've never slept in the same bed with someone before. I mean, besides my mother."

"Me too."

"Sorry, it's a bit cramped," she says.

"It's fine."

"I'm not going to have another fit or anything. There's really no need for you to be here."

Kevin laughs, "Bit late now."

"Yeah, I suppose."

"Just in case. I'm here. If anything does go wrong."

"I always sleep fine. Weird dreams though, sometimes."

"Monsters?" he says, laughing.

"Of course."

"Do you snore?"

"I don't think so."

They stare straight up, their necks stiff. There's a water stain on the ceiling and both have their eyes trained on it, silently making into something it is not. Pareidolia again. Laura thinks it resembles the head of a gorilla; Kevin hasn't decided, nothing comes to mind, unusually, for such a creative boy: perhaps it's the tension of the occasion.

"I suppose we should go to sleep then."

Being nearest to the lamp on the bedside table, Kevin moves to switch it off, but before he gets to it he notices a corner of magazine peeping out from under her pillow.

"What's this?" he says, pulling at it, knowing for sure that it is the pornography magazine that she has sequestered.

"I told you. It's study."

Laura doesn't feel the slightest bit ashamed. She might have before, she might have even a few days ago – but these two, maybe even more so since the funeral, are growing closer all the time, and she feels comfortable with him, her first cousin; she is lying in bed with him for God's sake, and he is in his prim white Y-fronts, they could not be any closer.

Laura props herself up on her elbow and Kevin copies her movements. She opens the magazine and they stare at it, wide-eyed, curious. She leafs though the pages, slowly, their eyes scanning together, as if each page is a revelation, something that they had known about but had never quite seen, some mysteries revealed, techniques or positions illustrated, fully, pictorially explained.

"Jesus Christ," she says. "I really didn't know they could grow to that size."

"Apparently they can. Although... I'm not quite there yet."

Laura giggles nervously at his joke; she does not want to picture what is in those white underpants – he's her cousin, they'd be much better off just going to sleep.

"Put it away," Kevin says. "I don't want to start... you know... getting all... hot and bothered."

"It's all right," she says, with a catch in her voice, "it's natural."

They fall back on the pillow, their heads close.

On the ceiling: the gorilla's scowl. Or is it just a water stain? A pond is a pond.

"I can do it for you... if you want," she says, the bravest thing she might have ever said to him, she has surprised even herself.

He gulps, his Adam's apple feeling stiff and lumpy in his throat.

"I've never touched one before," she says.

"I've never... been touched there before... except by myself... obviously."

He tries to make her laugh. Their laughs ease things. He likes when they laugh together, about teachers, Duffy or Mulligan, about Orlaith Crowley or lanky Helena, that long length of misery.

Every word he utters though seems to come out a stutter.

His chest pounds.

His knees have started to tremble.

Can she feel that next to him? The trembling? So much of her life is already just that: trembling, shaking.

"Is it going to be messy?"

"Yes," he says, "definitely, there is no doubt about that."

She giggles again, but it is more a nervous rasp than it is any indication of mirth. This is all unexplored territory. For both of them. And even the light is still on. They are so harshly lit.

Her hand moves under the blankets towards him, and the expression on his face shows that she has quickly found her way, has reached her target. She wants to see his reaction – they are harshly, inescapably, lit – and so she turns to him, his hazel eyes closed now, and a frown across his brow, more like he is solving a difficult algebraic equation than being pleasured.

"We shouldn't be doing this," he says, but his hand rebels against such a sensible thought. It has other ideas, and the look on her face says that this hand has found its target too.

"This is the only thing that has made me happy and excited in some time," she says, a surprising amount of anger in her voice.

He opens his eyes to her and she glares back at him.

"My mother just died, so don't you dare stop. Don't you dare fucking stop! We deserve a bit of fun in our lives after the shit we've taken for years. I don't give a fuck if we're supposed to or not."

He doesn't need any more convincing.

It is an experiment. For both of them. This is how they justify it to themselves. A learning process. Just as much as the magazines are. Education. The stout and the cigarettes too.

And so she keeps at it. And he does. Gathering pace. Both of them. But it doesn't take all that long. It is all far over quicker than she would have expected; as his breathless gasp calls the rhythms to an abrupt halt.

They hear the front door of the house opening and clicking again to a close. Tom's return. Nice timing.

Kevin reaches over again, this time succeeding in turning the bedside lamp off.

The blushed faces are hidden in the dark now.

The gorilla is gone.

And Kevin didn't lie: a mess has indeed been made.

"He's not going to check in on us, is he?" Kevin whispers.

"I doubt it. I'm sure he's got other things on his mind."

At the kitchen table, with a glass of Bushmills in front of him, Tom surveys the room with an air of satisfaction, an air of achievement, even pride. He is smiling to himself, and he cannot seem to stop it.

He switches the radio on, but keeps it low. He is sure the children are asleep already – they've been through so much, they're only kids still, innocent, God love 'em, they must be pooped out completely.

On the radio some political analyst is discussing Gorbachev and the changes he is implementing. The whole thing, the whole thing could come tumbling down according to the analyst. Tom is not sure what the "whole thing" is – he must listen further, pay attention. But he is sure that this Gorbachev fella is changing things for sure. Making a big difference. The entire world can change in a short space of time. Lives can change very quickly indeed. One minute it is one way, the next...a whole new other. He surveys the kitchen again, so many of the things in it are not his at all. Things that were left here, that he has acquired. Even the youths upstairs asleep, acquired somehow. But he will do his best to take care of them: that should be his sole purpose from now on, and whatever finances they need to get to college and beyond, take care of that. And as for that lovely lady, Maura. On her own these long lonely years. How could her husband have just upped and left like that? And Laura's father, his own brother. The cheek of them both. The downright cruelty of it. Was the place that bad that they had to up and leave? And the trail of destruction left behind. The debris of a broken family … and who is left with the pan and the sweeping brush to clean it all up?

The political analyst says politics is changing, that there are new ideas coming in to play, old forms being washed away. And walls, he keeps going on about walls, and bridges, figurative, literal, and now that Tom is some kind of father, he thinks he understands all this. Old barriers can come crashing down, or old curtains ripped and torn asunder and new brighter ones put up in their place, or no curtains at all. Let the light in.

Tom's metaphors get more mixed with each sting of whiskey in his throat: walls, curtains, a changing world. What does he know, really? He knows that he is a man that has fallen on his feet. And that is enough? Isn't it?

SERIOUS FOR THE WINTER TIME
TO WRENCH MY SOUL

9

He is musical. She has music too.
She is monstrous. He is monstrous, too.

The music is not theirs, not yet.
The monsters are not them. Not yet.

But monsters, monsters, monsters can be born and…

10

Dressed all in black. This is how he likes it. There is no funeral to go to, but still, black: his only colour.

He is sitting at his bedroom desk and he is fiddling with his synthesizer. It can do so many things: it can make so many sounds, just the touch of a button and an orchestra at his disposal. Beats too. Drums. Tom-toms. Snares. Hi-hats. Bloody bongos.

But he can't seem to make his songs work, not this day. He plays a few feeble notes and he hums a little. He writes some words in his notebook and then he scribbles them all out again.

He gets up and presses play on his trusty stereo. His mother had bought him this for Christmas only a couple of years ago. She knew he was a music fan – he would talk about little else – and so when she asked him what he wanted for Christmas the stereo was his only and obvious answer. She had bought him tapes too when he'd ask for them after a Thursday evening watching *Top of the Pops*.

His mother bought him the synthesizer the Christmas after – she would have bought him anything, anything to forget about the father that wasn't there. *Isn't* there. *Isn't*. She wanted to recompense. She still does, but money is a lot tighter these days, and she has to be careful. Kevin knows all this, and he is not a greedy boy, he is grateful for the things he has. The stereo and synthesizer are his most treasured things, and his tape collection of course, lined up alphabetically, properly, these are his things, *his* things.

Tanita Tikaram plays on the stereo, "Sighing Innocents". This one might seem like an odd choice but Kevin is well able to justify the selection. He thinks she's an excellent singer, an excellent songwriter too. He's actually very pleased that this album came along: it beats the shit out of the fluff that's in the rest of the charts. He's read that some of the rock critics are calling her "the female Leonard Cohen", and he can't really argue against that. The songs have something about them, something profound, spiritual, even the poppier ones have that hint of sarcasm, like the snipingly sardonic, "Poor Cow".

Kevin scratches his chin. Laura would take the piss out of him if she saw him like this, musing this way, "pretentious" she likes to say, cruelly, perhaps accurately. But he does, he actually does scratch his chin when he thinks, like he is assuming the manner of a critic of great renown, like he is a grand, erudite philosopher, when really he is just a nerd who likes to listen to pop and rock music. *Nerd*: the word is all the rage now, imported from America, popularized in movies like *Revenge of the Nerds*: it is common parlance, even in his schoolyard, even in his rural shithole; words like *dork* are gaining a foothold too, though thankfully *jerk* has yet to be met with any gusto. He prefers Irishisms, prefers *eejit* and *gobshite*, such terms seem to have more velocity when spat out. He's heard these insults from boys in school often enough, hurled at himself, at anyone weaker, any sensitive anyone in the firing line, or even Orlaith's scathingly vicious, unladylike tongue. She has nothing on Laura though. Orlaith is good-looking, and knows it, but she hasn't the charm of his complex cousin, couldn't hold a candle.

He scratches his chin again. Is there any hair growing there? He pulls a small hand mirror out of his drawer – sure, he can be as vain as the next boy – and checks to see if any follicle sprouts. He examines the chin, the upper lip, everything with the forensic detail of a scientist or a top sleuth from one of those detective dramas.

Hardly a thing.

Just a few light wisps that haven't yet the strength to toughen and blacken. He hides away the mirror again. Maybe next week.

He knows Laura loves this album too. One they agree on. A rarity. They listened to it together only a week or two ago – has it been that long already? Everything seems to have blurred with the funeral and the walk to the pond, and the night in the bed and ...

Is he supposed to feel bad about that? Is he supposed to regret what happened? The aftermath of a funeral. A stupid idea Tom had for them to get together and spend time as a family, a "new family", starting off a "new life", and the body hardly cold in the grave. The headstone not yet inscribed.

And he went in to her bedroom and he went into her bed and he knew something would happen. Two teenagers – with the hormones the way they are, rampaging through them – cannot be expected to lie next to each other and for nothing to happen, cousins or no.

Did he plan it?

How much had he thought through?

He hadn't been lying about the dust in the other room.

But did he know what he was doing?

And did Laura? Allowing it all to happen like that?

Are they both to blame?

Blame?

He didn't put his thing inside her. They didn't really *do* much, just fumbled around. That was the extent of it. Nothing to worry about … right?

It was only that one time. Kevin knows they both want it more now, but are they able to resist?

Or is it that they don't know how to orchestrate it? Find the right time to be together uninterrupted, without prying eyes.

Kevin thinks of the boy, the blond fella, Aidan Carty. What does she see in him? He wonders if he should try with one of the other girls, and chat up the gangly one, Helena … would Laura be jealous, would she care?

He looks out at the black sky. Tanita Tikaram plays. He does not know how to pronounce her name. Kevin and Laura have had several discussions about it and they've never agreed. But *Ancient Heart:* it had some fine songs on it.

He worries about her still: Laura. The name written above a poem with no words. A song with no lyrics.

But she has had no fits. Kevin is pleased about this. She has been calm in school. She has been calm with Tom – him cooking and looking after her like he is the father she never really had. This is all good.

She goes to the grave several times a week.

And she goes to the pond too, and stares out, waiting for something to happen. But nothing ever does.

Is she stupid to be doing that?

Kevin doesn't know. He wants to believe her and has been there with her twice since. But the water stays still.

The water rarely ripples. They sit on the flat rock and they eat a sandwich or they smoke a cigarette and they look out and then they walk back to their homes ... and that's it. No ripple. No rumble. No roar.

He has cast stones out there. He has flung rocks. But nothing, nothing occurs. Nothing moves in there. Just fish, he presumes, swimming there, or frogspawn when the season is right, or newts that swerve about. But no monster. He has never seen any trace of any monster.

In his quest to figure it out, to find a solution, to come to grips with his cousin's afflictions, he has taken a book from the library. A book about psychology, or neurology, the workings of the brain, something along those lines: it was hard going. There were so many words and concepts that went right over his head. But the book talked about "projection". And it seemed to make sense: it is like Laura's projecting this fantasy, projecting onto the pond, or trying to extract *from* the pond something ... that she's lost. There is no father. Lost. There is no mother. Lost. So, maybe, to make up for those *losses,* she invents a monster. Invents. Projects. A monster from the deep is more thrilling than the mundane existence of life in her country village. A dying village. A village of old people. And the young flit off to the cities as soon as they possibly can. Yes, invention. That's all she is doing. Inventing a monster. Something big and bold and brilliant that only she can see. It's hers. She's invented something that is uniquely *hers.* But she has wanted to share it too. She has taken Kevin with her to show him the monster. Saying: *look, look what I saw! Can you see it too?* Only the monster never appears. Is that part of the projection too? The need for it *not* to be there so that he will sympathize. It seemed counter-intuitive, but maybe there was something in that. The book made some sense. The parts he could understand. It got him thinking. It got him contemplating ... for a while at least. But he soon brought it back to the library and fell into familiar books, familiar territory, taking a book about David Bowie instead, more to his taste, and read and grew disgusted with this new Bowie, and wondering how the star-man so bright could have fallen so low, pardoning all puns. Bowie disgusted him now, to be honest, Bowie and that shitty blond hair a few years ago, looking so smarmy; the rot set in with that gay gobshite Mercury and ... and what the fuck is he doing this year, what the fuck is Tin Machine and ...

From monsters to projections to the thin white ...

That little blond fucker, just because he's got ...

Kevin needs some kind of distraction.

He looks up to Siouxsie on the wall, her bright red lips, her steely eyes.

He sits forward on his chair and thinks about playing some notes. But he soon abandons the idea and shuts the whole system off.

He takes down his notebook of lyrics, opens it, stares down upon it. It has her name on the top of the page, but it has no poem, has no song yet. What should he write? Should he even write? Why does he want to write a poem or song about his cousin? Because that's all he can think about. Because that's all he can do.

He did not kiss her. *They* did not. But why? They had touched their most intimate parts, to satisfaction, to climax ... but they did not kiss. Because you don't kiss your cousin. There are rules. Aren't there? But didn't it feel good to smash those rules? It did. It felt very good indeed. He feels no guilt. None. His father is gone. The absent fathers. *The Absent Fathers!* He should be entitled to do what he wants. There is no father figure. He thinks of the George Michael song. It's always on the radio these days. "Father Figure". Kevin is a fan of The Cure. Of The Smiths. Fuck George Michael. To kiss his cousin would be to admit something. To admit something that neither of them want to admit. What is that? What is it that they don't want to admit? That they both, need, want … need, want … what?

They had stared into each other's eyes, as their hands searched. The light had stayed on. She had not asked for it to be switched off.

The ceiling and the shapes it had there. A gorilla. Monsters?

The hands plummeting beneath the blankets. Feeling-finding. Finding-feeling. Pulling. Tugging. And it was all so fast. Over. Before you knew it.

No lips though.

No lips.

No mouth on mouth.

Eyes on eyes, yes, eyes on eyes, that much was true …

What did it all mean? And what is there to do about it now?

He plays "Preyed Upon" again, rewinding back to the beginning of the song and playing it all over again. It is a good song. It is a song for his mood. This is what he does, he seeks out songs to suit his moods, or often seeks songs to change them, to alter his way of thinking, to be someone else for a while.

There is a knock on the door.

"Oh, for fuck's sake!"

He doesn't even whisper this, he doesn't mutter, he just says it out loud. To hell with decorum. He's sure his mother can hear.

She enters with a cup of warm milk and a plate of chocolate chip cookies. She puts them on his desk, careful not to spill on the synthesizer (there would be hell to pay). She goes to the stereo and turns the volume down. She stands there for a moment, listening to the song.

"That's a nice song. Who is it?"

"Tanita Tikaram."

Has he said that name right? Does it matter?

"Never heard of her. Tanita. Like *Anita*. Foreign, I suppose."

Kevin is in no mood to explain anything.

"What's the name of the song?"

"He Likes the Sun."

He has rewound the tape back even further, it's the ninth track playing now and the singer is singing about growing old, and feeling down inside.

Maura O'Brien can relate. She can.

"You OK?" she asks.

"Yeah."

She goes over to touch the radiator under his window, checking to see if it is warm enough. She always wants him warm enough. The winter has been hard already, a steady frost most mornings, and they are saying that it is only going to get worse. Temperatures dropping all the time. The prospect of snow.

"You're not cold?"

"No."

Maura looks out the window at the blackness. She shivers a little, then draws the curtains. She thinks she hears a little cry out there. Sounds like an animal, a wounded one, or a hungry one, out there in the garden. They've been having foxes around. A spate. No, actually there is a collective noun for them, isn't there, she heard it on the radio quiz the other day – was it Larry Gogan that was going on about them? The group was called a *leash*, or a *skulk*, an *earth*, *lead* or *troop*. Take your pick. She would prefer an *annoyance* of foxes, more true to the situation. But surely they'd be hiding in a den somewhere, away out of this cold. Foxes get hungry of course, and go foraging, and need to bring food back to their young ones. When do the young get born? Is that a spring thing? She has lived all her life in the countryside and knows so little of how it works. Animals. Wildness. These foxes are that bit more urban though, aren't they, coming out of the woods and into the gardens, into the dustbins, looking for scraps, looking for anything sustainable. They are all searching. Hunger everywhere. She is hungry herself, forgoing the odd meal here and there, just so that he has enough. She likes to bring him treats like this. Especially when he is studying, doing his homework, or writing his songs. He might be famous someday, might be able to sell his songs. Or the Eurovision! Why not have a go at that! The Irish are damn lucky in the competition, having won three times or four times already this decade. And that lovely Niamh Kavanagh song, that surely was the best of the lot and…

"Anything else? I mean, thanks for the snack… but is there something…?"

She had been cast into aimless dreaming and he has pulled her back firmly into his bedroom, into the tension, and into confessing:

"Yes. There is something we need to talk about."

She is suddenly nervous. Visibly so. Why does she feel like this? It is her own son. Her one and only. Her beloved. They should be able to talk freely, openly; they should be able to talk honestly about anything. But they are not.

He is waiting for her to go on. This is like Laura and her ridiculous monsters. Is this going to be another thing he will be unable to believe? More nonsense. Or perhaps the mad mother has seen the monster too.

"There's something I'm ashamed of. Something I've been keeping from you."

She is facing him now. Straight on. She needs to get all this out. She is anxious but she needs to sort this out.

He can see her agitation and quickly blurts:

"If this is about Tom, I don't care…"

"It's nothing to do with Tom."

"What then?"

"It's your father. I've been receiving letters from him. From America."

There was a song, released only last year: "Letter from America", by The Proclaimers. It is a terrible song, but the title has come to Kevin now, and the melody too, and the Scottish accents. But he needs to concentrate on what she is saying. Forget that stupid Scottish song. Concentrate.

"The letters are actually for you."

"For me?"

Maura nods, already ashamed of herself, the concealing that has been going on for months.

"What? What do they say? These letters."

He is trying to sound surprised, affronted. He has never done any drama lessons in school. He would like to.

"I haven't opcned them."

"I don't understand. Are you saying he's been writing to me and you've never told me?"

She is nodding again, her shame growing, and her fear too, that he will explode right in front of her, have one of his awful tantrums. She hasn't seen any of that in a while. He's been so calm of late. Maybe he has accepted the fact that his father has gone and will not return, or maybe the glum music he immerses himself every evening, maybe all that soothes him. He can show so much maturity at times, like he is an adult and not the fifteen-year-old he actually is – just look at the way he deals with Laura's illness, so capable, so manly, so adroit.

"Why? Why would you do such a thing?"

His hurt seems so real, who would not believe him?

"I was worried … and angry. He left us. He didn't want anything to do with us. He went off and …"

She is trying to keep the anger and hurt out of her own voice, but she is failing.

"Where are they? These letters?"

She reaches into her apron pocket and pulls out a bundle. Kevin reaches out and snatches them from her, hurriedly, viciously.

"I'm sorry, I just want you to understand that …"

"Just leave me alone. Why don't you go and join the poker game as usual. It is tonight, isn't it? With all your boyfriends. Seems like you are enjoying your new hobby."

There is such venom in every word he spits. The letters he shakes in his hand; these letters from America, postmarked San Francisco. Songs start to creep into his head with that city in the title too, terrible hippy songs, songs he doesn't want in his head …

If you are going to …

Get out! Fuck off!

He is shouting silently at the bad song in his head. The bad bad song. He is also saying this with his eyes to his mother. *Get out! Fuck off!*

She has yet to hear this scream, the lid has yet to come off, but the pot is simmering all the time, simmering.

Maura doesn't know what to do with her hands. She wants to take his and squeeze them. She wants to run her fingers through his hair and softly apologize and explain everything and tell him that the future will be all right. But instead she is wringing her hands, and putting them into her apron pocket and then out again and wringing some more.

"I … I just …" is all she can stammer, feeling spent after mere minutes.

"Go," he says calmly, the lid stays on. "Let me read what's mine."

He is preternaturally calm. Almost as if he has been expecting all this. As if it had all been inevitable. A show-down. The letters. They had to come, didn't they?

"Just go," he says, calmly again, the malice all melted.

There is a tear in her eye as his mother closes the door behind her.

He is left here with the letters and he looks at them. USA. San Francisco. What bands came from there? He can only think of one he liked: Dead Kennedys. He can think of many he despises: Jefferson Airplane, The Grateful Dead, Creedence Clearwater Revival, the kind of old shit Lenny might listen to if he was in one of his ornery moods. Journey! Fucking hell, Journey, that's where they came from!

There is no fear or trepidation or wonder or excitement in what he holds in his hands. These letters. He knows all about them. Of course he does. He takes a deep breath. Maybe things do go according to plan sometimes. Maybe they do.

He goes to his cassette collection. Rubs his fingers across the alphabetised rows. D: for Dead Kennedys. The album: *Fresh Fruit for Rotting Vegetables.* The song, "Stealing People's Mail".

Tanita Tikaram will have to take a break. What he needs now is something more violent.

Tumultuous.

Chaotic.

Anarchic.

This.

For Dead Kennedys.

This is what he needs now.

Maybe his plan is working. He's a clever boy. Wasted in this village. With these idiots all around him. He might not be a good boy, but he's plenty clever. Wait and see. But this is what he needs now: loud music, something abrasive, something frantic, antic, and he puts the letters into his drawer, not bothering to open them, needs some manic music now, now, now!

11

Tom Dennehy. Ted Moran. Matty Staunton. Maura O'Brien. These are the card players: the sharks circling the kitchen table in Tom's kitchen. Their cards have been dealt and their hands pick them up and they inspect with avid interest.

There are grumbles. Sighs. Eyebrows rise. There are furrowed brows. There are clammy palms. The hands they have been dealt – are they good or bad? How will they fare? It could be a metaphor for so many things. But these people are not thinking in metaphors: they are thinking only about the actual cards, the queens and aces, the knaves, the pairs, and the moves they'll have to make, the strategies, the bluffs, the boldness, the mental grist and grind of the game.

Little stacks of poker chips are on the table in front of them. And they have drinks too. Bottles of stout (Tom could not find an opener and has to keep cracking them open on the side of the sink). Whiskey chasers, they have those too, should you need an extra kick, or a bit of Dutch courage. It looks like the real thing, this set-up, everything in place, and all seem pleased to be there; it is certainly one way to pass the winter.

There is a loud bang on the back door.

"Jaysus! What was that?" shrieks Tom, his voice loud and embarrassingly effeminate.

Sammy McCreary enters the house, his arm in a hard, white cast.

"Sorry folks. Didn't mean to startle you. It's this bloody arm."

"What on earth happened to you?" says Matty, his breathing still stertorous from a recent bout of the flu.

"Slipped, didn't I? On the bloody ice. That black ice is feckin' treacherous."

"When did this happen?" asks Tom, cracking another bottle open, his technique quite expert now.

"Last week. I'm a bloody misfortunate."

"Can you hold the cards?" asks Ted, the quietest of the bunch. "Or more like: can you hold your drink?"

Sammy takes his seat next to Maura, mystified at how the chair could have been left vacant.

"I can," he says, and he wiggles his fingers out the top of his cast much to the mirth of the others. "But I tell you what," he continues, "it isn't so easy holding the bloody paintbrush. And I've a job over at the school this week. Starting tomorrow in fact. Corridors need a bit of sprucing up according to the bould Sister Margaret. Why they couldn't have done it in summer when the kids were out of school I don't know. Maybe some little cunt was putting graffiti on the walls or something, that's all the rage now...I don't feckin' know."

He suddenly regrets his choice of words, appropriate no longer, not since there has been a woman present for months now.

"Sorry, Maura."

"Don't mind me," she says, taking a slug from her glass.

Sammy looks around.

"And Laura's not about?"

"Upstairs studying," says Tom. "She's a grand girl."

Sammy nods, and the others do too: no one could possibly be in disagreement there.

"I'm sorry I can't help you with the painting job," says Tom. "I'm off to the solicitor's office in town tomorrow. Clear up more of this inheritance lark. See what's to be done with … all this … what's the word for it … bureaucracy."

Sammy wiggles his fingers out the end of the cast again to let them know that he can manage, but the others have stopped looking at him and are more interested in the cards they now hold. The prospects. The unfolding of the game.

"Who's up or down so far?" Sammy inquires.

"Maura's up again. This beginner's luck thing is still going on. Getting a bit much to be honest. That's the sixth or seventh week of it now," says Matty.

"I caught on fast. That's all."

"Women's intuition," says Tom. "Maybe that's it. They can read things we can't. Very mystical creatures they are."

"You might be right there," says Sammy. "There might be something in that."

Tom smiles across the table at Maura, hoping he won't be noticed by the other men, and Maura, coyly sipping from her glass of gin, reciprocates his signs of affection.

Laura is lying on her bed, head propped on one hand, elbow sinking into the mattress, reading *Myths and Monsters*. This is the third time she's borrowed it from the library. Her diary is beside her also, a large red "Keep Out" adorning the front cover of it. She knows that Kevin likes to write stuff down, and perhaps this diary is an attempt to follow suit; maybe if she can structure her thoughts, maybe if she can put some kind of order on them, it might just help her mind calm down, and then perhaps the furious fits may gradually recede, more and more, she can but only hope; she knows this diary lark, the noting of everything, the reflections, it's all a bit of a nonsense, but still, what harm, what harm.

There is a tap at her window and Laura starts. She had been reading about Vlad the Impaler and his monstrosities – how could all of that have been true? How could someone like that have actually existed? – and now the fervour of her concentration is broken: it could only be one person throwing a pebble at the pane, really, couldn't it, it could only ever be the one.

She rises and goes to confirm, and just as she gets there another hits the window, right where her face should be. She flinches.

She opens the window to a cool blast of chilly air.

"What the fuck are you doing? What's this, Romeo and fucking Juliet?"

It is one of their texts at school, and they know the balcony scene well, who doesn't? Laura and Kevin both nearly peed in their pants one day when discussing the text: Helena O'Dowd had wondered aloud as to why Romeo hadn't just phoned Juliet. The class had erupted. *Just phoned her!* How the English teacher that day, Mrs. Fitzsimmons, had stayed serious, was testament to her professionalism, everyone else was thrown across their desks in hysterics.

"Come out a minute," says Kevin in a half-whisper/half-shout, trying to be tactful but not making a great fist of it. "I don't want my mother to see me."

Laura rolls her eyes, closes the window. She would have preferred another hour or so with her book, or maybe a scribble in the diary – it was a kind of therapy, clichéd, sure, but it had its charms. *Dear Diary, I have been studying men with huge dongs in pornographic magazines which my uncle has in his possession: a nice man but a dirty old devil it turns out, who lives with me now, because my mother is dead and my father is God-knows-where, and I pulled off my cousin in bed the other night. Am I a dirty bitch?*

It was more like a wild and salacious American novel, something bold and outrageous and untrue…except of course it was all gospel.

She rushes down the stairs as quietly as she can and out the front door taking care to leave it ajar – she wants to sneak back in just as furtively, draw no attention to herself, it is a good way of proceeding from now on, in everything she does, draw no attention to herself, keep her head down, get the exam results and get the hell out of here in a couple of years. And Kevin? What about…

Kevin is standing on the frosty grass looking addled and odd in his usual coat, a black scarf wrapped around his neck too to avert the cold. The freezing weather had come on quickly, and smoke rose out of all the family homesteads, and there were fewer fox cries, fewer things scurrying about, any insect long dead, any hibernating thing hidden away, you found your own snug corner and you tended to stay there, that was winter's way.

"What the fuck are you playing at?"

"Nothing, just wanted to talk."

"Talk? Could you not have waited till school tomorrow? And we do have a telephone you know."

Laura thinks of Helena and Romeo's telephone, it brings half a smirk to her still.

"There's a lot on my mind, that's all."

He pulls out a packet from his pocket and lights his second last cigarette.

"Thought you were giving up?"

"This will be the last pack. Unless Lenny gives me more of course. I don't want to buy them with my own pocket money. Need it for the music. You know how it is."

He offers her his last but she refuses.

"C'mon," she says, "it's bloody freezing, what's the matter with you?"

In her rush she had forgotten to wear a coat, a jacket, or anything of substance, anything woolly and warm, she shivers in the yard, her teeth literally chattering.

"Wear this if you want."

Laura looks at the trench coat first in disgust, but quickly she changes her tune when her teeth snap only harder and she has to hide the force of her nipples pushing out through her jumper.

"Fine. Give it to me."

"You should be dressed better for the winter," Kevin says.

"And don't you think you should be wearing something a bit heavier now too? I suppose this thing has never even been washed."

Before he hands it over completely to her, he delves into the pocket and takes out a bundle of letters.

"What are they?" she asks, already warmer from the hug of the coat, and the black scarf that he too has relented, and which she has tied tight as a noose around her neck.

"Love letters from Margie Cummins?" she asks. "Or has Helena finally learned how to write?"

Kevin looks like he is in no mood for jokes.

"These are from my father," he says.

Laura's leer darkly dies and she looks upon him with immediate and real concern.

Tom is at the fridge again. So often he is bending down to it, taking out bottles, putting in other bottles – no wonder his back is always playing up. It's the same at work, delivering DIY and hardware supplies, it was how he knew Sammy so well, a similar line of work, the same materials, paints, brushes, turpentine, ladders, rollers, buckets, hammers and nails and ...

"Anyone else?" he shouts, his back turned to them.

All hands shoot up. He doesn't even need to turn around to check, knows they'll all need re-filling, ever the gracious host, lets no one down, lets no one dry, good ol' Tom.

Sammy is examining his cast, "Jesus, it's so heavy just to lift the bloody thing up. Exhausting it is, bloody exhausting."

"Then lift up the other one, you clown," says Matty, and the others chuckle along with him.

"C'mere till I sign it," says Maura. "That's what the youngsters do, isn't it? Love hearts and all."

She winks at him.

Sammy beams broadly, "I'd be honoured."

Tom locates a black marker after rummaging in a junk drawer – every house has one of these drawers, where things get thrown in and forgotten, things thought one day might be useful, but rarely ever are: Dymphna's drawer was no different – and he tosses the marker to Maura. She catches it and writes her name on the snow-white, yet unblemished plaster of Paris.

"Now I must make my way to the little boy's room," Sammy says. "Another feckin' ordeal."

"Well, I'm not helping you with that one," says Maura. "You'll have to yank it out yourself."

"Ah, go on, Maura, be a pal."

They all laugh at this, though Tom's is clearly more strained than the others.

"Stall the game for a while so," says Sammy. "This could take some time."

"Upstairs toilet," says Tom. "The downstairs one is all blocked up. I haven't gotten around to fixing it yet."

"Not a good advertisement for a DIY man."

"I know, Matty," says Tom, "I'm letting the side down."

He was too young then to know anything. He still doesn't know the whole story in fact. Only scraps of what he hears. He shuts out what he doesn't want to consider. It makes him angry. His blood begins to heat up and he flings things, cassettes around the room, pencils at the window; he has stuck a compass in his own skin to make himself bleed. That is no way to be carrying on. He knows this. He doesn't mention it to anyone. Maybe only to Lenny when they talk about music. Because Lenny knows music is the great comforter. He hasn't even told Laura. He will though. He will tell her everything, when he can. She has revealed things to him, no matter how preposterous. And they have grown closer. They have shared moments. Sexual now. *Sexual now!* Think on that! How absurd. Two cousins lying in that bed, and feeling each other up, and not quitting until there were ... results!

Cousins.

Kevin and Laura.

They are close.

Sexually.

Spiritually.

Closer than him and his mother are spiritually. Closer than he ever was with his father: he hardly remembers him, a few nebulous scenes.

The absent father.

And these letters now: they are a plan, Kevin's plan.

Does Laura suspect...?

Does Laura believe...?

Laura can be gullible...

She folds the letters neatly back into their envelopes and hands them to him.

"Looks like you've got a lot to think about."

In the dark, in the dark, this cold garden, with no flowers blooming, in winter, the frost upon both of them, and he doesn't even feel that cold, too busy is he lost in his thinking, in his planning, his deviousness, not even feeling cold, just lost, in the night garden with the girl he wants to touch again, lost, but he'll find a way out, things will go according to plan. He'll not tell her yet.

Sammy flushes the toilet and has a gander at himself in the mirror. He checks his teeth; nothing stuck there, no green showing – he had broccoli for dinner, a few sprigs – no, nothing stuck, nothing embarrassing. He fixes his collar. *Not bad McCreary,* he says to himself, *not too bad at all.*

On the landing he checks his fly once more: it would be very embarrassing if he went down with his zipper undone.

But no, he did himself up proper, one-handed and all, impressive.

It is then that he notices Laura's bedroom door open. He hears no sounds from inside. Tom said she was upstairs studying, but there's no music playing in the room – and she's a great one for the pop music – not a rustle of paper, not even the sound of a bored exhalation. He pushes it open the tiniest bit, curiosity getting the better of him, and he peers in. Empty. Well, well. Where did the little scamp run off to? Wasn't it the trick of students everywhere, pretending to be upstairs hard at the books, when really they were gallivanting outside, having slid down the drainpipes or something, sure didn't he used to do it himself, the books never able to hold him for more than ten minutes.

He pushes the door open a bit further, and when absolutely sure there is no one there, he sneaks in quietly, careful of his tread on the old boards of the old house, and he allows himself a good look around.

So this is her little haven. This is where she spends her evenings. She's a grand girl all right. He had been watching her at the funeral. Watching her move around the room, all poise and ladylike, not bad at all for a country lass. More mature than you'd think and all. Looking way more than her years. What was she, sixteen? She looked nineteen or twenty. Grand big hips on her. She'd make a fella a happy man with those hips, he is sure of it. And the jugs on her too. She's all there. No little girl anymore. If he was younger himself. If he had the energy like he used to have. And she was a nice girl too, pleasant like, not the brightest in the world maybe … but he might be being a tad unfair there, he didn't know her all that well, but if she was a daughter of Dymphna's … and she had been rightly conned, hadn't she? The lad now, Kevin, he always seems much smarter, bit cunning mind, has that look about him. Couldn't trust him. Like his father before him. You thought he was one thing but turned out to be quite another. He wasn't the only one. They had 'em all fooled. Didn't they? The glad eyes they had for the wrong quarries.

He sees her books on the bed. Just lying there. As open an invitation as he has had in a long time.

One book is open: The Loch Ness Monster. A big greeny illustration of the famous mythical beast in Scotland. Well, fuck me, thinks Sammy, he was right, she's not the smartest kid after all, this book must be for ten-year-olds. The bloody Loch Ness Monster indeed. She must believe in all this stuff. Is that the case Laura, you little fooleen? Believe in monsters, do ya? Ha, ha, well wonders never …

And then there is another book. Wait now, one minute … this isn't a regular book at all. It is a diary. Well, now there's a find.

Keep out! It says on the front. I will yeah, says Sammy to himself, I will keep out and all, yeah.

He reads.

"And I could swear I saw something moving in the water, beneath the surface. It looked huge and dark. I'm certain there is some creature down there. Imagine, in our pond."

Sammy stifles his laughter. Fuck me, he thinks, this is great stuff.

He flicks a few pages forward:

"And we lay there in the bed, the two of us, and I thought this is all wrong. But then I said, fuck it, my mother is dead, I deserve some fun too. And I touched Kevin's penis and it was hard as a rock. And then he touched me, where I've never been

touched before, I couldn't believe how wet I was, and he stuck his finger right in."

Sammy gasps. He gasps so loud he puts his hand over his mouth in case he is to let another one escape. *Jesus Christ! I'm sorry, Lord, forgive me the blasphemy!* There is sweat all over his forehead, like he has just run a race.

Sounds then.

From outside in the garden.

Instinctively he hunkers down, crawls over to the window and peeps out. He can see Laura and Kevin outside, standing in the middle of the lawn.

What are they up to? What are they up to out there in the freezing cold? Everything he has learned about her tonight is cementing the fact for him: she is not the brightest tool in the box. Who'd be out in that weather? He wouldn't put Lucy out in it, not without her little doggy jacket anyway.

He sits back then, back on his backside, but just before he gets up from this low position, he spies something, under the bed. And what, pray tell, is this?

It is a treasure trove.

An empty bottle of Guinness.

Balled up rolls of tin foil.

And … sweet Mother of God … a pornographic magazine!

Sweat has broken out on Sammy's brow yet again and he feels suddenly feverish, like he might faint. He can't believe this. It is like it's not even happening, or happening somewhere else … is all this really here? Or have the painkillers the doctor had given him gone to his head completely and he's hallucinating, the old feckin' eejit.

No.

They're right in front of him. It's more like the secret stash of a dirty old man than the underneath of a teenage girl's bed. Fucking hell! It all seems wrong. Topsy-turvy like. Girls her age – what were they watching on the TV now? There was some Australian show they were all excited about – *Home and Away*: that was the name of it. Looked like a load of old shite. Sammy could hardly even understand their accents, those Aussies, and they were all way too tanned and happy-looking. But this! This from a teenage girl. Pornography! For fuck's sake. A dirty mag from London, Soho or somewhere. Under the bed of a bloody schoolgirl!

He takes a deep breath to calm himself down. Stop his pulse from racing. He'll have a heart attack right here in the room – and wouldn't that be some find, an old letch like him conked out on the floor of a girl's room surrounded by all this. They'd pin it on him, they would. That'd be some funeral, the whole village would have tongues wagging about that all right.

A right dark horse she is, that's for sure, Laura Maloney. The Loch Ness Monster, and monsters in the local pond, and men with monstrous dongs, there was a recurring theme all right – he didn't even know women could be so ... perverted. For that's what it is surely, isn't it ... perversion of the highest order? If it was Tom's old creaking bed you'd say something. Is he in the wrong room? No. He isn't. Sammy looks around. Girls stuff. Pinks and purples and pop stars on the walls. And, oh my, there's even a pair of her white knickers there and all, right there, peeking out from under the bed, right there, well take a look at that! His heart beats and heats like the engine of a rusty tractor overburdened, fuel-flooded. The itch inside the plaster has gone wild, sweat there of course, pooling, but he can't scratch it, can't get to it. He rubs at his crotch. He can't go downstairs like this, worked up the way he is now. He'll need one more minute to calm himself down, cool a bit, get his breath back.

A concerned voice then from down below:

"For feck's sake, Sammy, hurry up! How long does it take to piss?"

The other card players laugh raucously, alcohol-fuelled now, good spirits.

Sammy hurriedly shoves everything back under the bed the way he got them. He'll leave the scene of the crime, just as it was. He closes the page of the diary too, smiling lasciviously to himself.

He shouts back down the stairs:

"Coming, Tom! Turned out 'twas more than just a piss! And it's damn hard to pull up the trousers with one hand. I thought Maura would come to my aid."

"She would, yeah," shouts Tom back up the stairs, meaning of course the exact opposite.

That's the way it has been round these parts, these strange days, their strange ways: what you expect turns out to be the exact opposite.

Laura takes off the horrible trench coat – what did he say it was? *Bunnymen?* – and hands it over to Kevin.

"Thanks," she says. "You always take care of me."

"No worries," he says.

They both look at each other awkwardly. So ... what do they do now? Is that it for this evening?

Laura moves to him and hugs him.

Kevin puts his arm around her and holds her close to him, but he is nervous, out here in the open, if anyone saw ...

The strained embrace ends and they look directly at each other, eyes directly on eyes again, like they had been in that bed, that experimental bed, their moment of sin, of transgression.

Laura takes a breath, to steady herself. So much has been happening over the last while, it has all been moving at an incredible pace, but she doesn't want it to stop; if it keeps moving that way then maybe she will suddenly be older, grown, a woman, and ready to leave the place.

Kevin takes control. Just like he does when he holds her head from hitting the ground. Just like that. He moves in again, even closer this time, and he kisses her, his cold lips on her cold lips. The kiss is at first tentative, but the nervousness soon abates, and even though they know this is wrong, and it is wrong to be doing all this, he is going ahead and doing it all anyway... because it feels right. It *is* wrong... but it *feels* oh-so-right.

And she reciprocates, kissing keenly too. There is no right and wrong now. There is only this. There is no right and wrong now, no good and evil. There is no night now. Not even night. There is no lawn and there are no trees and no house and no moon and no families and no letters and no poker cards and no pond and no monsters. There is only them. The two of them. Kevin and Laura. They don't think *cousins* – because that'll ruin the moment. They keep that at bay. They just kiss. One on one. Leaning into it more and kissing back quick and keen.

There are no fits either.

There is no curse upon her; the epilepsy, even the word seems foreign to her right now. Another language entirely is happening right here. A simpler, truer language. Wordless. Saying nothing at all. What need? What need for words?

And don't think *cousins*, because that'll ruin the moment. And *now* is the moment. This is it, and this is them, another experiment perhaps. Testing the water again. How real is this? How real is any of it? Is this sin? Laura is as in control as Kevin is. He is leading her and she is leading him. She is leading him and he is leading her. It is two-way. They both want this. They both want this. They are sure they *both* truly want this.

A flash then!

There is suddenly a bright flash of light, seeming to come from behind a stand of nearby trees.

"What was that?" Laura says, pulling back, breaking the spell of the kiss.

"I don't know, lightning I suppose."

"I didn't hear any thunder."

"Might have been the lights of a passing car, from down the road."

Kevin tries to move towards her again, alive with the possibility of another, one more kiss, one more time he wants his lips right on hers: he wants his tongue sliding up against hers, more he wants, more – but she is not obliging now, she is pulling away from him, disturbed: this game is up, another one of their pastimes abruptly kicked to the side.

"I'd better get in. The poker game must be winding up by now. They'll notice me gone."

Kevin can't hide his disappointment, but they had been out there longer than was sensible, too long in that bitter, chastising cold. He wants her to know that there is nothing wrong with what they have done. Not any of it. There was nothing wrong with that time they were in the bed either, nothing wrong. He cannot speak any of this to her right now, he doesn't want to draw attention to it … and yet he does, he does at the same time, it's all he wants: acknowledgment.

"I'd better be off too," he says, "before my mother leaves; I'd rather be in bed when she gets in, so I don't have to talk to her."

"You'd better sort all that out."

"I know," he says, as if contemplating it. But the ruse is obvious, for his mind is still on lips, on tongues, on the closeness of their bodies, the bond, on her, on her, on Laura, his mind is always on her.

The poker players are putting on their coats and preparing to leave, their faces aglow from whiskey and the warmth of the house and camaraderie.

"Great game, lads," says Matty. "Maura, I think we'll have to politely ask you not to come anymore. We're tired of losing to you."

"The winning streak is bound to come to an end sooner or later. Beginner's luck, like I said before."

"Been a couple of months of it now," says Ted, "hardly the beginner. We'll be taking lessons from you."

Tom clears away the cards and the poker chips, the bottles and empty packets of Planters peanuts from the table, leaves everything by the kitchen sink. He's too tired now to clean it all up; maybe Laura might help out later, or in the morning. Tom could do with hitting the sack to be honest, stretch out those old legs, give that lower back a break. All that concentration, the concentration on the cards, the fond focus on Maura, well, it has clearly worn him out. Bed seems like the best idea.

"Thanks as always for the hospitality," she says.

"I can give you ..."

"No way, you've been drinking. The walk home will do me good."

They all sway to the front door, the hallway floor a lurching boat at sea, and they meet Laura coming in.

"I was just talking a breath of fresh air. All the study, gave me a headache."

She walks briskly past them all, hoping her excuse will be enough – it surely will, their brains are sozzled with booze – says her goodnights to the parting party, and she skips up the wooden stairs, lithe and energetic, a contrast to the tired legs below.

Tom is not in the least suspicious of her activities, and he is too flat-out tired to think straight anyway.

Sammy on the other hand watches her young legs flying up the steps and his eyes reveal nothing but suspicion, and of knowing, and there is something else in them too, call it greed.

12

They are at different sides of the classroom, but Kevin keeps his eye on her, she could have a tumble at any minute, so he keeps his eyes on her, and she looks over at him every so often too.

The other eighteen students are all looking at the blackboard, and Carl Duffy, the teacher, standing in front of it and leaning on his desk occasionally, searches their faces to see if they are listening, if they are paying him the attention he thinks he deserves.

Laura Maloney, clearly, is not paying any attention at all. Mostly she stares out the window and thinks of things that could have been. Or things that might yet be. What does the future hold? Where will she go? The episode with Kevin, this *relationship* with her cousin, as long as it is hushed and no one sees, as long as it is ...

"You'll not find the answers out the window, Ms. Maloney. A little more attention to your textbook and to what I'm saying and you'll find what you're looking for. Or at least what you'll need if you are to pass your exams."

"Will I?" she says, her tone replete with effrontery that sends seismic waves through the small confined classroom.

"I'm sorry?" says Duffy.

She speaks louder, more emphatically: "I said ... *will I?*"

Sharp intakes of breath. Audible murmurs. Fearful faces.

"Do you have a problem, Ms. Maloney?"

There is a sort of glazed look in Laura's eyes, as if she is not quite engaging in the conversation, her mind half on other affairs. She did take her medication in the morning, those new tablets that were recommended to her by Doctor Neelan and encouraged by Tom, and, she supposes, it does make her feel quite calm, but also it makes her feel like she doesn't give a shit about anything... because, well, she doesn't, really. The world could blow up right here and now; that bloody Ozone Layer they are all so bloody obsessed with could finally diminish to nothing and let all the sun's rays burn the bejaysus out of each and every one of them... is that what it did? The Ozone Layer. Reflected sun rays? Or *deflected*? She never listened properly; she doesn't even care.

And she doesn't give a toss as to what is happening in the class at this particular moment either. Doesn't care about history. Or Brian Boru. She only really cares about Kevin. And Tom now. But mostly Kevin. Because he always has her back. And because they love. They love each other. Is that weird to say? Is that completely fucked up? It is confusing, that much is true. They love like cousins love, like best friends... though... she'd still probably shift that Aidan Carty if the chance arose. Would she? Really though? Would she? The chance will never arise anyway. Not to girls like her. Not to the plain Janes.

And the monster will never arise out of that water either... will it?

She has to make do with her cousin, *make out* with her cousin! Jesus. That was an Americanism she had picked up.

Make out! Maybe they even said it on *Home and Away.* She really doesn't really...

"Well?" says Duffy.

"Well, what?"

She had thought he had moved on, but here he is, still staring at her.

"I asked you if you had a problem, Mrs. Maloney."

"Many. Many problems... actually."

Giggles from the classmates; Orlaith Crowley is all agog at the happening; Helena O'Dowd has woken from her post-lunch slumber and cannot believe her own ears.

"Right, well, if you could just focus on what you are supposed to be doing and..."

"What am I supposed to be doing?"

"Laura, if you're looking for an argument..."

"I don't know what I'm looking for."

She says this with true melancholy, it's actually heartfelt, not meant to provoke at all.

Kevin watches, worries. He had expressed doubt about her taking any new medication, she hadn't had any fits for some time, but her doctor was insisting that this new stuff would keep her calm on a more regular basis, would have a numbing effect, and would help her concentrate on her studies, but it seemed it was having the opposite effect: the way everything is around these parts; these peculiar people in their peculiar days: what you expect, turns out to be upended.

Duffy takes a deep breath and gives the class a moment to settle down.

"Aren't you supposed to wear your headgear in class too?"

Kevin is shaking his head, *oh shit, no, no, the teacher has really put his little foot in it now.*

Bitterly, Laura spits: "I don't need it."

Orlaith pipes up from the back corner of the class:

"She's on idiot pills sir, she'll be fine; she won't crash, and if she does, Kevvy's always there."

"All right, Orlaith, that's enough," says Duffy. "Well, Laura, I just hope nothing bad happens then…"

"*Nothing bad happens!*" she cries out, "*Nothing bad happens!* What the fuck would you know about bad things happening? Fuck you!"

And there it is.

Kevin half-suspected.

There'd been shit brewing for some time. She'd been mourning, or trying to mourn, her mother, her poor ever-sick mother; she'd been going to the pond to see if a monster would emerge, a fucking monster!

And she'd been kissing her cousin, her best friend.

None of it is good, none of it is normal. Something had to give… he knew it. And he feels half-responsible for it too.

Naturally, hysteria has broken out in the classroom.

Uproar.

Chaos.

"Right! That's it! Out!" screams Duffy, his voice higher and more girlish than ever. Sweat has broken out on his upper lip, glistening there just under his tidy pencil moustache, and he bangs hard on his own desk, clearly hurting himself in the process.

Laura gets out of her seat without any apparent hurry. She strides between the tight rows of desks, her wide hips bumping into corners of textbooks as she goes. She shuts the door with a thunderous bang.

The class reels to a stunned silence. They are wondering what Duffy will say next. All eyes are upon him. Just how, how will he regain control?

"And you can wipe that smile off your face and all, O'Brien," he says, giving Kevin a vindictive look.

Kevin shrugs, not wiping any smile off his face but instead holding his smirk in firm position, a Sid Vicious sneer, classic but effective. He holds it for a moment, then looks down at the story of Brian Boru, High King of Ireland, but he'd rather be with Laura; he'd rather follow her out the door, put his arms around her; most of all he'd rather be with his cousin.

Laura leans against the wall of the school corridor and takes deep breaths. Right, so that got a little out of hand, she could have dealt with it a bit better, but she was bored, and she is confused, she is so very confused, and she's not sure those pills are right for her – she'll have to talk it through with Tom and with her doctor.

Duffy's a little fucking snake. Everyone knows this. But she shouldn't have let him get the better of her. She should have just shut up and waited for the class to end and … then what? Then the following class would be just as boring. And then the one after that. She wants to escape. She wants out of this shithole completely. How is she going to be able to remain here until she is eighteen without completely losing her mind? And the stuff with Kevin, they'll get caught … they'll surely get caught and there'll be a fucking scandal, as if her family hasn't had enough of that shit already. Fuck it. Fuck it. Fuck it. If she just had a proper boyfriend, like Aidan, and a proper family, proper parents, and if Kevin was just her cousin and not someone who … Jesus Christ, fingered her … fuck sake … if all those things … if … and … but he is the one who is there when she collapses. He is the one who takes care of her. And though he is a pompous shit, still, she …

She can't continue with this. The thoughts are crippling her. She's just got to walk. Walk, walk, stop thinking. She throws her schoolbag across her shoulder and heads off down the corridor at a brisk pace.

When she rounds the corner she almost trips over cans of paint, rollers and brushes that Sammy McCreary has left on the floor.

"Fucking hell!" she exclaims, so close to having a shoe full of white creamy paint.

"Laura! Sorry, love. Just going to move these things over here. My apologies."

Clumsily, one-handedly, he begins to move his accoutrements, but he has more success with his foot, pushing them out of the main thoroughfare with his instep – they'll be out of classes soon and there could be all kinds of trouble if he hasn't got them aligned properly, close to the wall, out of harm's way. He needs a few warning signs too: *Wet Paint*, and even a bollard or two.

"What are you doing?" she asks him.

"I'm working. Isn't it obvious?"

"It looks like a mess, that's what's obvious."

"Place needs a lick of paint. Should've been done in the summer holidays, but look, if little brats are going around spraying things on the walls …"

She knows what was sprayed. *Duffy is a faggot.* It was funny. They scrubbed it off, or half-scrubbed it, but the smudge remains, it needs painting over to erase its memory completely – Duffy was livid, but Duffy deserves.

"What are you doing? Shouldn't you be in class?"

"Got kicked out. I have to go to the principal's office. Report for my … misdemeanour."

"Why? What did you do?"

"Swore."

Sammy's laugh rebounds around the corridor.

"Only that?" he says.

"It was enough."

Laura allows herself a little laugh too now at the memory, it was a bit hasty, her outbursts, and all for no reason really. Still, kind of funny.

"Which teacher?"

"Duffy."

"The little bender?"

Laura's laugh is heartier this time, relief to know someone has already taken her side.

"You can't say that," she sniggers, "and anyway, how do you know he's gay?"

Sammy gives her an *are-you-kidding-me* look.

"These little benders are everywhere lately. Since yer man on the TV, singing about the chameleon, a few years ago."

"Boy George?"

"And he's from Tipperary for feck's sake!"

Laura looks behind her, hoping no teacher will come and harass her and move her along to where she should be, in front of the principal, the dreaded Sister Margaret, as she readied to eke out her punishment.

"I hope Tom won't hear about this," Sammy says.

"Tom is not my father."

"Well … you better be getting on. Or you'll only find yourself in more trouble. You know what the Mother Superior is like."

"Don't tell Tom, please. I don't want to worry him. He's a good man."

"I won't," says Sammy. "Not a word; your secret is safe."

Secrets.

Safe.

She thinks of all her other secrets.

Are they safe?

If this man only knew.

They say nothing to each other for a moment, Sammy wondering how to proceed with his job, which side of the wall he should even start on, and Laura is wondering whether she should just go and face the music, the wrong kind of music, the kind of music she has no interest in, shouts and scolds from a withered old celibate hag … escape: that's what she's pondering too, not only out of the school on this day, but out of the smothering village once and for all. How many more years here? How many more years of this drudgery? This fucking mental torture. How many more?

As Sammy bends to his tins of paint she makes up her mind.

"That's it."

He has a screwdriver under the lip of the lid and he is trying to lever it off.

"Hah?"

"I'm not putting up with anymore of this shit. Fuck it."

She storms off in the opposite direction, not towards the principal's office at all, but towards the main exit, brazenly heading for the door, out of her confines, towards air at least, air, so she can breathe it in, breathe, breathe, give her some air, for Christ's sake.

"Laura, love!" Sammy shouts after her and follows as fast as his old legs can carry him.

She strides with purpose, strides like she means it. So many times in her life she has no control, sitting like a loon in those classrooms like she used to, with a fucking hurling helmet on her, when an epileptic fit could strike at any minute. Looking like a fucking gobshite, there for everyone to have a good laugh at. She's fifteen now for Christ's sake, not a child, if she bangs her head so what. Her fucking crown is thick enough. Kevin and Laura went up a hill to fetch a bottle of Guinness, Laura fell down and broke her crown and Kevin held her like he loved her more than anything else in the world, more than Siouxsie Sioux, or even Robert Smith. Kevin loves her. The notion hits her as she strides. Shit! He loves her! Does she love him? Well, does she ... really? How can she answer that? All she knows is that she needs more control, and thus this scarpering, out to air, to breathe, her thick legs fast down the corridor, blasting through the main doors and into a spell of freedom, bright freedom, birdsong, out to breathe, stand alone, her own two feet. Kevin had looked at her thick legs. He had gotten aroused. Ha! She had that power over him. Of course she had, *has*, she is female, the female of the species is more deadly than the male, giving off her pheromones to him day in day out, whether he knows it or not, and what is he to do the poor lad, only get his little willy hard and spend his desperate nights with a box of tissues. Her poor boy. Her perfect boy. Perfect. There's nothing wrong with him. Nothing at all. He's good. Slave to his hormones ever and always, like all of 'em. But he's good. He's good. Isn't he? He wouldn't ever do anything bad, would he? He's good for her.

"Laura, hold on!"

She stops at the side of the school, behind a wall that had also been given the *Duffy is a faggot* treatment, and scrubbed hard and now awfully smeared. She leans on it. There are a few tears rolling down her face, but they are not the tears of regret, nor are they the tears of anger, they are more of confusion, of wanting control and not yet having enough of it. Control. To be able to take life by the scruff of the neck, that's what she wants.

Sammy is breathless but catches up. He bends, his hands splayed across his thighs and takes greedy gulps of the sharp winter air. It's cold out here, he doesn't know how the girls do this every day in their short skirts, bless 'em, they are hardy out. He coughs up a great glob of green.

"You're not going to face her then? Sister Maggot?" he says.

He is trying to make her smile, and it works, sort of, but the tears are still appearing, wetting her cheeks, puffing her under-eyes.

"It's all just a bit much sometimes, you know," she says, her words in flutters and emotional stutters. "I just need a break, a break from ... myself ... I suppose."

She's gotten to the crux of it.

Sammy looks around, makes sure no one is seeing what is going on here – it could all be so very easily mis-construed. So many things were taken the wrong way these days. You could see two fellas having a walk together and what would you think? Seriously? Two men even, out for a stroll down by the pond – and what would you be thinking? If it was evening say, the gloaming ... would it be different? And no dog by them. And their bodies quite close. Everyone had their suspicions. If they saw Sammy and Laura out like this, would they think he was some kind of pervert, preying on a young girl? His mind suddenly flashes back to her bedroom, the magazines, the empty bottle, the white knickers he so wanted to slip inside his pocket and to hold to his face in a private moment, but he didn't ... she is no innocent angel this one, far from it, but her tears are genuine enough, vulnerable she looks, vulnerable, poor *crathur*.

"Look," he says, his tone warm, sympathetic, "why don't I drive you home. I'll say you were feeling sick or something, or a ... a fit came on again. Tom's away in the town anyway ... it'll give you time to think, time to concoct a story."

Concoct.

She likes that.

But she has doubts.

"We're supposed to sign out and ..."

"I'll take care of that when I get back here. I'll tell Sister Maggot you had a bit of a turn and took you straight to the doctor; there was no time to stick to the school ... what's the word ... protocol."

She likes these words: *Concoct. Protocol.*

She likes the idea too. It makes sense to her. She is not alarmed at his ability to think on the spot like this, to summon an escape route so quickly, effortlessly, off the cuff, as if he has practiced deception all his days. Perhaps he has. But none of it sends any warning bells. She feels safe with him. He is a friend of Tom's, isn't he? And she'd much rather be at home listening to music and lying on her bed than putting up with Duffy and his snarky old shit and Queen Bitch Orlaith lapping up the drama and only adding more to her arsenal of arseholery.

"C'mon then," he says, aiming for an avuncular levity, "I'll come back here as soon as I can and paint their scummy walls."

They drive along familiar roads. Every road is a familiar road in a village of this scope. Every bend. Every bump. Even the pebbles that sometimes get lifted up and spit against the windscreen, they have a familiar look about them, they could have names, and the standing Ogham stones in scattered fields, weathered, weather-beaten, but *un*beaten too of course, because they are still standing; and the stone walls that separate fields, the boundaries, and the hedgerows, all these are more familiar than people, because people change, but these things that surround them, these things that confine, they all remain unchanged, steadfast, they remain.

Laura has wiped the last tears from her eyes and is pleased when Sammy turns up the van radio: George Harrison's "Got My Mind Set on You", one of the biggest hits of the previous year and a song Sammy is happy to turn the dial on, to make it even louder, even if it does rattle his old speakers in their casings.

"I like this one," he says.

"Me too."

"This bloody cast is annoying. I'm sick to my teeth of it," he says, holding up the offending item.

"When does it come off?"

"Dunno. Another few weeks maybe. The bone must set properly."

They drive along in silence for a few moments and are soon on the pond road, which the locals like to call Lake Road.

But it isn't a lake. It fucking isn't. It's just a pond. Stop with all the lying, the fake bullshit. She thinks about this as she looks out at it. The water. Body. Body of water. It's just a pond. They always try to make things bigger around here. They are small, that's why. Small-minded. She'll get out. She will. She'll get out of here someday soon.

The van slows down.

"What's up?"

Sammy is looking out the window at the pond.

"Ah, you wouldn't..."

He pulls gently over to the side of the road and stares out at the water, shaking his head mildly, a faraway look in his eye, dreamy, like a man reminiscing, perhaps looking back on better times – were there better times around here?

"You're freaking me out now. What is it? What are you looking at?"

"Sorry, love."

He starts the engine of the van again, turns down the volume on Erasure's "A Little Respect", and drives along the pot-holed road slowly.

"What? What the hell is it?"

"It's..."

Laura's impatience grows and growls:

"Just say it for..."

"That stretch of water...there's something..."

Her eyes widen. Is he serious?

"Go on."

"It sounds a bit far-fetched I know, and...don't laugh now, I'm not a senile ol' crock of a thing just yet...but..."

She waits. She waits patiently. Waits for confirmation. For her to throw down her card and say: *Snap!*

"But a few times, I could've sworn…I saw…something…moving…"

"Oh my God!" she exclaims.

"What? Are you going to ring up the lunatic asylum? Book me in to the loony bin?" he laughs.

"Me too. I'm not joking. I swear. I saw it too!"

Sammy looks at her, completely shocked.

"Oh, sweet Jesus. I'm glad it's not just me, I'm glad someone else saw it. I thought I was losing my feckin' marbles. The fellas in the white coats would be coming for me…"

"No, really!"

Her chest is heaving now, butterflies doing loop-the-loops in her belly, school now couldn't be further from her thoughts, Duffy and Sister Margaret and even Kevin too and his Doubting Thomas-ness.

"One evening," Sammy says, "it was almost dark. This was a few months ago now. End of summer. Not long after your poor mum passed away, God rest her soul. I was out for a stroll. The dog, my little Lucy, she's as old as meself now, well, she was barking like crazy, and when I looked out across the lake, this big thing seemed to rise slowly out of the water."

They pull in to Laura's driveway, Sammy negotiating the turns with caution, softly over the gravel, Laura hanging on his every word.

"And, and it was like…like a dinosaur's neck, long and thin, and the dog was howling…and then, the thing just seemed to drop back into the water again. Plunging down like, creating these huge waves. To tell you the truth, I was terrified. I mean, in awe too, naturally, in awe I was, shocked, honestly, speechless, but afraid too, who knows what the hell it was?"

The van is parked now and the air between them fizzles from the tension of his narrative.

"Sounds crazy, doesn't it?"

"It's not, really. I think I saw something moving too. Under the water."

Sammy looks at her with interest; as if maybe he has an ally.

"I think the dog might have had something to do with it," he says. "Like you know the way they can hear stuff, like dog whistles, other frequencies and things us humans can't begin to fathom. I think the dog can sense when it is near."

"Let's go there. Let's go back."

"No, God, no. Not now. We can't. I've to get back to that job. It's too bright anyway: I get the feeling the thing only moves at night, or when darkness is falling."

"Tonight then. Bring your dog. I want to see it. I want to be sure it's real, and that I can't have imagined it."

Sammy mulls over her proposition.

"Go on," she urges. "We'll tell no one."

"All right then. But there's no guarantee it'll appear. And not a word to Tom of course, or to Kevin. I'll pick you up at around eight, down the road there, near that leaning electricity pole. You know the one."

It had almost come down in a storm once, that electricity pole, and now it leaned at an awkward angle, and no one had come around to straighten it back up again, typical, bloody typical.

"We don't want anyone seeing us", says Sammy, a giddiness in his voice now, a rising glee.

"I'll sneak out. Don't worry. I'm good at that," she says.

You probably are, girl, Sammy thinks to himself. There are probably a lot of things you are very good at. We'll see what the dark horse is like in the dark night with the dark monster beneath the surface of the dark pond. We'll see how good you really are.

13

In the near-dark Kevin makes his way along the lane, the journey home from another tedious day at school.

But Laura is not beside him. She is not doing a stupid, outdated Cyndi Lauper dance, and she is not yapping on about Kylie's new hairstyle or just how gorgeous Jason Donovan and Matt Goss are, and how Prince's new single "Alphabet Street" is actually quite good even though he's naked and looks creepy on the front of the *Lovesexy* album.

She is not picking blackberries and talking about Aidan Carty and how Duffy is a dick and how Orlaith and Helena are such wanton harlots and whether he wants to go back to her place because she is in the mood for some toast with loads of butter, real true yellow butter.

None of that.

There is none of that on this freezing cold December day on the way home from a barely-heated December school.

But headphones on. That as usual. And *The Head on the Door* playing in his ears – nothing unusual about that either; "Push" plays now, and he read in one of his music magazines that The Cure are to release a new album next year, and it is to be called *Disintegration,* and although no one knows much about it yet, Kevin is pleased that it has such a great title; there are rumours that they may tour Europe with one date set for Dublin in summer. Next year! Next year! He'll simply have to go to that. He'll simply have to. Laura will have no interest of course, but he might be able to drag her along with him anyway. He'll need the company. Someone to talk to on the bus or train. An ear for his excitement. He might convert her yet. She might be walking around with a big Robert Smith bird's nest hairdo next year, imagine that, he could change her look completely. Siouxsie eyes … black is the colour …

The silly cow: what the hell did she think she was doing in school today? What was the point in all that? Sure, Duffy is a wanker, but still, all she has to do is shut up and put up with it and they'll be out of the place soon enough. Another year or two. Bide their time.

That's what he is thinking. Out of there soon enough. He means *together*. Out of the place *together*. Patience. They could do it. Together. *All we need is just a little patience.* It is not such a daft idea. Why not? The two of them together. They get on well. They are all they really have, they need each other. Why not go to the same university together? Why not build a life somewhere else, somewhere foreign even, where no one knows them, where no one knows that they are cousins and the things they have done and the things that they will do again. They *will* do again. He wants it again. He wants her again. It is on his mind a lot. This is what he desires now, more than anything. He has had a taste of her and he has become greedy for her, and although his poem has not been written – the pages stay blank, the songs unsung – he has become obsessed. If that means that he thinks about her all the time, if that's what it means …

He knew from when they were very little, that she had problems. There was something wrong with her. The shaking, when he first saw it, it terrified him. They must have been only four years old, five at most, playing with cardboard boxes, building forts out of them – for him it was a castle under attack from a brutal battalion, the kind of thing he would have read in a war comic, *Commando* or *Warlord;* for her it was a castle too, but she was the pretty princess in it, and she badly needed rescuing. They had been adhering to the stereotypes; he knows that now of course, looking back, it was all so utterly typical, but it was the way it was: boys were boys, and girls were the fairer sex, and that was the way it should be – why would you go around thinking any differently? People laugh at Robert Smith and the "Cureheads"; the Goth get-up, but Robert Smith is not gay, just because he wears glossy (and comically smudged) lipstick, it is not about sexuality, it is just expression, freedom of expression, and that is what interests Kevin: expression, music, words.

And Laura shook.

And Laura trembled.

And Laura slid all over the floor.

And all he could do was watch, fascinated, scared but fascinated by the horrific episode unfolding in front of his innocent eyes.

And the next time it happened, and they were all alone, and she shook and trembled and slid, he went to her, and he cradled her, and it seemed to somehow help, it seemed to soften the blows.

And then the next time, and the time after that, the cradling, the helping, the soothing, the blows softened even more, and the love blossomed ... and the love has only ever grown.

She had allowed him in her bed. She had allowed him to touch her most private parts. And she had reached out for him. Privates. Private. They have always been a part of each other's private lives. The families: their tortured families. The dads gone: where did they go exactly? The absentees. Maybe a better band name. And how will they be found? He knows, he knows they will be found, and that they will be the ones to do it, Laura and Kevin, the plans are already in place, aren't they? Hasn't he already thought this through? Sometimes maybe plans…maybe things do go according to plan and things do…

Aidan Carty appears on a bicycle out of nowhere and taps him on the shoulder. Aidan Carty! The Swede! What the fuck is he doing here?

"Jesus! You scared the shit out of me!!"

"Sorry."

He cycles alongside Kevin, balancing on the bike, hardly pedalling. It is one of those expensive mountain bikes, bright, flashy, gears galore, and if Kevin were the kind of boy to be into such things he would be jealous. But BMXs never interested him. Mountain bikes certainly don't. Instruments, amplifiers, speakers, stereos, that's about his lot.

"Your cousin not with you? Thought you always went home together?"

"She got kicked out of class. I don't know where she went after that."

Kevin takes a sideways glance at Aidan, wondering where the hell he might be going. He looks at him standing on the pedals, as if in complete control of his machine, and he looks at his backpack, wondering what kind of supplies he's got in there – is he off for a fucking picnic or something … in the dark? On an evening with snow very likely!

"You going somewhere in particular?"

"Nowhere. Just cycling around. I often do this, after school. And on weekends. Taking pictures."

"Pictures?"

"Photographs, like"

"Oh?"

Aidan stops his bike and takes his camera out of his bag to show Kevin.

"Another little hobby I have. I'm a fan of gadgets. I like to take pictures."

"Pictures? Pictures of what?"

The music is still playing in the headphones that hang from Kevin's neck and so he switches the machine off, giving the blond boy his – albeit reluctant – attention.

"Pictures of anything. Sometimes I sneak out at night and take some shots then. Amazing the things you can see. Wild animals and so on."

"Right," says Kevin.

He is trying to think of what animals might be out at night, what could you see, what could you capture? Foxes?

"I saw a badger the other night. Very rare. It was much bigger than I had thought. I know where its den is now, might go back and see if I can catch it. On camera I mean. On film. Those things are actually quite vicious. Very sharp claws. Yeah, amazing what kind of animals you can see at night, when nobody else notices."

Aidan laughs, though Kevin can't see the joke. What the fuck does he care about badgers. Although, he could take pictures of those bloody foxes, scavenging round the bins at night, making a bloody racket, plenty of those you could *shoot*. And not just with a camera either. Maybe he'll have to borrow American Jason's gun. Get it sent over to him in the post. Blow the noisy fuckers to bits.

"Anyway," Aidan says, "thought we could do something … sometime."

Kevin is walking again; Aidan is slow-pedalling, balancing.

"*Do* something?"

"I hear you are interested in music."

Kevin is immediately suspicious, where did he hear that: Orlaith had been shooting her mouth off no doubt, taking the piss? *Kevvy is like Jean-Michel Jarre!*

"I do … I suppose … yeah …"

"I play guitar."

"Really?"

Kevin hadn't known that. He knows nothing at all about this guy. Knows only that Laura likes him because of his fucking blond hair, as if that was what made a person attractive. Hair. Seems like a bit of an arsehole to be honest. And how good is he anyway, on the guitar? As good as Kevin is on the keyboards? Kevin can play a few easy chords on the guitar, but he is a keys man, he tinkles the …

Aidan is looking at Kevin's schoolbag with interest.

"I think we might like the same stuff. You like The Pixies, Throwing Muses?"

"Yeah."

Kevin could expand on his love of Surfer Rosa, and The Pixies have a new album coming next year too – critics already claiming some of the tracks to be "monumental". But he says none of this, there is still an air of suspicion, Kevin dubious about this boy, coming up to him like this, out of nowhere, never before had they chatted, never once in school, and now, just like this, with Laura out of the way...

"We should play together sometime. Get together."

"Fine," says Kevin, though he's not at all sure it is. "Bring your guitar round sometime. Do you know where I live?"

He is half-hoping it is one of those wishy-washy invitations that never get picked up on, something said but not truly meant.

But Johnny Marr turned up on Morrissey's doorstep and the rest of course was...

Aidan smiles, "Yes, I know where you live, and Laura too, I know where you both live."

He suddenly loses balance on the bike and puts his hand on Kevin's shoulder to right himself, regain his balance.

"Sorry."

He smiles at Kevin again and turns and speeds off back the way he came, as if he had come and got what he wanted, had even stolen something somehow, nabbed, and fled with his loot, successful – why does Kevin feel that he has somehow lost out in this exchange?

Kevin looks at him tearing back down the country lane, the light at the front of the bike on now and searching out its path in the dark. Soon the boy and his bike are invisible. Soon the encounter over. But lingering, lingering with Kevin, a shudder, like a ghost is there still touching his shoulder, something that is not quite natural.

14

The front door of Laura's house is open and Kevin steps inside.

"Hello? Anyone home?"

He can smell toast. Someone's here. Guess who?

"I'm up here."

The door of her bedroom is open too and she is waiting for him; she knew he'd come to see her, how could he ever stay away? No doubt he has loads of questions about what went on in school, or he could come wanting something else entirely.

He sets his schoolbag on the floor and sits on the edge of her bed.

Laura is pacing, munching on the last bit of her buttery toast, and she seems a little agitated.

"Okay," he says, "out with it. What's the matter with you?"

"Lots going on."

He can see that. He can see that in the confused contours of her face, knowing every muscle and groove so well: every line she's ever had, he could always read, even between those lines. But he wants to hear it straight from her now.

"What the hell was all that in school today?"

"And what the hell was all that in school today?"

"He was annoying. Duffy."

"I know. He's always fucking annoying. But you don't walk yourself into trouble like that."

Laura stops pacing and sits on the bed beside him. She takes a couple of deep breaths and tries to steady herself.

"Sammy drove me home."

"Sammy?"

"Tom's friend."

"The old fella?"

"He's not that old...or maybe he is, I don't know...anyway, he said something..."

Kevin looks at her with mounting concern.

"About?"

"The thing in the lake. I mean, pond."

"Oh, for fuck's sake. Not that again. Look, there is nothing in the fucking pond. It's all in your head, all in your imagination. You've had mental issues since..."

"Thanks."

"You know what I mean. The epilepsy. The falls. I've always been there. Don't go all cranky on me now..."

He realises that his voice has been raised, and that she is on the verge of tears, that he is perhaps only causing her greater confusion. He is supposed to be the one on her side, always, this has always been his duty.

"Look," he says, softer, "you've had trouble, since you were young, and then your mother...look, all I'm saying is, it can't be easy, it's bound to take its toll."

"But..."

"There's nothing in the pond. I'm sorry to have to keep saying it, but whatever you are looking for it's not there."

He has been through this argument at home, when by himself alone in his room, his dark music playing, teasing it out. Could there be…? Nah. It is her imagination, it must be, surely. Whatever wires have got tangled in that brain of hers, she has created this monster. Monsters are created *by* people. Monsters are created *in* people. People may even *become* monsters – he is thinking now of The Smith's song, "Suffer Little Children", about The Moors Murders, Brady and Hinchley, complete monsters, he made her just like him, Brady made Hinchley a monster too, perhaps the most horrific monsters of the 1960s, the pair of them, or like Manson in America, monstrous. Monsters are not the things of lore, they are not objectively witnessed, not in ponds and not in forests anyway. It is all subjective. Subjective. Creation. Projection. That's what the library book had said. That's what Laura is doing, creating her own monsters, something to believe in, and maybe rail against. Kevin does know a little about the act of creation. That's all Kevin really is.

She is not giving up though.

"Well, maybe I need to see for myself. Tonight. Just to be sure."

"Tonight?"

"Yep. Tonight. Finally to see it for myself. And if I don't… then I will put the whole thing out of my mind."

"You're going alone?"

He suspects he already knows the answer to this one.

"No… Sammy is going to go with me."

"Oh, I see. Sammy McCreary. That old fucking drunk. He says he saw it too I suppose, yeah? On the way home from the pub some evening, was that it? With his miserable little dog?"

Laura stays quiet. Looks at her empty plate. She wants more toast, but she is too lazy to go down and get it. She should resist anyway, perhaps Tom would cook up something good again when he got home from his visit to the solicitor's office. His meals are good, better than her mother ever made. Tom is making life very easy for her. And so what if Sammy believes in the pond monster too. So what? Maybe it *is* real. Maybe it fucking *is*.

Kevin takes her silence for an admission.

"Thought so. The poor old fucker is probably dreaming of getting his wrinkly hands all over you. That's the monster right there. In his pants. That's the real fucking monster. Don't go near him."

Still she says nothing. Is she listening to him? Is she heeding his advice? Doesn't she understand how much he cares about her, cares for her, and has done, for how long now? How long is *always*?

"Seriously, don't go near him. Fellas like that are fucking dangerous. You don't know what these kinds of guys are up to. They're lonely. They're deranged. You can't trust anyone. And I can't be there to protect you all the time."

"Protect me?"

"Yeah, protect you."

She is fiddling with her hands and getting more aggravated; aggravated and somehow aggrieved; and she does not want an argument right now but he is insisting.

"Who has it been all these years, when you fall and bang your head? Your mother? Your father? Your friends? The fucking monster in the pond? Sammy? Tom? No! It's been me. All long. Me!"

He puts his hand out to take hers but she bats it away. She stands up and moves towards the window, looking out. Escape, escape, it is the only thing she has wanted, years now, how to get out of this barren place? Isn't she better off doing it alone, without him? Does he think he can control her? Does she, deep down, want to be controlled, is it easier that way? Control. It is the word that has been on her mind all day. Who has it? Who is out to get it? That horrible song Kevin teases her with. Joy Division: "She's Lost Control". When she falls and bangs her head, yes, yes, he is there. When she has no control over anything, her mind and body giving up on her, it is him who puts order on it, Kevin who tames the beasts, breaks the curse, it is him who cradles and catches her tears, soaks up her pity, makes her anew. Controls her. But hasn't it gone too far? Already. Too far? How much further can they take things? What is their relationship now? What does she want from him? To escape from him? Or *with* him?

The silence in the room is dense, tense. No music plays. She thinks about playing something on her stereo, but she doesn't. Let the tension stay, let it escalate … what then? Doesn't music just mask the real issues? Isn't their stupid pop music just a distraction from what is really going on? Isn't it all just rather … pointless?

And yet she would let him touch her again.

He has cradled her head and he has touched her intimately.

She'd let him do it again. She *wants* that too.

"Say something," he says.

"What's to say?"

He would prefer music on now. He would prefer something to fill the void. Something deep and heavy, rollicking and rumbling, to take his mind away from this awful moment, the suffocating room, winter outside and unrelenting. A cure for this moment of illness. The Cure. "If Only Tonight We Could Sleep". Has he been too harsh on her? But no music plays. It's all in his head. He has too much in there too, too much in his head. It's where they live. The two of them. Their own heads. And this place. It's this crushing place, too. They've got to get out. Escape. He shouldn't have been so … he'd been mean. He shouldn't have raised his voice to her.

"Talk to me."

"We are different," she says, still looking out the window; out at nothing. "We are different, you and me. We want different things from life. We can't even agree on what songs to listen to."

She turns to him.

She is looking at him now. Both have tears in their eyes, but the tears are not yelling falling, are suspended, the whole moment feels suspended.

She'd let him touch her again. She'd let him put it in. His little thing inside her even, yes, she would, she would. She knows it is wrong. *They* are wrong. But she deserves something. She deserves a little fun in her life. Who would deprive her of that?

And he wants her.

He wants her so bad.

But he is an imbroglio: anger, worry, a nascent rage.

He thinks of the high wire again. Balancing way up there on the wires. High up in the circus tent, faces upturned and watching – will *he* fall? Will *she* fall? Which one of these acrobats will be the first to tumble, the first to lose their footing and slip; don't look down now, there is no safety net; daring indeed. Derring-do.

She *would*.

He *wants to*.

"Shall we put on a tape?" she asks, sounding remote, as if she is talking to a stranger and not to her cousin, her mate.

"What do you think? Nah. Nah. See, I didn't think so. You'd just berate me for my poor choices, for my poor choices in everything."

"No, I wouldn't. I do everything for you. And I will continue, everything, everything is for you. You know how much you ..."

Laura shakes her head.

"Don't. We can't talk like that. It's not right. None of it. None of it is right. We are ... wrong."

They let silence fall for another minute. Bedroom silence. Music-less silence. It only grows denser. It chokes.

Eventually, miserably, he says, "I talked to Aidan Carty."

She does not appear in the slightest bit interested.

"He asked me where you were."

"Did he?"

"He's an odd one. Seems kind of ... secretive ..."

"Well, we all have our secrets now, don't we?"

"Yeah, but ... it's as if he's onto something the rest of us aren't. Knows something. Does that make any sense?"

"No."

"I can't understand him. Maybe I'm just jealous ... that's all."

She lets his admission hang, and then:

"He's just a boy. Just a fucking boy."

What does she mean by that? Kevin doesn't know, but it feels like it stings. Laura is not sure she knows what she means by it either. But it was what she said, and she sounded like she meant it. Perhaps that is the best way to drive through life: even if you don't have a clue what's going on, you look and sound like you mean it. It was what made those popstars successful: they had the look, the arrogance, but they were probably just as dim and lost as everybody else. Even the President of the USA, Reagan, he didn't seem to make much sense at times – Duffy railed against him regularly in class – but he is still where he is, President of the world's biggest superpower, and Duffy is where he is, being slandered by graffiti on a wall for all to see. *Duffy is a faggot.* When Jerry Clancy, a boy in Kevin's class, had seen the words on the wall, he even ad-libbed a rhyming end: *Just don't tell Sister Maggot.*

Kevin picks up his bag from the floor and slings it over his shoulder. Why does he carry around so much stuff in it? Stuff he doesn't really even need. He needs to shed some of this stuff. Get rid. That's what he needs to do.

He sees her book, *Myths and Monsters,* on her desk, and what looks like a diary too: *Keep out!*

"Are you writing a diary?"

She shrugs, non-committal.

"I best be off then."

She is facing the window again, the window looking out onto nothing. Just nothing-fields and nothing-walls and a nothing-sky that is dark with nothing. Down the road though is that pond, the thing they all call a lake, and maybe there is something in that water, swimming there, or resting there, or feeding, hiding away there all these years. Maybe not *nothing* in that pond, maybe *something*.

Kevin pulls his headphones over his ears and walks out of the room, The Cure's "The Perfect Girl" is playing in his ears, worming deep into him; he can trust his Walkman, at least he can trust those songs.

He switches off the machine suddenly before the singer reaches the final line and its conclusion. The song is about a "strange" girl and a "perfect" girl: they are one and the same. The rhythms of the song are jaunty, there is a sort of wooziness about it, almost dizzying, the synthesizers seem-ing to lurch, like they are seasick: he's not sure if he wants to consider the lyrics of this song at all. He will walk home in the dark and in silence, see what that is like for a change; a punishment perhaps, maybe that's it, but for sure he doesn't want to hear the last line of that song, because the singer thinks he's falling in ...

15

"You know in my day we used to say grace first," says Tom.

Their dinners are in front of them, and while Tom is not being severe with her, he does sometimes want to instil some manners into her, old-style – he's not stupid enough to think that times have not changed, it's the 1980s, he's well aware of that, but, it is no harm in letting young girls and boys know the effort that went into the preparation of such meals, and those receiving should be grateful, not only to the one preparing but most of all to the Lord God above in Heaven, who provided such bounty in the first place. The country wasn't blessed with riches at this moment, but Tom believes there are other places that have it a lot worse. The whole decade has seen nothing but famines in Africa on the Television, and yer man Geldof and his big concert thing a few years back, so look, they aren't badly off at all, and though many still take the boat to England or America, Tom is happy enough in his own house, and his girl is here with him now, and saying grace, it's only a little prayer of thanks, is it such a bad idea, saying grace, is it?

Laura stops eating, her mouth full, cheeks swollen.

"Grace," she says.

"Right, cheeky, I'm just saying, we had more respect for things in my day. You've had no wars or anything to contend with, should consider yourself very lucky."

"Sorry," she says, and she does mean it. He's right. He usually is.

She resumes, tucking into Tom's casserole like there is no tomorrow.

"Jaysus, Maura, you're like an animal there."

"Laura."

"Wha?"

"Laura. My name's Laura. You said: *Maura*."

"I did not."

"You did too."

"Well … sorry, love. Slip of the tongue."

"You wish."

Tom doesn't quite know what that is supposed to mean, and whether she is making fun of him in some way, gearing up for a round of mock-the-old-man, a game that she could quite easily play every night and win at quite easily too; it is all enough to make him blush, and as he holds his spoon over his own hot casserole – rich and thick and delicious if he is allowed say so himself – he hurries the conversation onto a different subject, an obvious deflection.

"Anyway, a growing girl like you needs her vitamins. Needs her strength."

"For what?"

"I don't know for what, study and stuff, making the brain cells. Stamina … just for growing up … and all that."

She makes him uncomfortable sometimes, she can see this. It is only because he is not used to living with someone, especially with a young girl. None of this had been planned, it all just happened, to the two of them, it was the last thing they could have expected, shacking up like this – and what were the villagers even saying about the odd situation? Its quick solution. The way things fell into place so quick. God only knows. And yet here they are, despite it all, eating together, making a go of it; they may have no choice in the matter, but they are getting on, that much must be obvious even to the most malicious of gossip-mongers who would have quite a lot to chirp on about after mass on a Sunday morning. She allows him his blushes, and he allows her to speak freely and to be the potential she is. Potential. He likes that notion. It comes to him often when he thinks of her. When he thinks of Kevin too. So full of youth. And promise.

"You know the night you let Kevin stay over? Was that really to protect me … if anything happened? A fit, I mean. Or … was it for you to get some free time with Laura … I mean *Maura*."

"God, but you are a cheeky one all right. Very *sarky* aren't you?"

He is laughing and he is blushing and this is all of course admitting to the very pertinent point she has just raised. She has nailed it: but how can he confess to it? Deflect again, his only form of counter-attack:

"You must have had a fight with Kevin or something. To make you so snarky. Is that it? Have the cousins been fighting?"

Laura shrugs.

Tom has become used to these teenage gestures, the rolling of eyes, the grins and grimaces – he must have had his own versions of these too when he was a whippersnapper out on the country lanes, chasing country love, and, more often than not, unable to quite snare it.

"I thought you were the best of friends," he says, aware now that he has stumbled upon something more serious than his ribbing had intended. He's hoping of course it is just teenage nonsense, a spit, a spat, storm in a teacup, something that can be forgiven and forgotten the next morning, nothing more than that.

But she has a look about her now, a sorrow in the dip of her eyebrows, that says she really has been put through the ringer, and she cannot be expected to sort everything out in a day, or in a week, months even; these sorrows take years to cauterize, if ever they fully do; her eyes, eyes that have both melancholy and a fighting spirit always vying for most display, they have wept, yes, wept, those eyes, but perhaps they have not yet wept enough.

Please, girl, he says to himself, when he sees all this across the kitchen table on an ordinary evening of an extraordinary cold winter. Don't do anything stupid now, stay on the straight road like a good girl and don't go sliding off. Please, love, let's keep it level, and don't go breaking all our hearts.

In another kitchen another pair, another *sort of* family, is eating through their sorrows and their sins. After a few minutes of silence Maura O'Brien cannot take it anymore and snaps the silence in two.

"So, how was school today?"

It has been the same question almost every day for the last ... she doesn't know how long, and almost every day there is a *fine*, or an *okay* response, clipped, curt. But her son goes in a different direction today; instead his lines drip with sarcasm:

"Very interesting. So much to learn, you know. It's so good to be a part of such an extraordinary and vital institution. Credit, really, to the education system: take a bow, Sister Margaret; you should be canonized for such sterling work, nay, miracle-working."

"Right," she says.

Got it.

It's going to be like that, is it?

So ... what does she do now? Does she add to his cynicism by asking more about school and study and exams ....
or does she just cut to the chase?

She leaves a few more mute minutes pass before she decides on the latter and candour.

"Did you read the letters?"

"Of course I did."

"What did they say?"

"They said lots of things."

He lets her hang with that for a moment, letting her stew, before continuing:

"The letters talked about the wonders of life in the U.S. of A. Fascinating place by all accounts. Spacious. Almost infinite. So much land there, where you are free to roam, like their own big and burly bison, and not feel confined. To be who you are. And with endless possibilities ... where lakes are huge lakes and are not little ponds pretending to be lakes. They are the real thing."

She is looking down at her plate.

Whiting. Fish she picked up in the village, from Mick Casey, the fishmonger, who she knows well.

Everyone in the area knows her well too.

This is the way it goes: everybody knows everybody else.

It is all unavoidable.

There are no great lakes. Not American size. Not supersize. Not mega. How do you compete with that?

Casey had said the whiting was fresh; but then he would always say that, wouldn't he? Would he know of great lakes and great fish caught in great lakes in the United States? The massive waters of where ... Michigan? She does not even know; when did she last open one of those encyclopaedias – she didn't even have the full set: that said a lot about her life.

These people, in the village: some people tell you what you want to hear, and others, like her son, will tell you exactly what you don't want to hear – how odd the dichotomy, as if there is no middle ground. She does not want to hear about the lakes of America, or the States of America, or the state of America, or anyone living and having a grand old time of it *in* America, or anywhere else for that matter. Especially not Tadhg and his lover. His lover! Think on it! How bloody preposterous it is to even *think* it. *Lover!* *Lover!* He was her own darling husband for a few short years, not all that long ago. He was around long enough to make a child, enough to see the boy take his baby steps and then ... skedaddle, right out of there, and never coming back. No, she does not want to hear about San Francisco and the wonders of life there, the freedom and the fortunes. She is weary. Maura O'Brien. Over her fried fish and a few measly chips with ketchup on the side. She looks, suddenly, achingly weary, and rather despondent too. The sense of bathos is all at once overwhelming. Yes, she is mostly weary. Mostly that. It is so hard to stay on and keep fighting.

Laura and Tom.
They could be father and daughter.
But they are not.
Thrown together like this.

Fated.

And here they are.

They sup and they stare at nothing sometimes. Tom still not used to his new environs. His old house was small, pokey, everything crowding in around him, no room to swing a cat. When Sammy ever brought his animal round, Lucy, she bowled around and wreaked havoc; things toppled, things tumbled, things broke, things smashed. This place is wider, more room to manoeuvre, room to stretch out his long legs of an evening, take it all in. He considers himself damn lucky, great fortune come upon him. He hasn't been all that lucky with the cards recently, their drunken poker nights, but the cards aren't all that important. Life is. The real hands you are dealt there, in life. That's what matters. And he's holding a fine hand at the moment.

He looks at the side dresser: Dymphna had an eye for nice collectibles, fine Delft – he had a habit of dropping things himself, had shattered many a plate in his time, easily as many as mad Lucy; he'd better be careful here. Even the cutlery in the drawers here is of high calibre; wedding presents he supposes, or she went out and sought and bought herself, when she was up and able and strong and not … the way she ended up. The poor love. God rest her soul.

"Turns out she left more money than we had at first thought," Tom says, half to himself.

"Oh?" says Laura, not expecting it.

"You need not worry about your future. College and stuff. There's more than enough to keep you well looked after, the solicitor informed me. And money that had been lodged in an account for you too, from America. There's money … in your name."

"From America?"

"Yes."

She knows what that means. It's not from Ronald Reagan, and it's not from Madonna to thank her for buying all her albums. It's from her father. Guilt money, she assumes. What is *blood money*? She has heard that term. Maybe in a TV show: *Miami Vice* or something, isn't that where she heard it? What does it mean? It sounds apt here; but maybe she doesn't understand. She's young. How can she be expected to know everything, be expected to deal with everything? How? How?

"A lot?" she asks; curious, keen, but trying not to sound gluttonous.

"How long is a piece of string … if you know what I mean? Enough. Enough, like I said, enough for you to go to study where you need to. To not be short."

"Right."

"Actually I learned quite a bit about the family, the finances you know, what with me being the guardian at the moment. He says the word *guardian* with such pride, and this warms the cockles, she wonders would he ever be brave enough to try on a different hat, not *guardian* or *uncle* but *father … dad*? Too much? Maybe that's a bridge too far. But they do have a future together. And if the other one, the absent one, never ever comes back …

He continues: "Your mother's grandfather, going way back now, he was quite well off. Linen, they said. There was always money in that, back in the day … but I won't bore you with the history lessons. Just to say that you will be all right. There's no need to worry."

"I'm not worried."

"Good. I'm glad to hear it."

He lets her take all this in, and distracts himself by noticing other things in his new kitchen: the lino could do with replacing, something he'll have to think about. He might drop soapy plates every now and again, but he's all right with general maintenance, his business after all, his *forte*, DIY. And oh! That toilet! He'll need to fix that bloody toilet, too.

Laura is miles away, a look of wistfulness about her.

"Do you miss her?"

She takes a moment before answering.

"Of course I do. But I'm not that sad. And I feel a little guilty about that. But she was always so sick. She had so many health issues. Like me, I guess. I'm glad that she doesn't have to suffer anymore. And now that I'm older, I can take care of myself... but yeah, I miss her. Of course I do."

Tom is happy to hear her talk about it. It's something the girl hasn't done enough of, opening up, explaining her feelings. She needs to get it out. Needs to vent. To complain. Throw a strop or two. Perhaps that was part of Dymphna's problem, the *not* getting it all out, the keeping of things inside, the bottling up; that was what was causing some of the illness at least, mental illness... there was a word for it... wasn't there, when you made yourself sick by thinking about stuff, overthinking, creating your own illnesses when there was nothing there to begin with, he'd read it in the newspaper recently. *Psychosomatic!* That was it! As far as he could garner that was what it was all about, anxiety, stress, manifesting in all kinds of upsets and ulcers and making the body ill and...

A little tear rolls down her cheek.

Tom rises, goes to her and puts his hand on her shoulder comfortingly, reassuringly. It is a gesture that says he is here, guardian, and that he will stay here for as long as she needs him, and that she need not be one bit concerned, this old codger now a permanent lodger, there's no getting rid of him, and when he does eventually die, someone like Sammy won't be able to say *way too young*, because he'll be a grand old age, a Guinness Book of Records entry, one hundred and ten, he'll certainly try and beat Sammy all the way.

The hand on her shoulder causes another tear to fall, a fine fat drop that makes it all the way to Laura's chin and hangs there. She wipes it away and tries out a little snicker, to show him that she does get it, all that he has done, and all that he is trying to do, and that she is grateful, and that they'll have to let this glumness go now and get on with their lives. Forward. Only on. Only on.

He takes her empty plate away and slots it into the sink of water.

"You made short work of that," he says to her. "I'm way behind. Don't seem to have the speed these days. I was like you when I was young, scoffing everything down, always in a mad hurry. Although the doctors say it's the right thing to do, to be chewing slowly I mean, to digest the food properly … there's a word for that too if I only could …"

He is just about to sit back down and finish the remaining scraps on his plate when the telephone rings in the hallway.

"Wonder who that could be."

He gets up again and makes his way out to the hall and picks up the receiver.

Laura can hear scraps of Tom's conversation.

"No, I didn't know anything …"

"No, not at all …"

"I will, sure …"

"Thanks for letting me..."

He puts the receiver back in its cradle and he takes a deep breath. He walks back to the kitchen and her eyes are upon him, eager.

She has an inkling as to what it might be all about.

There are butterflies doing their rounds in her stomach again, a bigger bunch this time, wider, flappier wings.

Tom sits back down at his place at the table and lifts the final half-rasher to his mouth. He chews it slowly, looking at her.

She is all anticipation, her nerves getting the better of her now; come on Tom, spit it out, and she doesn't mean that rasher.

"That Duffy... bit of a dickhead, isn't he?"

Laura scrambles out of her chair and throws herself on top of him.

"Yeah, he is, he is, thanks, Tom, thanks, thanks."

She lands a massive smack of a kiss right on his bristly cheek.

"Get off me, you silly girl," he chuckles. "Go over to the freezer and get us some ice cream."

Her tears have quickly dried in the sun of her smile: he has a knack, this good man, he definitely has a knack.

Maura is picking up the glasses and plates from the table and carrying them to the sink. She plops them in and watches them submerge, their sturdy frames overtaken by bubbles and suds, the grease sliding off to sully the water beneath.

Kevin is still sitting at the table, eating jelly and ice cream; half-pretending he does not care, but in actuality quite enjoying the treat.

Maura looks out the kitchen window, into the dark night, pensive, and a little pained.

"I never saw him write a damn thing, you know."

"What?"

"Your father."

"What do you mean?"

"I just think it's odd. This letter-writing thing. He just doesn't seem the type to put pen to paper. He never read a book. Would hardly glance at the newspaper ... never wrote a note of any description as far as I can remember. Certainly didn't leave a goodbye note, did he? I'd hardly even recognise his handwriting. I just think ..."

"Yeah, well, people change, don't they?"

"Do they?"

The night-time window does not reflect back a pop star on a glittering stage, not a shoulder-padded New Romantic all perfume and pout. She sees none of that. It is just the reflection of a housewife, or at least house*woman* now, the *wife* bit got lobbed off and replaced; an ordinary woman, on the verge of so much, ever on the verge of tears, for what has been lost and what she is in the process of losing, her son; on the verge of life's change too, her body gearing up, or is that winding down, at the window, reflecting, trying to figure things out, it is both a woman and a mother that stands here, and a widow of sorts too, though her husband is not dead as far as she is aware, most probably he is vivaciously alive; it was only her own sad sick sister was taken, but that was expected, a relief to everyone, if she has to be cruelly honest: wearing black that day felt like a betrayal, a lie, she was not that sad at all, it is only her son that makes her truly sad, this most of all, so here, still, still at this window, she reeks of love gone sour, of loss.

❦

"Let me ask you something," says Laura dipping her spoon into her ice cream, a triangle of wafer sticking out of it like a shark's fin.

"Fire away," says Tom, "as long as it is not something about Maura O'Brien."

"Do you believe in monsters?"

Tom lets out a surprised guffaw.

"Monsters? Jaysus! That's not the kind of question I was expecting. What kind of monsters? Duffy? What do you mean?"

"Like The Loch Ness Monster."

"Not at all, love."

Tom can see that she is taking the conversation totally seriously and does not think of any of this as a joke.

"Look, it's just bored little villagers trying to drum up a bit of business for their community. Which is fair enough. Some places don't have a lot going for them, so why not invent a little story, to draw in a few customers."

He pauses, searching her face, wondering if they are in agreement on this.

"You don't believe in all that old guff, do you?"

"I don't know what to believe anymore," she says.

"Well, don't you dare go looking for any monster in our lake. It's frozen over anyway. Iced over completely. But thin ice, I can assure you. It looks like you could skate on it but you wouldn't last long. You'd go right down through it."

"Frozen over?"

"First time in years. Have you not seen? And they say we'll have snow too. Strange ol' weather this year. Must be the ozo layer they're always harping on about."

"It's *ozone* layer. And it's not a lake. It's a pond."

"Well, whatever you say but ..."

"We should call it what it is."

"Just stay away from it. Whatever it is called. Until the spring at least."

Tom plops his plate into the suds, watches it sink.

"I'll do them," says Laura.

She nudges her uncle aside and searches for her mother's rubber gloves. He tries to edge his way back in but she hip-bumps him away, having none of it.

"No, really, you're cooking every night. Let me do it."

"All right then, love. Thank you."

He kisses her on the cheek and lets her get on with it.

"Go and sit down in the living rom. Put your feet up. Relax. You must be tired after all the business today."

"I am actually. Not getting any younger, that's for sure."

Tom leaves the kitchen whistling jauntily, "Heaven Is a Place on Earth," another tune he had picked up from the radio.

Laura locates the pink latex gloves and slips her own thin hands into the spaces her mother's once occupied.

She puts her palms together then as if in prayer, and she dives those hands into the murky water. Into the water she dives.

16

Menace.

There is menace in Kevin's eyes, there is some dreadful hatching; there is something mad now, something malign.

The jelly went down well, the ice cream, too; a pair always complementary. But everything else did not.

What had she been saying? That his father never wrote a damn word and…

His mother and him…a pair *not so* complementary. Not these days anyhow.

Kevin goes to the stereo in his bedroom. He slots in The Smiths' first album, and "Reel Around the Fountain" starts up: such a lazy beginning, such a laconic opening to the album. The song makes him think of Laura. So many songs make him think of Laura. So many things make him think…

But he's the one! He's the one who's always there, isn't he? Making sure she doesn't bang her head off the floor. He's the one who cradles her, her head resting in his lap. He's the one. He's the only bloody one! Would Aidan Carty know what to do if she fell before him, foaming at the mouth? Would he fuck.

Kevin sits back on his chair.

His bedroom.

His posters on the wall.

Siouxsie.

His music.

Because the silence would be terrible. The silence of no father. The silence of not talking to your mother. The silence of no friend. Only Laura. The silence of no girlfriend, only Laura. His cousin is his girlfriend! *Girlfriend!* Fuck. Let him not say that aloud. Let him not think…his cousin is his lover. They made love one night in her room…no they didn't. He didn't put it inside her. He touched her. Only that. She touched him. They fiddled. They fumbled. That was not love. No. Then what is? What is love? What is that thing they sing about?

That old fucker. Sammy McCreary. Tom's friend. He's up to something. They always are. Making children old. There is no monster. Not in that pond anyway. There is no monster. The monsters are elsewhere. The monsters are the ones who break order. The ones who do unnatural things. They are the monsters. They are the ones…

It does become a good metaphor: what lies below the surface.

He opens his notebook. Blank pages. Her name on top. Every page.

A good metaphor. He should write it down. He chews on the cap of his biro.

Below the surface there are…

What can rise up…

Things submerged…

He writes nothing though.

He chews on the biro cap; it's hard, uncomfortable in his mouth.

His hands go to his synthesizer. He touches the keys. No sound. It is not even switched on.

He looks at Siouxsie. *Help!*

The rock star glowers back. This is their relationship. Silence.

Submerged.

Hidden below.

He plays nothing: he writes nothing.

The metaphor is all a bit too obvious actually. That is why he doesn't write any of it down. He's better than that. He's far more creative than that. Kevin is an artist.

Is Kevin an artist? Or a pretender? A charlatan? A pompous...

The pages are blank.

Something cries out in the garden. Animal-like.

The fox?

He should name it.

Fox.

Fox comes almost every night, but every night Kevin does not see it. Just hears the mangled cries, or is that his own imagining?

Maybe it is the monster calling to him from the pond.

Or from the dark row of trees.

The dark row of trees.

The dark row of fucking trees!

A sudden thought then: a flash.

Yes: *flash!*

From the end of her garden: the dark stand of trees.

His eyes widen.

He stands up, away from the mute machine. He switches the stereo off too. This thought, it turns to flashes of memory, turns to illumination.

Flash of light from …

Not a passing car.

Not lightning.

As they kissed. The lovers. The kissing cousins. The taboo children. Embraced in the night. Garden. The cold night. The night unforgiving. Their bodies searching for warmth. Thin raincoat. Noose of a scarf. He told her about the letters from America and hoped she would believe him, he'd tell her the truth someday when they …

And what else? What *else*?

Silence now in the bedroom, a bedroom not used to silence.

Help!

Siouxsie says nothing. The rock star glowers. Is that all she ever does?

Close-up of Orlaith saying: "Love is tragic, isn't it, Kevvy? That's why people run away, with their real lovers. Doesn't matter even if they are the same sex."

Yes, *close-up*, like it is all a movie playing before him: he sees her right there, in front of him, Orlaith's snide-ness, her thorny teases. Orlaith: obnoxious.

Love is tragic, isn't it, Kevvy?

And Aidan. The Swede. Holding his shoulder for balance so as not to fall from the bicycle.

Flash of light again in those trees; the end of Laura's garden, and Aidan's voice: *Amazing the things you can see. Wild animals and so on.*

Sniggers.

And so on.

Snide.

They all had it. That fucking meanness.

Spastic girl: loves a bit of sympathy.

The hurtful things they hurl around. Noxious.

Burn in hell they will.

Kevin is standing in the middle of his bedroom. His *no sound* bedroom. His *music-less* room. His mouth is open. Revelations. That's what has come to him in the silence. In the *no notes*, in the *no songs*, in the fox-less deadness.

A knock on the door.

"Go away."

"Do you want a …?"

"No, go away. I'm going out for a walk."

"A walk? It's freezing outside! It might snow!"

"I need to clear my head. I've a headache."

No movement, hardly a breath, inside and outside of the door. Who goes next? He is waiting for her to say something and she is waiting for him.

Standoff.

Is this what they have become? This is not jelly and ice cream. These two do not go so well together. They cannot even face each other's face.

"Wrap up warm then," she says finally, and she heads back down the stairs, back to the kettle: she will make tea only for herself, for her only-ness, and maybe a dull biscuit too, the good ones are all gone, she had given them to him; she has not even been to the supermarket for a proper shop in ages, this negligence must stop. The kettle is put on. The comfort of the element heating. Soon steam rising. Snaking out of the spout.

Standing in the middle of the room: Kevin.

Help!

What happens next?

Siouxsie says nothing, but she doesn't need to. He has worked it out for himself.

He puts the stereo back on, the second track, "You've Got Everything Now", but he hasn't, he hasn't got *everything*, but he's got *some* of it. Morrissey sings of someone being his mother's only son, but a desperate one.

He goes to his bed and he takes a pillow from it. He places it in front of him, on the bed, and he beats it.

That's right.

With his fists.

Like he's done many times before.

He beats the pillow he beats the pillow he beats the pillow...

Because he can.

He beats the pillow because it is the face of Orlaith, because it is the face of Aidan; he beats Duffy and all the other teachers too; he beats Sister Margaret; he beats shit pop music, all this with his hard teenage fists; he beats his mother and most of all he beats his father. His father in the pillow, perfect, for he cannot call to mind what his father even looked like, the photos are few, and his mother tore up so many, so he beats a blank grey pillow, because that is what his father is: no image at all. Faceless. Faceless father. And he beats it some more, for good measure.

Exhausted he falls on the bed. He has not had such a workout in years. Perhaps ever. He is not a fit and healthy boy. Hard-bones maybe, tough enough, but unused to physical exertion, slow on the playing fields, for the most part uninterested. Too much of a brooder. Too much time ruminating. He should be out more with the GAA boys, and the soccer fanatics, the hurlers beating themselves across the heads with their big sticks – perhaps that was a metaphor too. Maybe it did make sense to him now that he thought about it, it never did before: yes, beat each other away boys, what else is there to do in the fucking village? Beat away to your heart's content, what's another bruise? What difference will that make? Unless you start a band someday. The Absent Fathers. The Absentees. What an ironic name! Wonderful! The Absentees... Live! It makes no sense. How can an absentee be live? An absentee is not present! Ha! It makes no sense. Perfect. Because life doesn't. Wonderful! Or Faceless Fathers? How about that? Live in San Francisco. Of course. Where else would the gig be? It would have to be there. Wouldn't it? There is only one city in the world that he truly needs to visit. And it is not for its rock and roll history.

He stares at the ceiling. Laura is not beside him. The last time he stared at a ceiling like this his girl was beside him. His girl. His cousin. His lover. Laura. The one he loves. Yes, he loves her. Why is it so hard to ... what is wrong with that?

And she is in trouble.

Yes, this much he knows now, too. She is in trouble. Must be. Something dangerous. Something dangerous about to occur. It's all there in the ceiling. Laura's ceiling had a gorilla. This is much worse. This is a whole ugly scene playing out. The ceiling is full of monsters. Like the pernicious Gremlins he saw on video only last year: what appeared cute and innocent suddenly turned malevolent if the rules were not obeyed.

The ceiling full of monsters.

Monsters in the pond.

Monsters all over the village.

All over the world.

He must go to her.

He must go.

Go … now!

He rises and takes a heavy coat from the wardrobe. The trench coat will no longer do. He must be prepared for harsh weather. Harsh times. This is heavy, this is a heavy coat, it will keep out snow, will keep out the severity of the winter winds, the monsters and their bilious breath.

He must go to her.

He must go to the lake that is not a lake. *It's just a fucking pond.*

But monsters there.

He must go to her.

Because he is all she has.

Because she is all he has.

17

Tom is snoring on the armchair. Laura watches him, making sure he is asleep, making sure he will not wake up.

It seems to be a deep sleep, he seems sated after an honest, productive day; maybe he is dreaming of nothing but good things: success in business, a good hand of cards, of massive fortunes down the road for him, or of Maura O'Brien, her tidy hand in his, or a shining new ring on her slim finger.

Laura puts on her coat and a woolly hat. She closes the front door gently behind her, quiet as a burglar, only instead of breaking in she's breaking *out*.

I'll sneak out. Don't worry. I'm good at that.

She is. She is good at that. And what does that say about her? What kind of person makes such a boast? Is that one of her best qualities? Is that something that will one day land her a job? Imagine if she puts it on her CV (they are already practicing and preparing these for future employment).

Interests and hobbies: *Sneaking out.*

Ambition: *Escape from the village of the damned.*

Hardly a sound as she creeps away from the house, hardly a sound, her booted feet tread softly on the gravel, trying not to crunch the stones beneath her. This spot she steps over now is the same place where she fell and tore the tape from her Walkman on the day her mother died. When she lost her mind and fell to her knees screaming and sobbing, when an ambulance passed, her mother inside it, leaving her for good – it wasn't so long ago, it wasn't so long ago at all. She didn't get to see her mother inside that ambulance – was she covered with a blanket or a sheet? Or was she zipped up in one of those awful body bags? She could have stopped the driver and asked to climb in and look at her one more time, to kiss her, to tell her that she will miss her. The thought didn't even occur. Not at that moment. She was caught up in the pointless battle with her fallen music machine, the mangled cassette tape, concerned with the ripping out of its innards. She hasn't properly mourned. This feeling gnaws at her. She hasn't properly given herself over to grief. But how do you go about doing that? If your heart's not in it. Where is your heart? Where is your fucking heart anyway?

She takes one look back at the house. The lights are on. She sees it as a building that emanates warmth. Has it always been like that? When her father left and her mother got sick … it always felt so chilly, the house itself even felt sick and dying with no one to properly nurse it, but now, new life had been breathed back into it. Tom. Tom is that new life, that new breath, resuscitator, new lease; it is hard not to like the situation.

Her bedroom is right up there: that is where she lays her head at night and dreams fantastic episodes. Dreams of what? Getting out. She dreams of not being here at all. Dreams a blind mole burrowing, a prisoner tunnelling.

And she lay with her cousin in that bed, too.

She did.

And they broke the rules.

They did.

You are not meant to lay with a member of your own family; society is pretty clear on that. It's even common fucking sense.

How many more rules can she break before she does get out?

Is that the way her life is to be? Is that to be the theme of it?

Rule-breaker.

Troublemaker.

Kevin closes the door hard behind him. He does not care how much noise he makes. His mother knows that he is going out, even if she has no idea of his actual destination. Does he? Does he know where he is going?

To fight with monsters? Is that it?

Are the monsters inside or out?

Within?

Without?

He puts on his woolly hat and his gloves as he takes his first steps outside. The night is hard and biting. It cares not for the softness of young skin and will cut right through it on a whim. It is unsympathetic to your needs. The world does not care whether you are in it or if you are on your way out of it. If you decide to depart, then fine, the world will still be here. If you sink down to the bottom of the pond it cares not one jot. Or if you die on stage, electrocuted by your own guitar, live in San Francisco, in front of thousands of your adoring fans, your green and pink Mohican hairstyle defying gravity … the world does not care all that much. Piss off. You are as worthless as anyone else.

The monsters will still be out there. Doing all their wrong things.

What if Kevin is just one more of them? The music monster, prone to tantrums, bursts of anger, close to madness – he beats his pillow, he does, he does that often. What about that?

He marches on.

His footfalls on the frosted ground say: *What about that? What about that? What about that?*

AND YOU MAY SAY TO YOURSELF,
"MY GOD! WHAT HAVE I DONE?"

18

She is …
He is …
They are …
All of them … perhaps.

Look hard enough into that pond: will you happen to see monsters there?

Or just take a glance, a glance askance.

On the surface, say. Eyes skimming like a flat pebble when expertly thrown at the correct angle.

Catch your own reflection there.

Will you find a monster?

Swear.

Swear on your life now: is that what you have found in there?

Deep.

Deep down?

Or just barely below the surface?

19

Sammy McCreary hasn't had it easy, but who in the village has? It is only a small farming community, they are hardly going to be flush with cash; times are tight, money for sure doesn't grow on the trees around here, hardly anything does, a few crab apples maybe, sour like the faces that try tasting them, bunches of bitter sloes – all the good stuff: the oranges, the bananas, they come from elsewhere, far away and elsewhere, Spain, Bolivia. The good stuff is always from far away and elsewhere. Grass is greener, ironically, away from the Emerald Isle. The kids are well aware of this and are always quick to point it out: the vox-popped youngsters on the radio tell of their great hopes for their lavish lives in London, New York, Sydney, Auckland. Anywhere but here. They take the boats and the planes, but the planes of course are better than the boats, because the planes are faster, way faster a way out of here, up up and away.

Sammy McCreary, for all his hometown pride, is well aware of all this. But Sammy stays positive. Despite all. He watches the nightly news and the thousands departing and he sees the movies too on his VHS recorder: the Yanks with their big bucks; Wall Street – *Yuppies* he has heard them called, *Yuppies*, now there was a term, it sounded like *puppies* to Sammy, him being a dog-lover and all, and he could picture the sharp-suited boyos with their briefcases, all of them running around with their tongues lolling out of saliva-stricken mouths, hungry for the green dollar bills. He'd like a bit of all that too if he had the opportunity: a bite out of The Big Apple, sure, why not? A man like Sammy would certainly have the charm to succeed, no bother to him at all. But he has never left the country. He has never owned a passport. Sammy has hardly even left the county. For a man with so little – a man barely scraping a living together with the paltry painting and dearth of decorating – you'd think he'd be more upset. You'd think it would get him down. You think he'd jump straight into that murky pond – well, not at this moment in time, the bloody thing is frozen over – but on an ordinary spring day say, you'd think he'd just attach some rocks to his feet, stones in his pockets as the tradition went, and jump right in, sink right down to the sandy bottom, give up the ghost entirely. But he doesn't. He doesn't do any of that. He sticks it out. He should be applauded for that, lauded for that at least, the putting-up-with, the seeing-things-through to the bitter end. *The bitter end*: there's a bloody phrase and a half. Do the Yuppies carry around a phrase like that with them when they're going through the revolving doors of a Wall Street building? *The bitter end.* He's seen quite a lot shuffle off to the other side, more coffins than you would care to remember, long brown ones with their shiny handles and plates, and even small white ones too, the saddest of all, doesn't bear thinking about, does it? But he's still here, having a go. He's no quitter. He has friends. He has his poker nights. He has ideas about things, and he mulls over them when he's out for a walk with his little Yorkshire terrier, Lucy. You might call Sammy McCreary an optimist.

He might even say it about himself. What's wrong with that? Bit of positivity. It's good to have that kind of outlook, the rest of them can be quite dreary, quite negative in fact; a lot of *ologon*-ing, and the news on TV every night doesn't help one bit, does it? Troubles. Troubles. Bombs and mayhem. Financial gloom. Words like *diaspora* – a new one for him. There's talk of them pulling down that wall in Germany, and maybe they will. That's positive, as far as he knows. There's changes all over Europe, if the clever fellas are to be believed. And the Russian fella with the mark on his forehead, he's making changes too. Fair play to him. Fair play to all the fellas having a go at trying to improve things. But in a small village in a rural part of this country, there's not a heck of a lot going on. That's why he likes to see the young ones, before they head off to wherever they decide to head off to. They have a spiky attitude, a sense of rush and push, and he likes that, reminds him of when he was full of vigour and vim himself, back in the day, chatting up the ladies on the way to a dance somewhere, standing with his back to a wall in some dance hall or other, some barn most likely, smiling away when he had a good set of teeth in him, pre-dentures, and an old fag hanging from his lip like he was a movie star himself, a Humphrey Bogart or Robert Mitchum, giving a girl a grain or two of his guff. Chances are few and far between these days, whatever guff he has he keeps to himself, to his own fantasies, unless it's a joke over the poker table with the lads, and that Maura O'Brien, fine woman she is too, surely Tom has his sights set on her, surely he is making proper plans. He's had a few women of his own in the past, Sammy has, oh yes indeed, he's had his fair share; he's not led that much of a sheltered life. But he never really had the opportunity for marriage, or if it had been there he was either not wise or not brave enough to take it on. Ah, what the devil does it matter now, he's still here and he likes being with the youngsters and the power he gets from them. They energise him. Even in the school, painting those walls and eavesdropping on their chat as they passed by, all joke and jostle, funny out they were, damn cheeky in many ways, and not in the least afraid to say what they wanted. That's the way it is with them today. Or tomorrow. *Tomorrow's World,* that's a show he often watches on the television. These are the kids of tomorrow's world. Fair play to them.

And that young Laura, well, she's a bit of a card all right. She's had her issues, the poor girl, but she's tough enough, tough enough for anything. And the things under her bed, well, *Holy God*, as Miley might say.

She says she saw the thing in the lake too but … now, hold on, hold on, Sammy McCreary … Sammy is not at all sure but …

He stands with his back to his own van, and he lights up a cigarette to help further his musing. It is damn cold but he'll stick it out a while longer. He is at the spot he said he'd be, the leaning pole, "the poor man's Pisa" Matty had called it, for those who will never get to Italy, which is probably all of them. It is mightily cold all right but he has a good thick coat on his old bones, and he has a good thick skin too, our Sammy McCreary; he laughs quietly to himself thinking on all this as he blows out Sweet Afton smoke into the harsh and hardy night.

Lucy runs around as if the cold has no effect on her at all, she takes not a scrap of notice. The mad old thing barks away to herself and is only ever keen on the multifarious scents of the world, the array of aromas forever assaulting her and needing to be teased out and comprehended. It must be great to be an old mutt, thinks Sammy, you can stick your old snout wherever you like and no one bats an eyelid, they just shake you off, or give you a pat on your shaggy head – would it were that way for humans, life could be so simple.

He spies a figure approaching. She's a little late, but isn't that the right way anyway, for a lass to keep a man waiting, surely it is the same strategy this silly world over. *Fashionably late*, isn't that what they say now?

"I wasn't sure if you were going to come or not. Bloody freezing it is. If you had decided to stay inside by the fire I wouldn't have minded at all."

"Well, I'm here now," says Laura. "Got your Ghostbusters gear?"

"Huh?"

"Never mind."

Sammy opens the door of the van for her – nice to show a bit of manners in this day and age, chivalry not at all dead, not for Sammy McCreary – and Laura climbs in out of the savage clime.

The dog jumps in too and straight onto her lap, not in the least unfriendly, used to all sorts, and her cold canine nose is immediately curious about the scent of the stranger. Laura tries to nudge it away from her nether regions, but the dog is having none of it, too wildly curious to give up just yet; she burrows as far as she is able before Laura gives her a clout on the top of the head, and the dog reels from its olfactory revelry.

"Take no notice of her," says Sammy. "She just gets a bit excited with someone new, that's all. She'll have your smell in no time, it'll lodge there in her memory, and she'll leave you alone then after that. She just likes making friends."

The dog remains in Laura's lap, the unclipped nails of the hairy brute jutting into her thighs.

"Back now, Lucy, back."

Lucy responds by leaping off the girl and into the back of the van, yelping with enthusiasm, frisky and electric on this awful night, a night when neither man nor beast should be out battling it.

"What's that strong smell?"

"Turps," says Sammy. "I suppose that's what you're smelling. Turpentine. Paint remover, you know. To clean off the brushes. That kind of thing. I'm immune to it at this stage. Don't even notice it."

"It's quite ... powerful."

"Another thing you'll just get used to."

Sammy looks a little nervous and he taps his fingers on the steering wheel as he drives, though he's not sure what part of the adventure is making him feel this way: is it that he has a fine young girl beside him in the van for the first time in decades? Or is it that they're on the way to see the monster, the lake monster, on this most inclement of evenings?

His cast feels heavy on his arm but the steering wheel becomes a kind of crutch. He stares out at the trees that bend in the woeful winds and the rains that get cast across the desolate landscape.

He turns the radio up when he hears the opening of Eric Carmen's "Hungry Eyes".

"I like this one," he says.

Laura says nothing in response. She hates it, but she doesn't want to offend the old man, and if Kevin heard even a second of this awful song he'd probably take the wheel and crash right into the nearest tree.

"*One look at you and I can't disguise…*" Sammy is sing-ing it now, badly, and the creepy croon sets the dog off in the back of the van; a dreadful duo now, a racket in the rickety van.

Laura feels herself blushing in the dark from the sheer embarrassment of all this, the awkwardness. She is begin-ning to think this might not be such a good idea after all, this coming here, butterflies in her tummy from earlier seem to have regressed, slimy caterpillars they are in there now, squirming.

The track finally ends and Madonna's "Lucky Star" begins, but Sammy turns this one down, he doesn't know it so won't sing it, and Laura thanks her own lucky stars for that.

"And Tom? What's he up to?"

"Sound asleep."

"Already?"

"He's had a big day. He's in his favourite new armchair now, snoring away. Dreaming about Maura, no doubt."

Sammy snorts, "Cheeky."

He lifts the sleeve of his coat to show the autograph on his white cast.

"She's a funny lady, that's for sure. Good to have her around though. She's brightened up our poker nights anyway, that's for sure. Cleans us out most evenings."

The dog has come back to settle on Laura's lap once more, but it seems more sedate now, as if used to the new person, quick to befriend; she is like Sammy himself.

"Does Tom know about what happened in school?"

"Yeah, I think so. Duffy was on the phone."

"Did he get mad?"

"Nope."

"He's a good man, Tom, sound out like. I hope you know that."

"I do. I know that. And ... are you?"

"Am I ... what?"

"Are you a good man?"

"Well ... I ... I ..."

"Hard to answer that one, is it?"

She is grinning, enjoying his sudden discomfort.

"Well, we all have our ... poor moments I suppose ... when we ... when we make bad judgments ..."

"Right," she says, stopping him from digging deeper holes for himself, even though, in truth, she wouldn't mind if he did go on and explain himself. Just who is this Sammy McCreary she happens to be in a van with? Who is he? And what does he want? Everyone in the village wants something ... don't they? And does he really believe in monsters? Is there something down in that pond? She'll find out some of these answers soon enough, won't she?

Sleet lashes hard against the windscreen. Out of nowhere it seems to have arisen, whooped itself up fast and has started strafing the roof of the van as they make the last part of their journey. The driving is difficult enough for Sammy with his bad arm, and now his eyes are being put to the test as well: bad weather, hard rain, cold, and the looming notion that he shouldn't be doing any of this, shouldn't be anywhere near this kind of situation, should be at home with Lucy at his feet, a fire blazing, a wee dram of something frank and fiery, and the television and whatever nonsense it was showing to dull the senses, *Dallas* or *Scarecrow and Mrs. King.*

Sleet hits hard again and the wind howls just as they pull up, as if the weather is telling them to not even attempt it, to stay inside, to stay dry, stay warm, turn around and go back to where they came from. Stay inside with the radio on: Climie Fisher have just started in on "Love Changes Everything", stay with that, it's so harmless, that singing voice so gossamer, so tender, it will not hurt or offend in any possible way. There's nothing for anyone out there in the cold, in the blackness. Nothing at all. Just gloom. Darkness, in every sense of the word. Go back, go back, just head on back.

Sammy turns the engine off.

They are not turning back.

They are here to see something. They are here to *do* something.

They have arrived.

Kevin stomps through the narrow streets and through the falling sleet of the village at night. His headphones cover his ears and his black woolly hat is pulled over them, the fabric stretched, making his head look odd shaped: an odd boy this fella, odd shaped, listening to odd music on this dirtiest of nights, unaware yet of all that is about to go down. But he's up for it. He's ready for action.

He bathes in the music of his Walkman.

The Cure: "A Night Like This".

He swims in it. It's warm in that musical pool, but it's cold, so bastardly cold outside.

Robert Smith is saying that he's coming to find someone, even if it takes him all night.

Cold, hard rain, beating sleet, beating bleak on every street.

And Robert Smith says it's getting darker, and darker still.

He walks fast, so fast that he is building up a sweat, he can feel heat and moisture there under his arms, and even a little trickle of perspiration down his right side, under his thermal garments – mother bought those, she worries about him in the winter; worries about him in the other seasons too, finding the right attire for each turning; but he only wants black, he only wants black, does he not make that obvious enough? Someday he might succumb to sentimentality, embrace all she has done (and continues to do for him), but he cannot think of his mother now. Not right now. There is too much going on at this moment. So much he has to do. So much to sort out. To set straight. He must stay focused. He strides. Street. Sleet. Bleak sleet on bleak street. He strides on.

He arrives at the front gate of a large house. It is one of the larger houses of the village and one he could very easily envy. But no time for that either. No time for any feelings like that. Not now. There are things to do. Things to sort. Unveil.

He struggles with the latch of the garden gate but eventually manages to get it open. It swings in the rising wind, a screech from its rusty hinges – for all their wealth they need a new gate, he should have a word with the master of the house, so many things need fixing around here. The whole village perhaps. The whole village needs fixing. The inhabitants. All need a little tightening of a screw here, a bolstering bolt there. Or do they all just need a Sony Walkman, and good music to listen to? That would be enough. Cure the world of its ills.

He stands at the door. He rings the doorbell. Turns his Walkman off. Waits.

The door opens to him, and Aidan Carty stands there, blond and beautiful, the hall light behind him seems to form a halo around his head. Kevin thinks of the Ready Brek TV ad, and the orange glowing children on their way to school, fed, nurtured, lambent. Warmth radiates from the house, and Kevin feels cold and alien outside of it.

"Kevin! What are you doing here?"

What *is* he doing here?

"Thought we could jam."

Kevin doesn't know why he says this. There is nothing more hideous to him than the idea of musicians jamming. Guys making it up as they go along, like those horrible prog bands, like jazz, yuck, the very notion sickened him. He likes his music tight. Bands that are practiced, that know their place, know each other well, a strong rhythm section, guitars that merge, no filler, no improvising, just play the damn songs, virtuosity stank, the punks had that much right.

"Jam?"

"Music. Play. Together."

Although his body feels hot under the wool, his face is cold and numb from the stinging wind and relentless rain, so much so that even his sentences are not warm enough to stretch out and link up: his words are more like icicles falling and smashing on stony ground.

Aidan Carty is looking at him bewildered, and not a little apprehensively.

"Right. Come in. Where is your instrument?"

Kevin steps inside, heat already hitting his face. Already his cheeks feel like they are beginning to defrost.

"Nothing. No instrument. I have my lyrics notebook though."

He pulls it out of his pocket and displays its front cover like he is at an airport and this is Passport Control and he has to prove his identity to enter a foreign state. "Lyrics" is scrolled across the front in thick black marker, scribbled ugly, no care given to artistry, a punkish scrawl; but it is what it says, a book with lyrics in it, or about to have lyrics in it. His titles do not lie. His as-yet-unwritten poem: Laura (it will be about Laura.) Or his songs (they will be about Laura, too).

Kevin looks around; everything about the glowing house is impressive: everything boasts money, boasts taste, boasts respectability.

"Place is very quiet," Kevin says.

"Both of my parents are away. Conference in Dublin. They'll be home tomorrow. I have the place all to myself."

What do they do, his parents? How come Kevin does not know? Everyone knows everyone's business around here. Or perhaps he is different, choosing to ignore them all, couldn't care less about any of them.

"How responsible you are. They must… trust you."

A popular boy like that would be sure to throw parties, invite girls round, he'd have a ball: that's what you'd think about Aidan Carty, take one look at his unblemished skin, his high cheekbones, his soft hair, his fancy clothes.

Kevin in an empty house would be… Kevin in an empty house. Or maybe his cousin would come to see him and touch him inappropriately. That is how is life is. A pond is not a lake.

Aidan shrugs. He was expecting none of this. He would've been quite content to laze around and do nothing all evening. Or maybe watch a video or something. He had rented *The Monster Squad* from the local video store, and even though he had seen it a few months ago, he wants to watch it again. He's not sure if Kevin O'Brien is interested in movies; he's not really sure of Kevin O'Brien full stop.

But look, Kevin is here now, and he feels he must entertain him somehow. A guest. A guest uninvited, fine, but a guest all the same. He has thought about Kevin, looked at him, yes, in class, when Kevin has been stealing looks at his own music magazines and not looking at what he should have been looking at. Everybody was looking at stuff they should not be looking at. Stealing glances. Furtively. Everybody distracted. Everybody living alternative lives, if only in their imaginations.

"Come upstairs. I'll show you my guitar."

Lucy bounds out of the car, taking no notice of the rough weather. She barks frenziedly and scampers back and forth, nearly knocking Laura over when she makes her way out of the vehicle and stands surveying the crepuscular scene. There's something mystical in the air, something premonitory, she thinks, it's in the grey hoarfrost, the sleet now softening and transforming to a light drizzle, and the shine of ice in the dimness, a glassy sheen that wants to break through the dark and be noticed.

"That barking, that'll raise her," says Sammy, wanting to sound optimistic, wanting to put Laura at ease and make her think her journey has not been in vain.

"Her?"

"All monsters are females," laughs Sammy, "didn't you know?"

"I did not. I was thinking the very opposite."

Sammy is excited by the conversation, excited by the drive that got them here, everything has been exciting him lately, the secret stash under the bed, the way he came across her at school, her brazenness, her assertiveness, disobeying the rules and telling them where to go; Duffy, the little quare fella (even though he knew he was not quare at all and actually had a fiancée, but he just acted that way, all limp-wristed, bent); Laura was feisty and fun and he couldn't let her down now, and he is excited, his heart thuds in his chest, and he is as frolicsome as his old mutt that yelps with glee, and Sammy is wanting to get closer, to get closer.

"Let's go down," he says, pointing to the pond; and she follows him, down to the edge of it.

Laura puts her foot out and touches the ice with the tip of her boot.

"It's frozen solid," she says.

"You could skate on it," he says.

"I forgot my skates," she scoffs, "did you bring yours?"

Sammy lets out a hearty laugh. For all the darkness and dreariness of the occasion she is able to make things light, it is no wonder Kevin likes being with her; she is a grand girl, a shame she doesn't even have a proper boyfriend to be courting. She might need a man to take her and show her what it is all about, better than any of them little fidgety boys, a man of experience, that's what she needs, she's mature enough for it at this stage – if the under-bed bounty told of anything it told of a girl of curiosity, a girl ready to learn, out to experiment.

She rubs her gloved hands together briskly, some friction to generate some molecules of heat. Anything. Any rub of heat at all to keep this icy bitch of a night from freezing the blood in their very veins. Her breath comes out in frosty clouds and then disappears like dreams unremembered.

Sammy bends to Lucy.

"Can you feel anything, girl? Any rumble down there in the deep?"

Laura watches them. This man and his little beast. How close they are. How trusting they are in each other. How odd that she is ever only close to her cousin. Touching. Touching each other. Wrong. Wrongly. Laura doesn't even have a girlfriend to hug. Not even that. Not one. Loners. Losers. Perhaps Orlaith has been right about the pair of them all along. Who else touches Laura? Who else gets any way close to her? Her mother used to stroke her hair, tie it back in plaits, when she sat on the side of her bed, back stiff and straight, and her mother wove like magic. No one else touches her now. No one plaits, no one placates. There's Tom of course, a friendly hug all right, yes, sure, avuncular, fine, but no one else has kissed her like a teenage girl should be kissed. Not properly, not on the lips. A proper TV drama kiss. Fireworks. A pop video kiss. Swoonsome. Imagine that. Fifteen years old. In this day and age. Fifteen years old and only ever been kissed by her preposterous, pretentious cousin. What does that say about her? What does that say about this place in which they are immured? And now she has landed here. With an old man and an old half-crazed dog. Out in the worst weather of the year. Just what kind of tragedy is she rooting for? Just what kind of gods is she tempting with this foolishness? Has she not had enough torment already? Has she not had her fill?

"Go on now, run along the edge and bark your head off. Let's raise that beast! Get the monster to stick her head out of that water! Let her burst up through that ice!"

Laura is watching all this: all Sammy's enthusiasm, the craziness of him trying to put ideas into the head of a daft dog. She grows suspicious, suddenly weary; whatever candle of hope she has within her gutters on the ledge of her heart.

Aidan's bed.

Kevin wonders if he has ever had a girl in there. Ever ventured? Ever gained? Ever brokered such an important deal. Probably not. If he has no one over on the night his parents are away, then why would he have ever had one in here ever? It doesn't make any sense. He is a popular boy. The girls make giggling comments when he passes in the school corridors, Kevin can often hear them. They could be falling at his feet at this very moment, worshipping his bright blue eyes, stroking his wispy blond strands of hair. But here he is. Alone at night. A made and tidy bed. It seems like such a waste.

Kevin is sitting on this bed and he is looking at the posters on the wall: Morrissey, Ziggy-era Bowie hugging Mick Ronson, Michael Stipe.

Kevin ponders this evidence: yes, it's all there; this is a rock music fan in his village. Most of the boys had no interest in anything other than brutal sports: Gaelic football and hurling, soccer, rugby, all of these rough and tumble things took up the bulk of their time and thoughts. Real music fans were rare, and his own Laura can hardly even be considered one, what with the shit she listens to.

Aidan moves to his stereo. It's bigger and more impressive than Kevin's, clearly more expensive, and he presses play on the cassette deck. His delicate turning of the volume dial is almost the same as Kevin's: soft, gradual, knowing pitch and tone, knowing when the best bits come in each track and probably able to explain what a graphic equalizer is too.

It is The Velvet Underground's "The Black Angel's Death Song", and it is a wild and uncompromising riot, certainly not the stuff you'd be kicking back and relaxing to. It is not background music. It is grab you by the balls … bombast … it stirred, it made you full of … something … existential dread or a readiness for a feral fight … whichever way your heart was veering that day.

"This stuff is out there," says Aidan, and Kevin can't help but agree, remembering the first time Lenny pulled out the famous banana record sleeve in his shop one day: the album that launched a thousand other bands, some of which even turned out to be quite good.

Why had these two boys never become fast friends? Who was the one shying away? Who shied from whom? And why now? Why had they not been forced together years ago; they've grown up a stone's throw away, why all now on this peculiar night?

Aidan picks up his red Fender Stratocaster which was leaning insouciantly against the wardrobe, daring anyone good enough to come and caress it.

"This is my baby. Go ahead. You can touch it if you want."

Kevin shakes his head, alarmed at the phrasing.

"I don't play. Not guitar."

Aidan sits on the edge of his own bed, places the guitar beside him, leaving it there leaning in between them, the long neck of it, the frets shining in the light, an uncut silver string-end sticking out over the tuning keys.

"How come you are out on a school night? Have you got your homework done?"

Kevin sits, statue stiff, his mind, his thoughts, deadened all of a sudden, fallen flat, as if whatever was clear at the outset has been dulled.

"No," he says, mirthlessly. "I came here to figure something out."

"Figure out?"

"A few things bothering me."

His thoughts are muddy now, and the Velvets' unruly din only makes his lack of clarity more apparent. Yes, a few things are certainly bothering him ... but how does he go about setting them right? He looks at Aidan's pillow; it is roughly the same size as the one on his own bed. Aren't all pillows roughly the same size? Aren't all fathers? No, they aren't. They come in different sizes, different shapes, different make-ups: some are even normal and stay.

Maura O'Brien paces the rooms of her house. Whichever room she finds herself in seems to hassle her, unsettles her. She can hear the wind howling outside and things falling and crashing, lids off dustbins, the poles of washing lines cracking, the whipping of electrical wires high up over the little streets she imagines coming down at any minute and plunging the whole village into darkness: live wires spitting sparks out on the wet ground, live wires, live wires. Why is she going to these places, to these dark imaginings? Is it because she is addled now, upset that her boy has gone off into this nasty night when he should be home getting ready for bed? She should be bringing him a cup of warm milk and settling him down, settling herself down, but instead she is all riled up. Quite the opposite then. She blames herself, for the way she has handled everything. She blames Tadhg for leaving like that, for making a mockery of her, bringing shame on her in front of the whole community. She blames herself for not putting on a proper display of mourning for her sister; she could have pretended that she even liked her, just a bit. She blames Tom for ... for just being so bloody nice when she doesn't deserve any of that. She is embarrassed, flirting away the way she does during the poker games. And the lies she told them all. The blatant

lies. Of course she knows how to play fucking poker. She
has known how for years. Her father and his father before
him all knew how to play, could play any game you cared
to mention. Even sleight of hand tricks. Conjuring cons.
Pick a card. Hold it close to your chest. Always your cards:
close to your chest. These were the days before television,
what else had they to do when the working day was done?
Of course she watched them. Hungry for lessons in life. Of
course she learned the rules. She knows her way around a
chess board even. Backgammon. Bridge. You name it: she'll
match you – although she might give Happy Families an
obvious miss. So why did she lie to them? Well … why not?
Wasn't it easier just to pretend? To pretend to be someone
else rather than admit to who you really are? Your husband
left you. Isn't it a whole lot easier to don a different robe,
play a different role? And the sympathy they keep offering her, shoulders to cry on, and the way they took her in
and gave her a distraction, before she was driven to it. She
likes it. She likes all that attention. Of course she does. She
has been neglected for far too long. Who else was going to
give it to her? No one. Only a few lonely old geezers with
nothing else to do. Doddery bachelors with way too much
time on their hands – they were sure to send a few compliments her way. Why would she *not* lap it up? She'd take
every ounce of it. It makes her feel like a woman again, a
woman attractive. Nothing wrong with that. She should
not have to scrounge around for scraps of happiness. She's
glad they'll all serve it up to her. It all passes the time. When
your own husband, the man you fell for, turned out to be
something else entirely and left you in the lurch. Left you
languishing. Left you lonely. Left you a fucking laughing-
stock. When your own son hardly talks to you and blames

you for everything. Blame. Blame. Blame. It is the only word, the only concept that keeps coming to haunt her on this treacherous night. Blame. Blame. Blame. How much of it does she really deserve? How much of that?

She darts from room to room restlessly now, a rattled wraith in some manic melodrama, wringing antic hands.

She finds herself in Kevin's room then. Out of bounds, she knows it, but there she is, trespassing, rooting through his drawers and finding them, holding his letters in those antic hands, fingers twitching, heart a-pummel, dizzy with dilemma.

Tom snores so loudly he gasps himself awake. He coughs and splutters and needs a moment to get his breath and for him to get his whereabouts. Ah, it's his new house, his new armchair, his new life, that's where he is, and he smiles the smile of a man content.

The house is quiet. The TV is on and it's that Boy George fella again. Tom shakes his head disdainfully: those kinds of men – are they really men? – shouldn't be left near the public, not to mind putting them on TV with kids watching them. A bad influence. Parents shouldn't even allow their young ones to watch such aberrations. Girls should dress as girls, and boys as boys. Simple as that. Why confuse matters? The world was confusing enough with its prickly politics, its rounds of endless violence, factions and fractures. It was all much simpler when he was growing up. The lines of demarcation were abundantly clear. There was none of this nancy-boy flouting around. Dresses. Wigs. Make-up. A man in a feckin' dress! And he's Irish too. For feck's sake. Bloody disgraceful.

Tom gets up out of his chair and switches the TV off. The house is deathly quiet. She must be studying away the poor girl, hard at the books. She'll make something of her life all right, she will surely. The right attitude, even after all that she's been through. She'll surely have a great future. Will make no mistakes.

He goes to the stairs, stops, listens. Not a peep from her up there. Maybe she has fallen asleep, worked herself into exhaustion. Perhaps he should check in on her. See if she's all right, see if she needs anything. He might make a cup of tea for himself. Only the one, mind. He doesn't want to be up peeing all night. The tea goes right through him these days. No bladder control at all. The prostate – whatever that is – enlarges as men grow older, that was what Sammy had told him. What kind of evolution was that? Was it God playing some cruel trick? For what purpose? Wouldn't you think He'd be kinder to men as they got older, as they got more infirm? Wasn't baldness and bushy eyebrows and feckin' ear-hair enough to be dealing with? Bloody hell. Sometimes life made no sense at all. Tom sighs. Growing old, growing old: no two ways about it, no walk in the park, and God not much help in matters. He sighs once more to put an end to these dastardly thoughts.

Tom does mount the stairs. He does go up and knock softly on her door.

Nothing.

He knocks again, and when he hears no sound he opens the door ever-so gently, peers into the pitch-black room.

"Laura, are you there, love?"

The bed, he can make out, has a bump in it. She's in there so. Tucked up. The poor lass, she's probably pooped herself out; hours poring over the textbooks; took an early night. She's a good girl, this Laura, will make no mistakes in life.

What Tom does not see is that the bump is a couple of pillows made to resemble the outline of a sleeping body, blankets pulled up high and covering the "head".

He does not see under the bed either and the mess she has still not cleared up, the "find" that his buddy Sammy stumbled across. He sees none of this in the forbidding dark.

She's a good girl, he says to himself, softly closing the door, trying not to wake the grand girl who is not there.

The beast is a small one. It is a Yorkshire terrier and it runs around madly, tirelessly. There is no large beast, nothing has risen from the depths of the pond, things are only dropping: the temperature, their hopes.

They watch the little dog run from side to side like they're watching a tennis game; back and forth the little mutt runs, barking wildly to the vacancy.

Sammy shakes his head. He whistles and the dog comes running to him and leaps. He gathers her up in his arms, a circus trick clearly done many times before.

"Never mind, Luce. We tried. We'll raise her some other evening. Maybe when the weather will be better."

The dog barks a response as if she understands her master, but Laura is unwilling to bend. If anything, the cold air has cleared the mud from her mind, and she is thinking more lucidly, and her eyes, accustomed to the dark, are beginning to see everything a lot more clearly.

"Don't you think that if the pond is frozen, then the beast would be frozen too?"

There is logic to this. Hard logic. Surely irrefutable.

"Maybe," says Sammy. "Been the coldest winter in a while."

He coughs, lets the little dog down again, and gathers his thoughts.

"Maybe she has frozen and sank to the bottom. Or maybe she has buried herself way down in the sand and silt, only to rise again in spring, some kind of hibernation … or something."

"Or maybe there was never anything in there at all, ever, and the two of us just have wild imaginations, or have nothing better going on in our lives but to invent such ludicrous stories."

She almost feels Kevin's words coming out of her, his influence, his tone of certainty.

Sammy laughs, nervously: "You could be right. That could be it too."

Laura looks out across the pond. So, what next? What do they do now? They've come this far. They've come this far on this horrendous night, and … for what? Everybody wants something. If you go out on the worst night of the year, you must surely be after something. Surely you don't give up that easily. What's at stake? What's at play here? What indeed, is the game?

"Why don't you step out yourself, on the ice I mean … maybe the monster might come up that way? To meet you. Perhaps it's hungry."

Sammy pats his belly, "Ah, now, I'm a bit on the heavy side. I doubt it would hold me."

"The ice or the monster?"

Sammy looks at her, unsure now as to whether she is joking or not. There is a sinister edge to her words, a dangerous vibe emanating from her. He seems to have lost control of the night. They had been in the nice warm van, with the radio on – they could've enjoyed that a lot more. He could have put his arms around her, given her a little cuddle and tell her she's a marvellous girl and that everything would be all right, that she has a great future ahead of her, encourage her. That might have been the way to go.

Laura is still staring out, trance-like, deep in thought. She doesn't feel the bite of the weather at all now, seems to have become as accustomed to the cold as she has to the dark. These things don't knock a feather out of her, she stands, powerful.

She decides to move closer to the pond. And she does so, slowly, like she is a professional dancer being filmed on a stage, the camera focused on her soft tread, deliberately slow steps, slow, but closer, closer.

She steps onto it, delicately, taking an intake of breath, and exhaling slowly again, calming her heart rate right down, her pulse right down – she does not want to get herself all worked up, it might wake the monster below, ha, or the monster inside her.

"Ah, now, love, I think we've gone a bit too far. Overstepped the mark. I think we should just abandon the project and head on back home."

The project?

She doesn't turn to look at him, but she speaks anyway, not caring if the words vanish in the wind, or dissolve in the mist, or get sucked right into that far away but somehow near moon.

"Have you?" she says. "Have you gone too far? Or have you not gone nearly as far as you wanted?"

She takes another slow step. Her foot slides a little but she manages to maintain her balance. If she does slip she will have nothing to hold on to. Where's Kevin? When she slips he's usually right there.

She stands, two feet planted on the ice, defying it.

Girls just want to have fun? Is this the simple truth of it? Or do they want a lot more from life? Do they deserve a little more? Not to be treated like they can be used and abused, ruled, fooled.

A step further.

It holds her.

So far.

All this ice holds her – frozen water, it's only that, so simple, so natural, and it's *right*, in winter. So many things in her world are *wrong*, but ice, in winter, seems just *right*, seems like it makes complete sense.

Slowly she steps.

Delicately.

So far … it holds her.

As yet … nothing breaks.

Kevin gets up from the bed and faces Aidan. He should not be here, he is in an unfamiliar province. He is looking down at Aidan and the expensive guitar – is it a copy? – he does not even want to hear; he doesn't care how good the guy can pick or strum, he could be Johnny Marr, so the fuck what? That's not why Kevin is really here. He is here because he has some very important things to sort out. If he does not sort these things out, then things … might leak … right across the village, and he does not want these things coming out: his secrets. Secrets have a way of hurting, of destroying. It all depends on who holds them, of course. All depends who decides what to do with them. Secrets are weapons. Secrets destroy. Who knows *what* in this village? Who holds what information? How many know about his family? He does not want the idlers gossiping about him. He will leave this shithole as soon as he can, but he will leave cleanly, so no one can say a damn thing about him. And when they see him on TV in the future, or on some strobe-lit stage – no, not strobe-lit, Laura, just illuminated – they will only say "I remember him", and they won't be able to add a second clause.

Up from the bed, Kevin goes to the stereo and turns it off. The Velvet Underground need to be appreciated: you need to open your ears and your mind. They cannot be heard like this. They should never be relegated to background noise.

Facing Aidan.

Close to him now, so close as to be uncomfortable.

Face to face.

But the faces are *too* close.

Personal space inhabited, defiled.

"Wh-what do you want?" Aidan stammers.

"I could ask you the s-same question."

"I don't understand. If you want to play music then maybe…"

"I don't want to play fucking music. Not with you. I play by myself. I compose by myself."

"Then why are you here?"

"To ask you a few questions."

Kevin takes a step back, relieving Aidan who takes a big breath. Kevin goes to the window and closes the curtains. He does all this calmly, as if it were his own room, as if he were now entitled to be there, entitled to be anywhere he damn well likes. He is a good boy; he has to remind himself of this. He takes care of his cousin. He does. And he will write. When he gets the next chance…he will. A poem. A song. Laura.

Aidan watches him, surprised at his effrontery, worried about his intentions.

"Questions about what?"

"Photographs first."

"What photographs?"

"You know. The ones you took of me ... and my cousin."

There had been a flash that night, when the cousins stood in the centre of the garden, a bright flash of light, seeming to come from behind the nearby row of trees.

Lightning? No, none at all.

There had been no crash of thunder.

The lights of a passing car from down the road?

They had heard no engine, no wheels on the road. None.

"I ... I ..."

"Why did you take pictures of us? What did you see?"

Kevin's voice is cold, as cold as the night they are in, as cold as the world that they are in, and he will not let up.

"Well?"

"I didn't mean to ... see you. I was out taking pictures of other stuff. There's a badger lair. One often comes out at night, f-f-foraging. I just happened ..."

"What did you see?"

Terrified Aidan.

Trembling Aidan.

Trembling like Laura.

That's how she starts, before she falls. And Kevin is always there to pick her up. Good boy. Kevin is a good boy.

"Well? I'll ask again, what did you see?"

"I saw ... I saw ... you both kissing."

Kevin moves closer to him once more. If he talks now he will ruin it. If Kevin lets out his true feelings ... yes, a little bit of subtlety is required here. Say nothing. Let the quaking boy squirm. Let him quaver. He is a boy who goes out at night and spies. He is a spy. He has been spying on Kevin and his cousin, that's what it boils down to. And what had he been sniggering at?

Sometimes I sneak out at night and take some shots. Amazing the things you can see. Wild animals and so on. Yeah, amazing what kind of animals you can see at night, when nobody else notices.

The boy looks sad now, guilty, and Kevin's temperature starts to rise. He can feel it inside him. He cannot stop it. It is just like Laura's fits, unstoppable. He can never control his anger.

His face is red, red from his inner roiling rage.

Aidan's face is red too, from shock, from fear, and from the scald of a few escaped tears.

"If you are stalking my cousin…" Kevin huffs.

His eyes have taken on a crazed look; nothing now will prevent him from getting to the end of this, to the end of this night, the reason for him being here.

"If you are stalking…"

"I'm not stalking anyone," says Aidan, whimpering, "I'm not interested in your cousin."

Kevin feels hot all over. He is in his winter clothes. He still has his winter gloves on; his hands are hot and sweaty. He still has his woolly hat on too and his scalp itches.

These are not the answers he was expecting.

He wants a fight, a big one, but this slight, beautiful boy will not fight anyone, he just backs away, alarmed, afraid.

"Then … why?"

Aidan clutches the duvet on the bed, both fists gathering up the soft material. He doesn't know what to do. He doesn't know what to say. How to explain himself? Some things you have to keep secret, for fear of...

All of a sudden Kevin moves swiftly to his bed. The blond boy flinches, for one terrified moment thinking that he will be pounced upon.

But Kevin doesn't.

Kevin doesn't as much as touch him.

Instead, bizarrely, Kevin starts to pound with his fists on the pillow. He just ... incredibly ... starts beating it.

Aidan's look is of complete bewilderment; just what the hell is going on now?

Kevin pounds. His fingers bunched into tight fists. Pummelling the pillow. Just like had done in his own bedroom.

He pounds.

Punches.

Pummels.

He pounds his father's face. He pounds the village. He pounds the pillow ... because he can. He pounds the pillow because ... because it is the face of Orlaith and because it is the face of Duffy and all the other teachers too. He pounds Sister Margaret. He pounds shit pop music with his hard hands. He pounds his mother and most of all he pounds his father, again and again and again. It always goes back to that. To *him*. The absentee. He cannot call to mind what his father even looked like; the photos are few, and his mother tore up so many, tatters, into the dustbin they flew, or fell like snowflakes. So he beats Aidan's blue pillow, because that is what his father is, no image at all. Faceless. Formless. And he beats on it some more.

Aidan watches all this in utter horror. He has never witnessed so odd and so devastatingly brutal a scene. It almost makes him want to laugh, though not because it is funny, it isn't, it is absolutely terrifying, but because he does not know what to do. How do you respond to such a scene? What do you do? What do you say? *I'm sorry for your troubles?*

Kevin is far from finished. He has not exhausted himself this time. He is too full of an all-consuming power now, a rage, from deep down, from the core of him, and so his adrenaline continues to pump, keeping him going, and he is only wanting more.

"Why? Why did you take those pictures?"

Kevin has abandoned the pillow; his focus is on his enemy now, eyes still crazed, face hot, nostrils flared.

Aidan picks up his guitar, hands trembling as he does so. Again he does not know what to do, knows not what to say, but the guitar is a crutch, it is what he always goes to, something he thinks he has control over. He plays a few random notes, but because it is not plugged in it sounds tinny and weak. It sounds like him. It sounds just like Aidan, tinny, weak.

"You," he murmurs.

"What?" asks Kevin, scratching his itchy head.

"I was never interested in taking pictures of Laura. I … I … was interested in taking pictures of you."

"I don't get …"

"I've taken pictures of you before."

This is how you explain yourself.

You just blurt out your secret – and you wait for the inevitable blows.

Aidan takes his face away from the guitar and looks at Kevin. It's a bewildered Kevin now. Kevin who has attacked a pillow. Who has pummelled, pounded, punched. The whole village was in that pillow. The whole village got what was coming to them. But it is Kevin who does not know what to do now. His heart still beats hard, yes. And still there is a raging sea inside of him. Within. Within. And he scratches his head again, confused.

"Me? Why? For what?"

He gets a sudden flashback of Aidan on that fancy bicycle of his, losing balance, and his hand going to Kevin's shoulder, the slight squeeze of the fingers.

And then, from out of nowhere, from the darkest corner of his memory, another flash, an incident: Kevin is a little boy, and he is walking in the woods, and when he turns around his father is there, smiling, and Laura's father is there too, and their hands, their hands... are joined!

Laura is standing about ten meters out on the ice. Wind whirls around her. Her eyes look glossed-over and she stares at the moon, an almost-round white, acne-scarred moon, which has ventured out from behind the purple clouds. They say you are not supposed to stare at the sun. It will damage you. But the moon? Is it okay to look at the moon for a long time? To dream of different outcomes?

Maura O'Brien reads the letters. This is all so unusual. Her husband had never been the kind to write anything, not even a shopping list, certainly not a goodbye note. And now these letters. It is just too strange. And his word choice: cool, trendy, as if he is appealing to the boy, trying to connect... but it feels all so contrived. Are these the words of a middle-aged man?

Tadhg practically begs for Kevin to come and visit. He says he will pay. He says life is good in the USA. He talks about freedom. About being yourself. About the music gigs he could take Kevin to. Great gigs. Festivals. Maura is no match. How could she compete with any of this? But still ... it all seems wrong ... all a little ... off.

Tom thinks about calling Maura. Should he? A quick call ... just for a chat? The house is empty. Laura is fast asleep. He's a little lonely. But he thinks it might be too late. It is probably rude to call so late, people panic, they expect the worst.

He goes to his bedroom. He has a box of magazines. He bought most of them from a fella in a pub once who was offloading them, wife found them and got angry, was going to kick him out. Tom got them for a right bargain. He rakes through them now. There is a magnificent one of this sexy black girl, strong and athletic with large purplish nipples, the most exotic thing he has ever seen. Now, where could that be ...?

Kevin paces the bedroom of Aidan Carty like a caged animal. The trapped gorilla of Laura's ceiling. His mind is in spin, a cyclone. What is going on exactly? He had come out of his own house so purposeful, so sure of what he needed to do, but now, now ...

"What do you want with pictures of me?"

He may as well at this stage: Aidan may as well admit it all.

Confess.

He's already halfway there.

Blurt ... then take the blows.

"I thought that … you just looked cool and …"

Kevin stops his pacing and looks hard at him. The blatant fact of it now, fully dawning. He's another. Another fucking one of them!

"You're a faggot?"

Aidan hangs his head. He stares at his guitar strings, rubbing them anxiously. He wishes he could go down to the garage and to the big amp his father bought for him and plug it in and drown out the whole fucking place in noise. The whole world in racket. Velvets-like drones. Punishing feedback. Ear-splitting. Thought-breaking.

"Is that it? You are a fucking bender? A Boy George? A little Marilyn?"

"I just … I …"

Kevin laughs maniacally.

Another tear trickles down Aidan's cheek.

"Give me the fucking film," says Kevin.

Aidan rises, wiping his tears with the cuff of his sleeve. He throws the guitar down on the bed, goes to a drawer and takes out his pricey camera. He opens the back of it and ejects the roll of film. Shaking, he puts out his hand to Kevin, offering the incriminating evidence in his open palm.

Kevin leaves Aidan like this for a moment, hand outstretched, shuddering. Then he snatches the film from him and stuffs it in his pocket.

"How were you going to use this? Were you going to blackmail us or something?"

Aidan, with shaking hands, is putting a new roll of film in the camera, avoiding eye contact; he is still teary, still a-quiver.

"You shouldn't be doing anything," he says. "Not with her. Gross."

Gross. It was a word picked up from American TV, and it maddens Kevin even further.

"I don't think you are in any position to tell me what I should or should not be doing."

Still avoiding eye contact, still shaking from the entire episode, Aidan nevertheless opts for last-ditch bravery.

"She's your cousin. It's fucking disgusting."

Kevin fumes. His eyes wide and his nostrils flared again.

"Is it now? And you the one interested in other fellas' cocks. And that's not disgusting at all, is it not?"

"No, it's … I can't help … and anyway, look at your own family!"

The rage now. The red-hot rage. The pillow had only been a warm-up. The rage it comes now, full-throttle. Amped up. Like a full force gale. Kevin reaches out and grabs the guitar from the bed. In one swift move he swings it by the neck and the edge of the guitar's body hits Aidan right across the side of his blond and beautiful head. The camera falls to the floor, its lens shattering. Blood sprays in an arc across the poster of Bowie and Ronson.

Maura packs away the letters, back safely where she found them. It makes no sense. None of it does. Her life. None of it makes any sense. Playing poker with a few randy old bachelors, for fuck's sake, is that what she has been reduced to?

She looks out the window, searching the darkness, worrying about her son out in it: this bad night, this bad night, the rain, the rancours – why is he not coming home? This bad night. This bad life. Why don't they ever come home?

Sammy watches Laura out on the ice. *The feckin' hoyden*, he says to himself.

The dog, for once, is completely still, as baffled at the proceedings as its owner.

"Laura! Come back, love! Let's get you home!"

But Laura does not respond. Although frozen to the spot, the heat of life burns hot inside her; she could fall right through, a perfect circle, like those ice holes fishermen make in Norway or Finland or wherever, and plunge to the depths. Meet her monster. But hasn't she already met it many times before? It was in every paroxysm, every ataxic attack; her creature, her curse, not yet caught or cured, not yet fucking castrated.

He could not find that magazine – it must have dropped out somewhere. Perhaps it is in the back of the van. How embarrassing if someone finds it? He hopes it would be Matty, or Sammy, and not anyone else. What would they think? He is a respectable member of the community. A small businessman.

He doesn't bother with any of the other magazines: if the black girl can't be found then there's no point; that's what he is in the mood for, always in the mood for her, the exotic girl; he's too tired now anyway. He would be much better off with a nice hot bath and just to hit to the sack, more in his line; he's too old for that carry-on: Roxy from Birmingham (22).

He doesn't do what his conscience tells him though: he fills no Matey bubble bath. Instead he picks up the phone in the hallway and dials the number he can't put out of his head.

"Sorry, I hope it's not too late."

"It is late. And Kevin's not here."

There is frustration in the voice of the woman on the other end.

"Where is he?" Tom asks.

"Out with Laura, I presume. They're always together those two, up to something, aren't they?"

"No, no, Laura is in bed, sound asleep."

"Right. But I wouldn't be too sure. Of either of them. Something is wrong. These families. Us. *Us,* I mean. There's always something fucking wrong."

It is the first time he's heard her swear like this. He is immediately concerned. It doesn't sound like her at all.

"Do you want me to come over?"

"No, I don't."

"Are you sure?"

"Yes, I'm sure."

She is.

She is very sure.

After giving a whole night of thought to it, she is very sure. She doesn't want anyone. The whole village is wrong. It's the only label she can think to apply to them all. She imagines them as empty tins, like you'd see on an assembly line, tins of beans, or thicker than that, cans of paint, unlabelled. And as they pass by her one by one she slaps a sticker on their bellies. Tom is *wrong.* The poker is *wrong.* The absent husbands: very *wrong.* And those two cousins: aren't they just a little *too* close? What was Tom thinking even letting them stay over that night? And why did she go along with it? And those letters, what kind of change could come over a man to make him suddenly pick up a pen and write such drivel, such childish sentiments? What could change a man to be *that way* in the first place? Wasn't a woman good enough? It was all wrong. And the sad thing is, there is no way of putting any of it right.

"Good night Tom."

She puts down the phone, firmly, finally.

And whatever cards Tom has been dealt in that conversation, he knows now that he simply has to fold.

A rumble.

A rumble from the depths.

From the depths of depths.

What kind of monsters have awakened? Is the whole place just one pernicious beast, sleeping for all these years, peacefully, serene, now become demented, cantankerous, mean?

Is that what gives?

Is that what cracks though the ice on this most perfidious of nights?

Ice and fire.

What opposing elements at play.

The heat of bodies, of seething minds. The frozen frightening winter.

Men. Women. Boys. Girls.

A battle.

Age-old.

All on display here.

But where do they go now? Where do they go?

20

Blood on Bowie. Blood on Mick Ronson. Blood on bed. On red guitar. Blood on unconscious Aidan. Out for the count. Not getting up.

Kevin: blood on his black shirt, spatters of blood on his face, one drop under his eye like a tear.

He needs to scream this out. Scream this all out first before he can proceed.

He presses play, The Velvet Underground once more. This time it's "European Son", and it is deliriously derailed. He screams along with it:

"AAAAAAAAARRRRRGH."

It is so cleansing.

It feels so good.

A perfect purge.

He understands why John Lennon was up to that kind of shit on *Plastic Ono Band.* Made sense. The Primal Scream. Shout it out baby, shout it out. Even Tears for Fears knew that, to shout, to let it all out.

His eyes are wide, as if they will never close again; they have seen so much already, shocked by what he has done. What he is capable of.

Sterling Morrison: wild guitars, Lou's too, he must stop the music on the stereo, stops it in his head too, it's all clashing. He has thinking to do; he must make plans. What has been done has been done, yes, what has been done has been done. There is no going back now. On with this. On with all this: his plans. He will emerge clean. Like he has not put a foot wrong in anything; he will set the proper scene. He will put things right. Oddly, even with adrenaline still pumping through him at a startling rate, he thinks he knows how to get through the rest of the evening. He has plans for his future, great plans for his great endeavours, great, great . . .

Set the stage then.

With Kevin himself in the centre of it.

Screaming fans. Gushing with love and admiration. Shrieking with abandon at just catching a glimpse of him. He is illuminated. He has been transformed.

Ten meters out on the ice. Wind whistles around her still. And yet she stares at the moon. Yes, the moon is all right, it will not blind you no matter how long you decide to stand and look at it. It is welcoming. In its constancy it is a comfort there, high above and soothing. And the tides it brings. And light; sailors have set their sights on; it has guided, a compass, and light now, light now, it is a spotlight on her. She will have an entry for her diary for sure. *Dear Diary. Listen to this.* Or no. Just straight into the tale. Cut to the chase. Tell it like it is. A pond is a pond. *A girl on a frozen body of water and looking at the moon while an old man and an old dog bark from the shore and and and . . .*

Kevin could probably write it better. He has a gift, that boy. She wants to see his poems. He talks about them. And his songs. But he does not show them. Perhaps they are not all finished. He has high hope for himself. High.

He is her cousin. Is he looking at the moon too? Is that what he is doing?

She loves him.

She loves him not.

Start again: *A girl on a frozen body of water looking at the moon while an old man and an old dog bark from the shore* – it is an image almost too good for her diary. A lost girl in a story. That's what it is. Lost girl. Story. An ill-fated girl who has lost her father and her mother, an orphan, yes, lost, luckless, an orphan, that's what she is, she has just realised it, an orphan, and sent to live with a wicked uncle. Only he's not wicked at all of course, poor Tom, he's a nice old devil, even if he does have a box of filthy magazines. The story might not work then. It would have far greater impact if he was a nasty piece, and tried to fondle her breasts, or worse, tried to pin her down and rape her some evening with the theme of *Glenroe* playing in the background. That'd be something, wouldn't it? But he just makes dinner and he just looks after her, just looks after her well. Maybe there is no drama after all. The only shenanigans going on are with that Dick Moran in *Glenroe,* the wily businessman, all smooth palaver and ...

Maybe there is no drama ...

Or maybe there actually *is.*

Because Laura begins to shake.

She knows when it is coming and it is coming on now. Is it coming on? Or is she *making it* come on? She has been in this position before; she can feel its quick trigger: it's on, it's on, she has been in this position before, plenty of times. Is this for real or is she creating it? Does she summon it ... or does it summon her?

She begins to shake.

A few cracks appear on the ice.

Hardly anything at first, just tiny hairline fractures, no thicker than the lines of a spider's web. But these lines get thicker and whiter as they part from each other, the left side of the ice losing its hold on the right side of the ice, almost like they are saying goodbye to each other, crying at their tearing apart, love will tear us apart, and the ice splits into narrow channels at first, she's lost control again, narrow channels at first, but widening just a little, with water coming out now over it.

She slides on this.

She falls.

Febrile.

Falls.

The Fall: one of Kevin's favourite bands. Ornery. Provocative. Loud.

The fall: America's autumn, never as severe as winter, never that cold in Ireland.

The Fall: Adam and Eve in the garden, they should not have touched that fruit: they had been warned, but they went along and did it anyway.

Falls.

Falls.

She falls.

But the pond still holds her.

She is not sunken yet.

The ice is cold on her clothes, the wetness leaking through her, sending shivers down her. And her own shake gets bigger, and then it gets bolder yet. She takes all the right medication. She does all the things the doctors tell her to do. So many pills down through the years. Various colours. Various shapes and sizes. Various degrees of success. Side effects too: headaches, blurred vision, poor coordination, fatigue, dizziness, nausea, skin rashes. But still they come, these fits, these seizures. Such an alarming word. *Seizure!* Sounds like *Seize her!* Sounds like *Caesar!* A despot inside her, ruling over her. Governing. She needs a Brutus, stab in the heart, take out your dagger, stick it in now, give it to me, give it to me, stick it in now, give it to me!

She has been seized by something, something *in* herself. Yes, from *within*. Of course there are monsters. *Seize her! Caesar!* There have always been monsters. Every era. Every age.

She is in the throes now. Her body sliding on the glabrous surface. A glabrous glee-less glide.

Not sunk yet though.

Soon ... soon surely, she'll go under.

Sammy is in a wild panic.

"Oh, shit! Oh, fuck! Oh, no!"

He is a painter and decorator. He paints walls and ceilings. He will paint for you indoors or outdoors, no bother. He has painted the bathrooms of rich folk and the fetid, sweat-odoured changing rooms of the GAA. He'll paint anything you like as long as it is stationary. His job is comfortable and he likes it very much. It is a nice way to make a living. But he doesn't know anything about the situation he is in right now. He doesn't know what to do in an emergency. His lonesome life in the lonesome village has been devoid of things like this. Give him turpentine and an old radio playing and he'll get the job done. A bit of Bruce Springsteen. "Hungry Heart". Or "Hungry Eyes", like before, in the warm van. His slip on the black ice which resulted in this fecked-up arm of his, well, that was the height of emergency in his eventless life, and he was sure it ended there. No such luck. He has something else to deal with now. Something very different and much more serious. Perilous even. Nothing you can do with your cans of emulsion here. Your Dulux range of colours. No chart for this. A girl on thin ice having an epileptic fit. Girl. Thin ice. Epileptic fit. He would not have scripted that were he asked to. He would not have had the imagination to come up with something as outrageous as that. He would only have gotten as far as getting a young girl into his van and maybe a cute cuddle or a kiss. Harmless. Harmless. Or was it? Shame on him: if that was what he was after. Is that what he was after? Who knows? Sammy won't admit it to himself. He won't even tell himself the truth. What was he playing at? What was he doing here all along?

And what on Earth is he to do now?

His broken arm.

His heavy cast.

He is a useless man: he castigates himself.

But there's no time for all that. No one to hear. No one to call for help. There is only that mocking moon above, doing nothing at all. He has to be brave. Do it himself. DIY. No other choice.

He steps on to the ice and starts to slippily-slidily make his way towards the gyrating girl.

The dog is having conniptions on the shore, spinning in circles, losing its small mind. It has been told to stay but it cannot. The dog slides onto the ice too, her four legs flailing, independent of each other, directionless, never having had to negotiate such a medium before. It would almost be funny if it weren't so dangerous, and if all of them weren't going to fall through the ice and drown or freeze, or freeze and drown, whichever came first – it would be very funny indeed.

"I'm coming! I'm coming!" he shouts, and the hope in his words seem to get lost in the wild winds, and he's not sure if they even reach the stricken girl.

Kevin looks up at the posters one more time before he leaves the room. There is nothing at all wrong with having Bowie, Morrissey and REM on the wall, nothing at all. The choices are commendable. But honestly, the wall could do with a bit of Siouxsie. If he were in his own room now he would ask her for help, for prudent advice, dear prudence, but perhaps her eyes would say he needs no help. She has a habit of doing that to him. Being utterly silent on his wall. Saying nothing. Her mixture of insolence and aloof-ness: that was the attraction. Kevin can get by on his own, he doesn't need anybody. Maybe that's what her eyes are saying. No father. No mother. No matter. Don't need them. He's a clever lad; he can get by on his own. He's a good boy. Deep down. He knows he has just hit a beautiful creature across the head with a hard, heavy guitar, knocking him unconscious, but Siouxsie, really, Siouxsie, he's a good boy deep down, wants only the best for himself and his cousin. Their future together. A life. Out of the village. Away from stone walls, livestock, bramble, away from cow pats, faces they see every day. A life together. Now, a big city, that's different. Record stores. Hip coffee shops. Hand in hand with Laura at live concerts. Or maybe she's up on his strong shoulders. Smoke and alcohol and loud guitars. Maybe a puff of something illegal. That's not asking too much, is it?

Siouxsie says nothing. She is not even there. Won't come out to play. She is not even there.

Down the stairs of this house at terrific speed, his feet hardly touching the steps, he soars.

He leaves the front door open – part of the plan, see – and looks around frantically as he exits. Does anyone see him? Of course not. Who would be out on a night like this? They are safe inside with their fires and their electric bar-heaters and their television sets and maybe Mike Murphy is on and they are chuckling away at him and his smooth patter, cup of tea on the lap, and maybe a Penguin bar, or a Club Milk coming out of its silver foil.

He sees the front wheel of Aidan's bicycle peeking out from the side of the house. He goes to it and grabs it. He drags it over to the front gate and again has trouble with the latch, but after cursing it and continuously tugging at it the bloody thing finally gives way and opens to him. There you go now, Kevin. You are ready. Climb up on that saddle. There. Off with you now. Ride it like a stallion. You are a strapping cowboy. There is a fair lady in need of assistance. Go. You have lots to do tonight. Lots. Ride! Ride like the wind, Kevin. You have so much to achieve. For the night, the night is only beginning.

21

Sammy is making his way towards Laura.
Easy does it now.

Despite the wind, he can actually hear the cracks of ice underneath his feet, giving way. But they are not sunken yet. It still holds. Just get to her and bring her back. That's all he has to do.

Laura still trembles and buckles. She sees nothing from her lowly position, just greyness and glass, even the moon is out of shot now – has one of those ugly clouds come over and hidden it again? And where's Kevin? Her cousin. Kevin. She loves him. She loves him not. You get used to things. You get so used to things, so much so that is hard to imagine things in other ways. He's always there to pick her up. She buckles, she shakes. Where's Kevin?

Closer. Sammy edges. He is a heavy man. All those pints in Cronin's Bar, all those greasy burgers he fries in the pan, are they going to let him down now? Those things have put fat on him, those things have put flab on him, spare tyres around his waist, are they now to be his undoing? Surely the ice cannot maintain all that weight. Surely the ice cannot hold.

It doesn't.

When he is no more than a metre away from the girl the ice gives a loud crack, loud and definitive, *this is it*, it says, *this is what you get*, the ice says in its laughing, like it is cracking a joke, and here's the punchline: *this is what you get for all your lies and deceit; get down through it now, get yourself down into that cold water, baptise yourself, wash your sins away.*

Is that the voice of the ice?

Is it Laura's?

Is it God's?

Hard to tell. With so much going on. With the wind blowing and the dog barking and the ice cracking and laughing laughing laughing at them all. What are they even doing here?

Kevin pedals furiously through the streets of the small sleepy village. He takes corners dangerously, not caring for his own safety; he is beyond all that now. He almost comes off the bike when a red fox darts across his path with what looks like a small kitten in its mouth, or is it a mouse, or is it a shrew? Too quick to see properly, both of them, Kevin and Fox, they are far too quick: the animal scurries away and Kevin rushes on.

On.

Furious pace.

Pedals.

Getting there.

Pedals.

He will.

He will find her.

He will get them both where they need to be, to safety.

Sammy McCreary sinks.

Ice-breaks.

Falls.

Down.

In.

His whole body.

His whole body, his whole self falls through the hole created by his whole weight. Whole into hole.

His pub-weight.

His easy-greasy-beefburgers, his fatty-chips-and-fish-fingers weight. Down through.

It is a hole, an almost perfect circle, like those ice fishermen make in Norway or Finland or wherever, and he has gone right through it and Laura can see him, his big head bobbing and screaming in the quiet night.

The winds have died down dramatically, as dramatically as they started up, and the rains have stopped and there is only the sound of a man screaming and a dog beside the hole, slipping, sliding on four legs, and beside itself with anguish.

It would be funny if they weren't all going to die. It would be hilarious.

Freeze or drown?

Which will come first?

Doesn't seem like much of a choice, does it?

Laura is quite calm now, watching all this. She sits up. Her throe has let her go. She is sitting and she is composed, a metre from the hole where the sinner has fallen through and, well, it is some sight to behold. The hole mirrors the circle of the moon shining gloriously up above them again, out of the cloud again. It comes and goes. If someone could only paint it. An artist. Not a painter/decorator. If someone could only photo it ... or write about it. Poetry. Where's a poet when you need one?

"Laura! Law!… Help! Hell!…"

Sammy's screams are fractured like the ice, breaking off in gasps, how much more of this can he take? It is some sight all right. The ice cracking up, laughing at them.

She is curious. She is wondering about it all. She is sitting with her rather large bottom on the ice and is not feeling particularly cold, strangely enough. You just get used to things. The body is able to adapt. Amazing, isn't it? Amazing.

She is suddenly distracted though. A voice calling her.

"Laura!"

It is Kevin, who has appeared on his bicycle. Of course! Kevin is always there, always there to pick her up. Why does Kevin have a bicycle? That's not his, surely. But he is here anyway. He has arrived. He always does. He does not let her down, ever. She'll have her head in his lap soon enough.

The two voices shouting her name seem to converge and merge, it is the most remarkable thing on this night, almost as good as the moon shining down on them, spotlighting them; she smiles at it all, this terrific picture, and she stands and waves to him. The ice is holding her where she is. She must be light, despite her rotund rear. Isn't that strange too? Or luck, at last? But it didn't hold Sammy, look at him, inside in it. He's actually inside in it, in the freezing water!

Kevin tosses the bike and runs to the pond, skating right across it.

Sammy's plaster of Paris is sticking out of the hole. It is rising up there like a dinosaur neck. It is like a monster. Yes, at last! We have it! We have it! Laura's eyes widen in surprise and delight. There it is! There, look! The monster!

The monster from the pond! It has come to her. She had been right all along.

Kevin gets to the hole and the white plaster and his mother's name written across it. Is this significant? He has no time to consider it. He begins to pull the man out.

"Laura," he says. "Wake up! For fuck's sake, help me!"

The dog has stopped its demented yelping: perhaps it understands that help has arrived, a rescuer; it watches eagerly on; and Sammy's head comes out of the water, and Sammy's torso is bent now over the edge of the ice, and they heave at him, and they pull and drag him, and soon the man's knees are able to get over the ledge and soon his whole body is lying on the surface.

But the ice still cackles, like a witch now, clapping her hands in wanton glee: oh come on through, come on through, meet me at the other side.

They better all get off it pretty quick, because now there is even more weight on it, and bigger cracks appear; it is having a grand old laugh at them, these stupid humans in their stupid endeavour. Why are they even here? What took them to this place on this awful night? What is the point of it all?

They drag him with all their might.

Laura holds one arm and Kevin holds the white cast other – holds his mother's name – and they drag the sodden man away from the pond and on to the hard stony shore where he shivers and splutters and gasps, unsure yet as to whether he is alive or has found himself in a cold cold hell, not the wickedly heated place he has heard about in Fr. Kavanagh's Sunday morning sermons, but the exact opposite: life has a way of fooling you, why would death be any different?

Kevin speaks to him in a loud, commanding voice.

"Can you get up? Can you walk?"

Sammy moves his head to offer an affirmative, his face pallid in the waning moonlight, features deathly, grim. He must be alive though. He hears voices, and the voices make sense to him.

The three of them stumble to the parked van. Kevin opens the back door while Sammy leans on Laura. He manages to get a leg up and Laura and Kevin both push him until he is fully climbed in and lying shivering on the floor of it, Lucy lapping at his face in what looks like an effort to revive him.

Kevin jumps in after him and wraps a paint-encrusted blanket around the struggling man, wondering if he'll make it through the night, wondering if that pond has already been the death of him.

"Get the bike!" Kevin shouts to Laura, and immediately she runs off to get it, the austerity in his voice not something to be argued with now.

Kevin rushes around to the front of the van and starts the engine with the keys that had been left dangling there. He mutters to himself as he starts it up: what did that old fool want? What the fuck did either of them actually want?

The van starts and he switches the heating on as high as it will go, he revs the engine, his foot to the floor; perhaps this will turn into a movie scene after all and he will indeed have to *step on it*. He does, revving the engine even more, causing Lucy to bark riotously.

Laura is having trouble lifting the bike into the back of the van, but she finally succeeds after heavy grunts and cursing. Part of the bicycle falls on Sammy, the handlebar actually punching into his gut, as if he hasn't suffered enough already.

The old man groans.

The young girl giggles.

She slams the back door shut, runs around to the front and climbs in beside her cousin.

"You can drive?"

"Tom showed me how. This one can't be that different, can it?"

He studies the pedals and the handbrake for a moment before releasing it. His foot is way too heavy and whatever lightness of touch he lacked in Tom's van he lacks again here. It takes a couple of lurching attempts before he gets the thing in motion, and the vehicle shudders along, though it is far from a smooth ride as the groans of man and dog testify from the rear.

The driving is treacherous but they make progress. Kevin tries to steer as straight as he can, but on rounding one corner he nearly drives straight into an oncoming car. Lights! Fuck! Of course: lights! He forgot to put the lights on. The other car blows its horn in angry protest.

"Where are we taking him? Home? To a doctor?"

Doctor Neelan would be shocked to see them turn up at her door like this, but she was the generous, helpful sort, would surely be able to rescue Sammy from his most-probable hypothermia.

Laura herself still feels almost no cold at all, miraculously, and the heater in the van warms her further, blowing hot air currents out of the black vents.

"No," says Kevin. "We're going to Aidan's place first."

"Aidan's?"

Kevin's steely concentration is on getting the van to keep moving without getting them all killed; it is his only focus right now. He'll have to explain it all to her when they are on safe ground again. There is so much he'll have to explain to her, so much to clear up, not just of the events of this night but so much that has preceded it. And the future too – he looks out the steamed up windscreen, how do you clear that? He must look to the future too, out of this mess, and into the good life, their life: no murk, no monsters.

The drive culminates in Kevin awkwardly hitting the kerb outside Aidan's house. Laura bangs her head against the side window.

"Fuck sake."

"Sorry. It was my first full drive. Forgive me."

They do not look at each other. They have no time for eyes to lock onto each other, no time to decode grins or grimaces, to deflect leers or allay fears. There is still a hell of a lot of work to do.

Kevin opens the back door of the van, the dog leaps out and Laura goes again for the bike.

"Put it at the side of the house. It's Aidan's."

She does as instructed, glad at least that someone has some idea of what is going on; she has been trance-like for most of the evening, and staring at the moon was far more relaxing and meditative than the motions she is going through now. But Kevin is in charge, clearly, and she is vaguely impressed.

Sammy is unconscious. When Kevin climbs into the back of the van to pull the old man out, he notices that while he is still breathing, he is sound asleep, or most likely passed out.

"What is it?" Laura asks.

"He doesn't seem to be awake. Shock, I suppose."

When his feet touch the ground Sammy wakes a little, but he is groggy, his eyes rolling around, his left eyelid

ticking, flickering uncontrollably, he mutters and he moans.
The cousins take either side of him and drag his cold body
into the house.

They get him to the downstairs living room and lay him
right down on the plush carpet.

"Why is there no one here? Why was the door
unlocked?"

"Come with me. Upstairs. We need to drag Aidan
down."

"Drag?"

There has been nothing but dragging all evening. What
has happened here? Why would Aidan need to be dragged
anywhere? Where are Aidan's parents? What the hell is
going on?

She follows him up the stairs and is shocked when the
door is flung open and Aidan Carty, boy beautiful, boy gorgeous, is lying on his own bed, unconscious too, a halo of
blood on the bed around his blond hair, and spatterings of
blood on the posters on his wall.

Laura looks around flabbergasted, hardly able to
breathe. What the fuck has gone on here? Is all this Kevin's
doing?

"Is he … is he …?"

"No, he's not dead."

"Did you kill him?"

"I said he's not dead … at least I don't think he is."

Kevin goes to Aidan and puts his finger to his neck.

"A pulse. We're okay."

"Okay?"

Laura is shaking from fright and confusion, just how
do you compute all this? How do you put a narrative on
what has happened? It is a crime scene. Is it the second

crime scene of the night? There is nothing but tragedy in this fucking village. The whole place stinks of violence and death and … of utter fucking lunacy.

"Trust me. Calm. Calm. Stay calm."

These are the words he uses when she is in the midst of her curse. These are the consoling words that he uses to such great effect, and they are working again for her here now. On this foreign soil. This alien place. She is in Aidan's bedroom. Perhaps she would have dreamed that she would have been invited here one day. That the beautiful boy would fall for her charms and lead her here.

What charms?

"Okay," she says, somehow convinced. "But what now?"

It is the question of their lives.

Kevin goes to the drawer and takes out Aidan's camera. He straps it around his neck.

"What …?"

"Just trust me."

She follows his lead and they lift the boy from the bed. Together they drag him downstairs – drag again, the night has been such a drag – their arms are sore and tired from all the exertion, but adrenaline still pumps, it will not let go, it will not let them down. Who said a village could not be exciting? Who said this shithole was actually a shithole? You can make stuff happen. You just had to think outside the box … and a little insanity and violence helped matters along quite nicely.

He doesn't wake up.

When they lay the boy on his own living room floor, next to passed-out Sammy, he does not wake up.

"Look at them, our sleeping beauties," says Kevin, a look of fairy-tale menace in his eyes, wolf-wickedness, goblin-grisliness, witch-wantonness.

"What should we do with them?"

"Pull down their trousers."

Laura looks at him; she does not know how many more times she can be gobsmacked tonight.

"Are you fucking serious? Why?"

"Back-up. Safety. Just do it."

"I don't get."

"Just do it."

Plans. Sometimes they do work out, don't they? Sometimes you put something together and all the pieces just fit in the right way. He remembers a jigsaw puzzle when he was young. A Disney scene. Perhaps it was the Disney castle, with those sparkling stars above it, or there were rainbows, fireworks, something like that. Anyway, he had finished it and he had felt proud, and he had dismantled it and packed it away into its box again. The next time he took it out and tried it, he got right to the end ... but there was one piece missing. Had it fallen under the couch when he had last tidied the pieces away? Had it slipped away sneakily into another world just to mess with his mind? Some joking portal? Who knew? But the jigsaw was ruined. It couldn't be completed. One missing piece ruined everything. And so the little boy had felt heartbroken. He would spend the rest of his days looking for that missing piece. It never turns up.

But this ... this satisfies.

This all fits.

Things into place.

Connecting.

The full picture.

Things seem to be going according to ...

Laura unbuckles their belts and pulls down their trousers.

"Their underwear too," Kevin says.

She still does not know why she has to do this, but she does what he says, pulling their underpants right down to reveal their most intimates, right there, incongruously, in this posh and proper pricey home.

For a girl who has lived a rather sheltered life, she has had more than her share of penises over the last while. There were those smutty magazines and the men with their mighty appendages. There was Kevin in the bed, his smaller one in her grip, small but hard, so hard and so eager and so quick to complete its transaction. And now this. Two men. One old with greyish hair bushing around a sparrow-like entity, and a younger one, a one she might have fantasised about, one that might have entered her innocent (innocent?) dreams, now flaccid and useless and quite unimpressive, quite pathetic in its soft and curled-up sleepiness.

She still thinks they might be dead. The two of them, lying there, they might be completely dead. She rattles inside at the thought, and the thought that both she and Kevin are somehow murderers. Is that possible? But the two on the carpet, their chests move up and down. Thank God for that. Their chests are moving up and down.

Sammy's eyelids briefly flutter and he groans. Yes, he is certainly alive. And he might even be thawing. And if he is sick from his minutes in the pond, if there are physical repercussions … then let him be sick, let there be repercussions. He should not have been near the pond, should not have been near a young girl.

Kevin sees his mother's name again, snaking out of the man's sleeve. How is he to process that?

He is not.

Ignore it.

They are not finished yet.

Much still left to do.

"Place Sammy's hand over Aidan's genitals. Quickly. Before they both wake up."

This is a horror show. Or a demented comedy. But she is part of it now. Part of this grim, seedy, nutty drama, and there is no backing out of it now. She had climbed into that van. She had sat with him as he drove. Why? She does not know how to answer her own questions. She had stared at the moon. A mad she-wolf.

Laura places Sammy's clammy hand over the young boy's privates.

"Turn their heads towards each other."

She does this too, angling their heavy heads and causing another moan from Sammy, as if he is coming round.

"Okay. Stop there. Now get out of the way."

Kevin starts to shoot, clicking and clicking with the camera from different angles. He is not used to this kind of technology – give him a stereo or a synthesizer any day; but he knows enough to point and click and get the shots he needs and when he finally stops he opens the back of the camera and snatches the film out and stuffs it in his pocket.

Laura is nodding. As if she is starting to understand that there are methods to all this madness. That he has his reasons and looks like he knows what he is doing.

"We've got to hurry," he says. "Get some cloths or paper towels or something from the kitchen, fast."

She flees to carry out his decrees, now eager to please.

Kevin looks down at the two prostrate men on the floor.

"You won't fuck with us again, boys. That's for sure."

Laura soon returns with two dishcloths and hands them to Kevin.

"You take one. We can't be too careful. Get wiping. Wipe everything down. Wipe the guitar upstairs, the stereo, the bicycle handles outside, the van's steering wheel and door handles. And the handles of doors here too. Everything you can think of."

Kevin says all this while wiping down the camera.

Laura's nerves jangle with the excitement of it all and again she takes in his every instruction, nods to his needs.

The dog has entered the living room and goes to its master, licking his face again. The dog's eyes seem to have prayers swimming there, praying for the man to wake up, but is God listening? He has been nowhere in any of this. Nowhere in the village for years.

"They will be all right, won't they?" says Laura, the last of her wiping done.

"They'll be fine. In time. They both will. They're just taking a nap that's all. Though they'll be surprised when they do come round."

"I'm not sure I understand it all … I mean, I …"

"There will be time enough. There will be time enough. I'll explain it all when …"

It is best to just get out of here. It is best to just get home and to the two worried guardians.

Maura is pacing the floor wondering why her boy is not home – why do they never come home?

And Tom, does he know that Laura is not in bed, that two pillows under covers are not actually her? That people can be dreadful, deceitful. That people can be what you least expect.

Tom is sleeping soundly in his own bed, and he dreams of nothing much at all, maybe just his hands putting his cards down on the table and saying *I'm out*, and someone else taking all the winnings.

Laura will wait for the explanations.

It will all make sense at some later stage.

It will.

It will.

Of course it will.

Won't it?

There is still a future, for both of them, of course there is, they are young, they are young and in …

Deep.

Before Kevin goes into his own house he notices blood on his coat. He takes it off and goes to the side of the house and puts it straight into the dustbin. The arm of it sticks out a little, dangling over the edge; like a person might leave fingers skim along a pond if out sailing in a gentle punt.

In his room he puts the camera-film on the shelf, hiding it behind his cassette tapes: The Cure. Of course.

He goes to his desk and flicks through his notebook, the one marked "Lyrics". He flicks through empty pages. Only the name Laura appears on every page right at the top. He finds his pen and while chewing on the cap of it he writes "and Kevin" on every page too, so that every top is now labelled "Laura and Kevin". What about that? What about that? What about that?

He gets a black marker then and scrawls out the "Lyrics" title on the cover. Underneath it he writes "Laura and Kevin." And he flicks once more through each page and each glorious page heading.

Laura and Kevin.

Laura and Kevin.

Laura and Kevin.

Suddenly there is a clattering sound from outside his window. He goes and looks out and sees a fox at the dustbin. Fox! It has smelled the blood. How keen its senses. How keen its ever-search, its ever-strive. It pulls on the arm of the coat until it is completely out of the dustbin. It sniffs at it. It sniffs at Aidan's blood. Aidan who has woken up with a man at his side. Aidan who does not know why there is a dog looking directly into his eyes and an old man at his side and why both males have their trousers down. It could be a comedy. There could be canned laughter sounding somewhere. It could all be televised and the audience is having a good old whoop and holler at the whole thing behind some hidden screen. But there are no laughs. There is just an eerie silence. And it doesn't feel like comedy. There is nothing funny about this at all. Nothing at all. It feels more like tragedy, a grotesque, ugly and mystifying tragedy. How do you get your aching head around this one?

The man beside him is just as stumped. He is just as sore. He is just as sore and just as puzzled; will they ever find that missing piece?

Ice cracks still in the far-off pond. It cracks up still.

The moon. The moon is still there. It never goes away fully; it comes back every night – you can rely on that much.

The fox takes the coat in its mouth and drags it: more dragging.

It runs off as fast as it can with its bounty.

What will it use the coat for? Bedding in its hidden den? Kevin does not know. He would need a library book to find all about foxes, wild animals. Perhaps the beast just likes the taste and smell of human blood. Perhaps it is a vampire. A monster. You can get a taste for things; you get used to things.

"Go," says Kevin at the closed window, out the closed window.

He does not see his own reflection this time. He sees only the fox. A scamper of brush. He does not see himself on stage and the masses of fans in front of him gushing, shrieking with joy at his very presence. There is none of that.

He sees only the wild animal, and it is running fast.

"Go now. Run! Run!" he says. "Get the fuck out of here, Fox! Run! Run! You don't want to be stuck here, run, run!"

Ostinato.

I TOLD YOU THAT WE COULD FLY

22

Their bottoms on the hard, cold slabs of rock. They are at the pond again. Has it shrunk? Or have they gotten older, wiser to it? It looks smaller. Everything looks smaller to them now that they have grown some, and they are still growing, yes, in size, yes, in wisdom, growing, naturally. How could anyone ever have said this was a lake? Look at the size of it. It's tiny. This place where they've grown up, it's so bloody small. How could anyone have ever said otherwise?

A pond is a pond: if this is all they ever take away from village life, if this is all they have really learned . . .

They like summertime. They liked the slow walk that got them here today. They are not carefree, they cannot be, not now, but they enjoy the ease of the zephyrs on their skin, the sun and its warmth on their upturned faces; school is out and they are waiting for exam results and they are waiting for their lives to change in extraordinary ways, this couple. So much of their lives has been all about waiting, a waiting around for something, for something to be over or for something to get started, and now their wait is with tremulous trepidation, knowing what is to come, but fearing for the responsibility and all that will entail.

On the gentle stroll to this frequented place they had passed Orlaith Crowley and she had given them a scintilla of a smile and she slung no insults their way; she had just grinned goofily – she is happy, they suppose, that Aidan Carty is now her steady boyfriend and they've been going together for quite some time.

Orlaith might not know it yet, but Kevin and Laura know it to be all a lie. It's *wrong*. Again. So definitely *wrong*. Aidan is no girl's boyfriend. How could he ever be? He is pretending. He is a charlatan. It is not the real him. He lives a complete lie, though he is doing his best to play his part – you need a part to play in a village: the creepy man in the van, that's a part, or the village idiot, or the effeminate teacher who is not gay but forever will be stained, or the part of the intellectual trapped and trying to find a way out: *Help me, Siouxsie Sioux. Run, Fox, run!*

Kevin explained all this to Laura, about Aidan's photos, the *surveillance* he called it, spying on them like that; the garden that night, the flash, the flash from the bush. He explained too about the admission of homosexuality, Aidan Carty, not what you had expected, the confrontation in the bedroom, too, he told her about that, and the swing of that red guitar, and the blood spraying and landing like an extra lightning-streak on Ziggy's face.

He painted that picture for her.

And she did not judge.

She did not gasp or guffaw.

She just listened, staring out at the pond.

Was that the reason for Kevin beating him so severely? For the photos of the kissing cousins in the dark garden? The flash of the camera's light. *Amazing the things you can see. Wild animals and so on.* The possibility of blackmail?

Was that the reason for the brutal beating? Or for just being gay? A faggot? A bender? A queer? Some of the villagers are, and some of the villagers are not, but you can get beaten either way, your name scrawled, your good name sullied. Reputations crumble so easily in a small place with mouths that have nothing better to do. Families fall. Kevin hasn't quite worked out the answer to all this yet; there is a lot that he hasn't quite decided.

He listened to Kate Bush the previous night, who sang about being a coward and not knowing what was good for her. There was such honesty in all that.

Maybe he needs more time gazing out at this now more-than-familiar body of still water, and the nothing that ever happens there, maybe he needs more time. Time goes slowly in places like this. But it will speed up for them soon, with all that is coming, all that is due.

From her meticulously clean and un-scribbled rucksack Laura takes out a bottle of red wine. She has stolen this from Tom's recently installed drinks cabinet, and she's hoping that he will not notice it gone; although there is no slide yet into anything like senility – how old is Tom anyway? – she will still capitalize on even the slightest moment of forget-fulness: it is cruel, sure, she knows this, but that's the way the world is, cruel, uncaring, she fully knows this too: when does life ever really deal you that good hand? When? Tell her. Just when?

The poker nights have stopped. No one can be bothered anymore. Sammy McCreary one day got into this van with his little dog Lucy and they were never seen again. Perhaps he went somewhere warmer, finally got a passport and went overseas, to a warmer clime, sure, why not, where there was no treacherous ice, to a less treacherous life, where you didn't slip and slide and break things as you fell. Perhaps he no longer paints walls and rooms, maybe he paints *pictures* to hang *in* rooms, framed pictures of ice and moons, why not, stranger things have happened.

She pours a plastic cupful for her cousin – she's got a whole stacked pack of these plastic cups, bought in the pound shop – but she does not pour for herself; she just tucks into a ham and cheese sandwich that she made that morning, and she's cut down on the butter: she should be commended for that. It isn't easy, a life without real and proper things: butter, a normal boyfriend, a mother and a father; but she's got to start looking after herself now, be more responsible for herself, her body. She has to grow up fast.

They have spent months together, these two, this couple, months in private moments, on these quiet tracks through the quiet countryside: Kevin delighting in the release of The Cure's masterpiece, *Disintegration,* but unhappy that he was not able to get to the concert at the R.D.S. in July: responsibilities encroaching, life, life took over, money, or rather the lack of it, life, life, and their new life starting. They have spent months, yes, walks, jaunts, kicking stones along the paths (Kevin also proclaiming that it was a toss-up between *Disintegration* and *Doolittle* for the album of the decade, and both coming so near to the end of the decade, and Lenny agreed, though Laura thinks the former a miserable pile of bullshit and the latter just a shouty-screamy load of nonsense), or strolling through the woods, slowly, ambling, leisurely, or just idling right here, at the pond of no-monster, the beast-less pond. They both nearly wet themselves with laughter one day when they spotted a newt at the edge of it, not even fully formed, a mere eft, creeping there, comically crawling.

"Is that it?" they wondered. "Is that the culmination of all our dreams and fantasies, all our arguments? Is that the monster from the deep?"

They have spent months in bed together too. Under covers. They like that, the connotation: *undercover* cousins, living like spies, incognito, double lives, secrecy, cloaks, daggers, clandestine encounters, coupling. When Tom is out, and they are left alone on Saturdays, they have the run of the house, like they are a married couple, in each other's pockets, but gladly so, but mostly in her narrow bed, time there, the joint stare up at the gorilla on the ceiling, making plans, moulding projects, talking about the future, their lives. Together? Well, that simply has to be the case now, doesn't it?

They have discussed the past. Naturally. They have waded through it, like anglers with myriad sea creatures skimming round their feet, and they have tried to catch these shimmering things, hold them in their hands, the past, what has led them here: understand this; it has led them here again.

They have become each other's therapists, one listens while the other rants or raves or moans or marvels, and the other nods or sighs or does whatever is requisite: they have dispensed with the childish notebooks, torn up the dumb diaries, and they have just spoken, plainly, honestly, no frills, no fabulations.

This is what I did.

This is what I felt.

These are not the lyrics of a song.

This is just how they operate.

This is what they do now.

Kevin told her all about seeing them, Tadhg and Declan, the fathers, the two fathers that day – what season was it? Memory has to embellish, fix or fabricate – but how they held hands on a walk once, that much was true; it struck him once, years later, and stuck with him, memory, the meddling of it, the rising of it, out of nowhere, a flash in the dark: the middle of a forest, it was a clearing, and the sun unable to get down through the canopy of leaves to shine on the two men; the men stayed in that shade, close, but in that shade, shaded from the world's glare, as well as the sun's … but not the son's.

She has told him about her fits. How they have become fewer because of the medication, how she has it all under control. This delights both of them. Cured?

And that time on the ice?

Had she been pretending?

Mostly, yes.

Though she couldn't say why. She couldn't say whether it was that she wanted to damage herself or damage Sammy McCreary; she couldn't really be sure of anything.

Pretending.

Yes.

The seizure was not really real. Not like before.

So what was the reason?

What was her motive?

Why does anyone do anything? She does not know. She just did it. As Sammy watched. As the mad, maddening dog manically barked.

But the moon had looked good that night: it shone, and it had been enough, bright when unclouded, limning, she had been satisfied with that.

He has told her about the letters. The letters from his father. That weren't really from his father at all. This had completely shocked her.

What?

"Letters from your father that weren't from your father?"

They were written in Jason's hand, his pen pal, copied from Kevin's own notes and sent back, postmarked San Francisco. Kevin's plan. Kevin's thinking. All his own doing.

Ingenious?

The idea had been to stir up enough momentum to get Kevin over to the States, to leave his home, leave his home-town, this "shithole". But it didn't quite pan out. He's still here. Other things have taken over, new life, growing.

"That was such a stupid plan, you dickhead. You think your mother wouldn't have seen through it?"

He blushed with shame at his lack of finesse. He was no criminal mastermind, that was for sure. But still, the intention was there. He had been planning. He had wanted it. Had wanted out. Was that not enough?

Perhaps Maura did see through it all; and where would they even get the money; he needed to get to college, not to America. Maura was not going to fork out for a trip to see the man who rejected her, *fuck that,* she swore at Kevin right in the kitchen, letting loose, letting herself go mad for a change, lashing out instead of always taking it; their frost continues, as yet un-thawed: it is always winter in their kitchen.

And the fathers, the actual fathers, Declan and Tadhg, somewhere in Haight-Ashbury most likely (how did they ever gather the money together to get there: would that mystery ever be solved?) or locked up in Alcatraz: how would anyone ever know? Is Alcatraz still up and running? Imaginations run riot, always, when there's nothing much to look at, when life is bare. They do not want to be found, that couple, they do not want you to come looking for them. They got out; in many ways, they made it, what is the expression, no, not *got out … came out.*

Maura would not bend on money. She told Kevin times were tight. She had to take on second and third little jobs around the village, whatever needed doing: the butcher's floor needing the sweep of a broom, shirts needing ironing, ends to be met, pennies needed to be rubbed together, ever-errands to run – he'll know all about this soon enough.

So … college?

Still on the cards?

It's all so doubtful now, all so doubtful.

He listened to Kate Bush last night, and she consoled and she comforted and he wished he had a mother that wise.

As yet, un-thawed.

Kevin hadn't told Laura about what he would do when he got there, to the Unites States, if it had all actually been realised. But he had fantasised about it. Countless times. What would he have done? It would have gone something like this: he would have tracked down the two men, the two homosexual fathers, he would have found them shacked up somewhere, in a little house on the side of one of those hilly streets. And Kevin is carrying a gun in this dream, a shotgun, Jason's of course, and it is hidden in a guitar case: no one would ever suspect. And he tracks them down and they open the door to him, and they are shocked, speechless, but they invite him in, huggingly, back-slappingly. And when they are all seated and drinking casual beers he breaks the spirit of this fond and unexpected reunion, and, slowly, he opens the guitar case, with the ruse of playing a song he wrote for them, and he takes out Jason's fine and polished hunting gun and he cocks it, this deadly weapon, this firearm, having learned, having been taught by his pen pal, Jason, his accessory, and he focuses, eye to the eyepiece, aiming, and he fires, once, twice, and two gay bodies are blown to pieces. The sound is bigger than anything you could get from a music amp, and it rings, rings loud in the ears. Blood on the clean walls and on their trendy un-Irish furniture. This is what Kevin has thought about. As he gazed into Siouxsie's eyes. As he gazed about the strictures of his own room, his fingers playing silent notes on a turned-off synthesizer. This is why he wrote no poems, no songs, because this is all he thought about: this story. And Laura, of course, Laura first, Laura foremost, naturally. But this story, this story, he has thought about it a great amount too. It still runs across his brain. Technicolor. This gruesome ending.

There has always been violence in him.

There has always been rage.

Red rage.

But none of this grisly scenario will ever play out. Because Kevin will not ever get there. He will never get to San Francisco in the same way he will never front a band on stage with green or pink gravity-defying hair. He is stuck. Responsibilities now. He is stuck more than ever.

Laura, her turn: she had told him about never really being interested in Aidan Carty in the first place. It was just that he was the best looking boy in the school; it seemed like the most obvious thing to say, the most obvious way to behave. The other girls in school said it, with whispers, with giggles. She just followed suit. No real reason. No motive.

Why does anyone do anything? She just did it. It felt like the right thing to do. She does not want to follow anyone anymore.

But she loves her cousin. He's perfect.
She loves him not: the pretentious fucker.

Kevin loves his cousin. She's perfect.
He loves her not: she needs a proper musical education.

And their monsters, their monsters, their monsters will be...

Under the gorilla they have gotten closer. They have united. No fear. No experimentation. It is just the thing they do now. Routine. No fuss. But close, so very close, taking time, doing it right. But it is *wrong*, isn't it? It goes against all the rules of society. Well...fuck society. These two are rule-breakers, troublemakers. They have stood on the ice and it did not break. Against nature? They have so far defied it.

And no one catches them.

And no one ever knows.

No one is taking photographs.

They are left to do all this in peace.

Everybody has enough to be getting on with: making money, chasing away the red foxes that ransack the bins and that seem to get ever closer, ever closer, those animals. Amazing the things you can see at night. Badgers. Sharp claws. They could rip off your arm. You don't get too close to them. In a village, in the countryside, this is the balance you have to achieve: this is the danger, close ... or *too* close?

Kevin lights a cigarette and blows the smoke away from her, in the other direction, he must be responsible now.

They are at the pond.

Kate Bush had sang about taking her shoes off and throwing them in the lake.

It is nowhere near a lake. How could anyone ever have mislabelled? A pond is a pond. How could people have gotten it so terribly wrong?

Laura throws the empty bottle into the water. She says she should have put a message in it.

Saying what? *Help?*

Saying: *never gonna give you up.*

Saying: *we could live for a thousand years.*

Kevin's Walkman is broken so they use hers: the "L" earpiece is for him, the "R" is for her. They share.

The tape that plays is no longer *Hounds of Love* which he had been insisting on: it is now INXS' *Kick.* The song that plays is one they both actually agree on: "Never Tear Us Apart". How could anyone *not* like that song? Even Lenny, so mired in the previous decades, Lenny, in the musty thrift shop, even he likes it and predicted great things for Hutchence and co., the world theirs for the taking.

Just then a rumble…from deep down.

Turning down there…in the deep.

Surrounded, protected by liquid all around, in safe, warm fluid; it only grows there, it is only getting bigger, day by day.

It moves.

It moves!

She can feel it.

And when Kevin puts his hand on her belly, he can feel it too.

Author's Note

You have come to the end of *My Perfect Cousin*, and, much as I thank you for sticking with it, I must apologise too, not only for making 1988 a very hot summer and cold, chilling winter – they weren't – but for also, as you will have noticed, a not altogether happy ending: Laura and Kevin seem to be stuck in their ruts, stuck in their village, stuck with each other.

Was it all of their own making? Perhaps. You might think that they deserved what they got, but I can't help but feel sorry for them; they did not have it easy, right from the beginning, life, its tribulations, seemed somehow insurmountable.

So, no happy ending then, I really am sorry. That's it. Off you go now, dear reader, to ...

But wait. No. Hold on there just one second.

The more I think about it, the more I'm beginning to feel that ... yes, actually, there is a happy ending here after all. Yes, there is, and that happy ending is of course: Ireland today.

In the 1980s gay-bashing was a far more common occurrence, not only in Ireland but in many so-called liberal countries all over the world. There was no such thing as an LGBT community in Ireland back then, and if there was (then LGB, before the T was added in the 1990s) it was very much underground. The word "pride" was not often tagged on to the word "gay", and no one would have dared parade, certainly not in country villages; rainbows were just natural manifestations in the sky and represented nothing else; there were no gay marriages and there was definitely no way you would have even considered a gay Taoiseach to lead your country.

How times have changed.

Kevin's struggles to understand what his father really was – indeed all of the villagers' struggles to understand, or relate – and his brutal beating of Aidan Carty, would be, thankfully, very unlikely in this liberal, more secular, progressive country that Ireland has become, and this is something that should be consistently celebrated.

A happy ending then, after all, if not for the fictional characters, but for the real people of Ireland, thirty years later, but not *too* late … and perhaps *ending* is not the word we should be using either, for long may this continue, this sense of inclusion; we want no ending ever to that, not to kindness, not to acceptance, not to love.

ACKNOWLEDGMENTS
AND THANKS

As ever, to my wife Yuki, and to my children, Reinan and Nina, who have supported me in all my writing endeavours; all of this would be impossible without their love, understanding and encouragement.

To my family in Ireland, who have always given me the freedom to express myself as I saw fit, much appreciation; Dad, especially, for taking the time to read these books and for staunchly sticking by me.

To my publisher, Svetlana Pironko, who keeps championing my work, and for having the uncanny ability to identify, steady me, and make me believe in myself during those wobbly moments when I am most in doubt.

To friends who read my work and always offer honest criticism (and, thankfully, more often than not, favourable reviews): Bill Blizzard, Chris Oleson, Vikki Williams, Jennifer Bucke – thanks for always being there.

To Sean and all my other perfect cousins, big thanks, big love.

To Niall Griffiths who gave me a big leg-up on a very high wall.

To my partners-in-rhyme, mentors, friends: John W. Sexton and Eileen Sheehan, two astoundingly talented poets, who helped set me on my way and have always been spiritually alongside me in every step … can you believe we're still doing this stuff after all these years?

And to The Undertones of course, for that wonderful song.

Much love and respect to you all.

ABOUT THE AUTHOR

Colin O'Sullivan lives in the north of Japan with his family and works as an English teacher.

Colin O'Sullivan's first novel, *Killarney Blues*, captivated critics and readers alike and has won the prestigious Prix Mystère de la Critique in France.

His second novel, a literary dystopia called *The Starved Lover Sings*, was published in Russia to critical acclaim.

His third novel, *The Dark Manual*, is due to be made into a TV series.

O'Sullivan's short fiction and poetry have been published in various print and online anthologies and magazines.

To learn more about Colin O'Sullivan, visit *http://osullivancolin.wordpress.com* and *www.betimesbooks.com*

Printed in Poland
by Amazon Fulfillment
Poland Sp. z o.o., Wrocław